A Book Of Short Stories

Robert H. Austin

iUniverse

A BOOK OF SHORT STORIES

iUniverse books may be ordered through booksellers or by contacting:

iUniverse
1663 Liberty Drive
Bloomington, IN 47403
www.iuniverse.com
844-349-9409

ISBN: 978-1-6632-3622-7 (sc)
ISBN: 978-1-6632-3601-2 (e)

Library of Congress Control Number: 2022903406

Print information available on the last page.

iUniverse rev. date: 03/09/2022

DEDICATION

I am dedicating this Book of Short
Stores to The Miller Connection
For their love and support

Funny Things My Granddad Said

One of the story tellers.

He was funny all right. My Granddad Austin. He meant to be funny sometimes and other times, he made us laugh when he didn't understand or hear something clearly. He was a very happy person and truly enjoyed life to the fullest. He could find humor in most situations. He loved to laugh and hear and tell jokes. Some of his jokes were just for the "men folks". They were never very dirty, but were always funny and hearing him tell them made them funnier.

He would always start by asking, "Did you hear the one" .... and we would usually say we had, but that didn't stop him and we would hear it again, and again. He would laugh just as hard as the first time he told it.

My Granddad was a barber by profession. He cut hair at the Helm Hotel in Bowling Green, Kentucky for forty years. After retiring, he worked part time barbering for another ten years. Altogether, he worked as a barber for fifty years. Most of his jokes came from the barber shop.

He always wore a hat. It set a little to one side of his head and just back a little. The brim was always turned up and seemed to be smiling just like he was. He was always smiling. Boy, when he got dressed up, he was at his best. He loved to wear a suit and all of his accessories. He had a diamond stick pin and diamond ring. Usually wore cuff links. They were not diamond. He truly looked like a very successful businessman. And boy did he like to smell good. He not only wore shaving lotion, but he wore cologne and powder also. I can remember him telling me that a man should not only look good, but smell good also.

His dressing up was usually for Sunday and church. He and my grandmother were very active in the First Baptist Church. He sang in the Choir and she belonged to every woman's group available.

He was a person that always enjoyed the outdoors. Every year, until he was too old, he had a garden. Just as soon as he came in from the barber shop, he would change clothes and go straight to his garden. He was happy there in his private world and did most of the work himself. He was plowing, weeding, harvesting or just checking it over every evening. My grandmother did help some, but it was his garden and he did most of the work. He not only had vegetables, he also had beautiful flowers. Roses were his favorite and he had every color and variety you could imagine. During the winter months, he would read seed catalogs and magazines pertaining to gardening. Every time he found a new variety of rose, he would order the bulbs and plant them in the spring. My Granddad was one of the first people in the neighborhood to have a gasoline garden tiller. My Dad set it up for him and showed him how to operate it. I can see him now, walking behind that Sears tiller and smiling with every step. He grew up with horses and mules pulling a plow, so this tiller wasn't only a tool for him, he was thrilled just to operate it. No one could have had more enjoyment than he did walking behind that tiller. His garden was the thing he enjoyed most about outdoors. He did have another activity he loved about as much and that was fishing.

My Granddad loved fish. He loved to catch them and he loved to eat them. I never knew for sure which he loved the most. I always thought he loved catching them the most when he was fishing and he loved eating them the most when he was eating them. He used cane poles. Cane poles were the best and the simplest to use. No line to get tangled and you were ready to fish when you got there. Just unwind the line, put a worm on and start fishing. He had a way of slinging his line in the water very much like someone using a whip. He let the pole back over his head and with one motion swished the pole over and hitting the water so hard that his bobber would go under the water. He would always tell me that we must be very quiet so we would not scare the fish. I use to think that the way he churned the water with his bobber, nothing would scare those fish. It never seemed to bother the fish. We usually caught enough to have a good fish fry. This was also a big part of the fishing trip. The cleaning and cooking.

It seemed that we ate the fish the same night we caught them. I think mostly because Granddad talked all the way home about how good they were going to be and we were hungry for them when we got home. He would talk about a skillet of fish with cornbread and hot coffee. I will never forget him saying that he could tell which fish we were eating and who had caught it. He would say, "Oh, yeah, that's that big old cat you caught over by that stump".

After my Granddad had completely retired, he and I had some more fishing trips. I will always be glad that I was there to take him. He never drove a car and had to depend on someone for his transportation.

I was so pleased that my wife and our two children got to know my grandparents on both sides of our family. They were great grandparents and so very great for our two children. They had many opportunities to be with them during the holidays and sometimes actually babysit for us.

My wife and I just became great grandparents for the first time. One of our grandsons and his wife had a little girl over a year ago and are expecting a little boy in just a few months.

It happens to all of us if we live long enough. We start with our parents and then grandparents and if we are lucky, great grandparents. Then, years later we are looking at ourselves and thinking, "How could we be great grandparents?" Well, it's going to happen if we marry have children and live long enough. It is a true blessing.

STORIES TOLD TO ME

BY MY

GRANDPARENTS.

Jesse James

Told by my great grandfather

My great-grandfather was born and lived during the time that Jesse James and his gang was robbing banks and trains throughout the south and mid-west. In the early 1800's, Jesse and his gang robbed the Southern Deposit Bank in Russellville, Kentucky. This was only about thirty to forty miles from where my great-grandfather was raised. Just a little history to make this story sound real. After all, he did tell all that would listen, that this was a true story. And it happened to him. I was about seven or eight when we would visit with my great-grandfather and great-grandmother. We would always make the visit on Sunday afternoons and sometimes get there in time for Sunday dinner. (Dinner was the mid-day meal; the evening meal was supper). Anyway, after all the meal was finished and everyone gathered in the living room. He would begin. It seemed these stories were always told in the winter time and a fire was going in the fire place. The kind that has a grate. It could hold coal as well as wood. He would have his cane bottom chair setting in front of

1

the fire place so he could spit in the fire as he chewed his home-grown tobacco that he had made into a twist. After he sat for a few minutes and had spit a few times in the fire, causing a spew of steam each time, he would look at the grandkids gathered around, setting in the floor and then ask.

"Well, children, have I ever told you about the time I saw Jesse James"?

Even though we had heard the story many times and would say, "Yes sir, you told us about Jesse James", he would continue as if no one had answered. "Well, I was in the field watering our cattle." As he started the story that we all knew by heart, it captured our interest and we all listened intently as he continued. "We had a well in the middle of a big field, must have been twenty- or thirty-acre field." "I was drawing the water up with a rope and bucket when I heard horses coming." "There must have been ten or twelve men on horses." "They road up to me and ask if they could have a drink of water." He would pause and spit in the fire. We all sat there waiting for the story to continue. He would lean back just a little in his chair and start again.

"Well, after I gave each man a drink from the bucket, the last man handed the bucket back to me and said." "Young man, do you see that man in front of our group on the white horse?" I looked and watched as he rode in front of the rest." "His horse was a fine animal." "I told the man, yes sir." Then my great-grandfather would look around the room to be sure that everyone heard what was coming next. Then he would say in a very quiet, almost whisper, "You can tell your grandchildren that your grandfather gave Jesse James a drink of water".

As I said, he did live during the time that Jesse robbed the bank in Russellville. Could have been true, or could have happen to someone else. Anyway, it is a good story and I have now told it to my children and grandchildren. I even told it in a Dale Carnegie class in public speaking. And yes, I did win the best speech that night.

This same great-grandfather was a story teller about ghost and told us that he had seen many. His son, my grandfather carried on the same tradition with his stories. He added more to his stories by reading short stories. Some of these included Tom Sawyer and Huck Finn. Mark Twain tales. Uncle Remus stories about Brer Rabbit and the sly fox that was always trying to catch the rabbit and being out witted each time. I can remember asking my grandfather to just tell the story. It was always more exciting and with his ability to ad lib, made it more interesting also. He would add an extra twist or a new character when he just told it from memory.

The Chicken Foot Lady

Told by my grandmother

My grandmother Hudson on my mother's side (maternal) was also a story teller. She specialized in the scary stories. Her favorite one was the Chicken Foot Lady. This story was like the Jesse James story in that we had heard it many times, but was always glad to hear it over and over. She would always tell it just before bedtime, and would remind us to listen after we went to bed for the Chicken Foot Lady. The Chicken Foot Lady would come into homes at night and get little kids that had been bad. Being bad meant that they had not minded, or have misbehaved in some way. My grandmother would come in the bedroom where I was sleeping and tell me the story. I can remember her making the sounds of the Chicken Foot Lady. She would say, "You will know when the Chicken Foot Lady is about, by the sound." "You will hear a squish and bump, squish and bump." "The squish is the sound of her chicken foot." "The bump is her human foot." I would lay there after she and my grandfather had gone to bed and listen for the "squish and bump, squish and bump. Sometimes I was sure I could hear it, and would cover my head and finally go to sleep.

Panther and the Woods

Grandfather Story

Another story from my grandfather is the Panther in the Woods. Again, it was told many times and each time he would add just a little extra to make it more interesting. This is one story that I found out later in life, was told by others. I had some friends that told the same story about their parents or grandparents. Anyway, here is the way it goes.

This man lived on a farm and had a lot of wooded area. To make extra money, he set up a sawmill in the woods and sawed logs to sell to his neighbors. The mill was about one mile from his house. On this particular day, he was going about his business of sawing logs when his two dogs came up close to him. This was something they just did not do. He petted each one and scolded them. They would not leave his side. Concerned, he shut down the sawmill. The dogs were whining and tucking their tales between their legs. Just then, he heard a scream. The scream was like a woman screaming. It seemed to be deep in the woods. After waiting for a few more minutes, the scream came again. This time it was closer. The dogs were more scared and tried to get under the pile of logs near the saw. The farmer was now starting to be concerned. His horses were grazing nearby. He always unhitched them from the wagon when he worked at the mill. Now, the horses began to flair their nostrils and arch their necks. He thought I must do something. The scream came again and convinced him that something was coming toward them and very fast.

There was no time to hitch up the wagon. He ran to one of the horses and leaped on. The dogs were just behind him. They raced toward the house. The other horse led the way, making more speed without a rider. The scream was louder, closer. Soon, the farmer could hear the sound of the pounding of feet, just behind him. The scream was now so close, he was afraid to look back. His house was now in sight. The white picket fence was about four feet high. The gate was closed. He knew there was no time to open it. Racing toward the fence, the horses jumped the fence and stopped just short of the porch. The farmer jumped from his horse and pushed open the front door to his house. As he looked out the window from the safety of his house, he saw a giant black panther ripping the sides and hind quarters of his horses. This panther was almost as large as a horse and had long, sharp claws. Greenish yellow eyes glared at the farmer through the window. The panther screamed one last time and jumped back over the picket fence and returned to the woods never to be seen by anyone again.

The Haunted House

Another Grandmother story

Another story by Grandmother Hudson. This one is about a haunted house. In the days when my grandmother grew up, it was customary to set up with people when they were near death. No one should be alone when they died. Doctors would tell the family that there was nothing else they could do. The family knew it was a matter of time before death came. Neighbors would help the families in times like this. It was my grandmother's duty to help on the particular night. The lady was old and very ill. She had been in bed for many days and everyone knew that her time was very close. My grandmother sat next to the bed and watched by the light from the fire place as the old lady breathed very slowly. The house was quiet. All members of the family were sleeping.

At about four in the morning, the daughter of the old lady came to my grandmother and told her that she would take over for her. It was still dark and as my grandmother left the house and started for the road in front, she looked back at the house. Just above the roof of the house was a white sheet, floating very gently over the house. It hovered there for a few seconds and ascended up in the sky. Just then, my grandmother heard the daughter crying inside the house. She returned to the bedroom and was told by the lady that her mother had died. My grandmother said, "Yes, I saw her soul going up to heaven."

Years later, I have thought about this story and have concluded that the white sheet must have been smoke from the chimney, or fog over the roof top. I am sure that my grandmother thought it was really the soul or some kind of spirit.

Rising from the dead

Stories by my great uncle

I had a great uncle that was also a story teller. His stories were of the strange unusual type. He was the brother of my grandfather and the son of my great-grandfather that saw Jesse. Here are a couple of his stories. These are also first-person happenings and sworn to be true.

Back in the early 1900's people were seldom embalmed. The deceased were kept at home, or displayed at the local church. In this story, the lady was laid out in the church in her finest dress. The casket was open for all family and friends to pay their respect. This lady had not been embalmed. As the preacher began the service and started to discuss the life of the deceased, the lady slowly raised up one arm from the casket. Everyone in the church gasped. She raised up, opened her eyes and looked around at the members as they were rushing from the church through windows and both doors. The lady recovered and lived for many more years. Obviously, she had been in a coma and was thought to be dead by the doctor.

My uncle's other story tends to confirm some of these mistakes. My uncle was hired by the local church to move some grave sites to the new church site. They exhumed many graves and relocated the caskets to the new graveyard. Most of these had solid tops on the caskets. Some however, had glass windows from about the chest up. This was done because no one was embalmed. The deceased could be viewed. So, one of these caskets had the glass window. As my uncle and his helper removed the earth, the person inside was completely turned over. They found others with their clothes torn and scratches on their faces. So, according to his story, some people in those days were buried alive.

Both of these stories could have been true. May not have happen to my uncle, but do make good stories to tell around the fire place on a cold winter evening.

I HAVE WRITTEN THE
FOLLOWING STORIES
OVER THE YEARS.

The Truth about Samantha

July 2002

It was a cold winter day when the Robinsons' moved into their old house they had just purchased from a local realtor. Allison was not very happy as she carried the first load of items from their moving truck up the winding staircase. Just as she entered the curve in the stairs, she thought she heard a voice. She couldn't understand what it said. She carried the items of bed clothes into the spare bedroom. As she started back down, she thought she could hear a voice again.

She met Charles, her husband, at the bottom of the stairs and said, "Charles, I think I just heard a strange voice going up and coming down the stairs.

"What?" Charles asked.

"A strange voice. It was so real sounding Charlies."

"Honey, you are just tired and need to rest. I'm sure it's just your imagination"

"Well, I know one thing for sure, this house is very cold. Please go down to the basement and check the furnace."

Charles agreed and went to the basement to check out the old furnace. Allison picked up a load of towels and washcloths and started up the stairs again. This time the voice was louder. She raised her arms completely shocked and the towels and was clothes fell over the banister rail to the floor below. She looked around and then at the towels and wash cloths on the floor below. She then screamed for Charles.

Charles heard her and ran back upstairs to find her shaking and looking at the towels and washcloths lying on the floor below.

"Charles, I want to leave this place," she said as she pointed down at the pile of towels and washcloths. "This house is haunted, and I do not want to live here."

Charles and Allison had been married for just a year and were planning on having a family very soon. In fact, Allison was expecting her first child in three months. They had wanted to have a large older home to raise their family with lots of room to romp and play. This old house had caught their eye, as they were house hunting. It was an old two story and needed a lot of repair. Charles had said that this was the type of fixer-upper house he really wanted. Allison was not too sure and after being there for just a few hours, she was pretty sure they had made a bad decision.

Charles knew he had to comfort his wife. After all, she was six months pregnant and did not need this kind of stress. He looked at the towels and washcloths then back at Allison. "Honey just remain calm. There has to be a logical reason for this." He took her in his arms and held her close.

Allison began to cry as she continued to tremble with fear. Charles continued to hold her and rubbed her back with one hand. "We just need to sit down and talk. Okay?"

They sat down on an old trunk in the hallway at the top of the stairs. It had a flat top and would make a nice coffee table; Allison had thought when she first saw it. Now sitting there with Charles, she wasn't thinking about how nice it was. Her thoughts were about leaving this place. She knew Charles thought it was just an accident, but she knew what had happened. She thought something or someone had jerked the towels and washcloths out of her arms. She wasn't sure, but it sure seemed like something did it.

Charles waited until she seemed to be back to normal then said, "Honey, do you mind if I go back to check on the furnace? I was just about to get it going when you called me."

Allison looked into his eyes and said, "Sure, I'll be okay now. But please stay no longer than you have to."

After Charles had descended the stairs, Allison stood up and turned to look at the old trunk they had been sitting on. She opened it and found a small book. It appeared to be a child's diary. Samantha was the name on the front cover. As Allison opened the diary a picture fell to the floor. She picked it up and could not believe her eyes. It was a picture of her as a child. Running down the stairs, she called to Charles, "Honey, come here quick."

Charles was just coming up the basement stairs. "What is it", he asked, concerned that she had had another experience with the unknown.

"Honey look at this. This looks like me when I was about eight or nine years old."

Charles took the picture and said, "Really?" Charles had not seen any pictures of Allison as a child. He took a few seconds to look at the picture. Then said, "Allison, I know all of these events are upsetting to you and I'm sorry." He hesitated then handed the picture back to her. "Why don't we try to get some rest tonight and discuss this in the morning when we are not so exhausted. Maybe you can have one of your sweet dreams.

Allison knew he was right and agreed. She thought maybe it would be better tomorrow. Anyway, they would be more rested. She did plan to talk with Charles about leaving this place. She had a bad feeling about this old house. They both went to bed and were both soon asleep.

The first night in the old house was not a good one for Allison. She thought she heard a voice. "You and your baby will never see each other if you continue to stay in this house," Alison had always had dreams and wondered if she dreaming now or actually hearing the voices.

It was a beautiful day the start of the first full day in their old house. Allison looked for the coffee and pot in the boxes they had stacked in the kitchen floor. A good cup would sure taste good now, she thought.

Charles came down from the bedroom and saw her looking for the coffee and pot. "Allison, I have already made coffee" he said.

She looked at him with sleepy eyes and said, "Oh, really? How long have you been up"?

"About two hours. I have also made some breakfast for us."

She knew this was not the best time to talk about leaving the house. After all, he had made breakfast for her. She would wait until later in the morning to talk about leaving. After breakfast, Charles cleaned his plate and went to check out some of the boxes. Allison also looked through some boxes and found and old picture of her when she was young. How she looked like the picture she had found was so unreal. She calls out to Charles.

"Honey, come here and look at this."

"What is it, Allison?"

"This picture, I can't believe I looked so much like this little girl."

"Yes, that is very strange that you could look so much like her when you were younger."

"Let me get that diary and do some more reading." She was becoming excited. Charles thought to himself, "I wish she could get this off of her mind."

"Look Charles, there is a lot more in this diary than we first thought. Listen to this." Allison read from the diary, "I tried to warn Samantha about the stairs, but she would not listen. She was very head strong and did not listen to anyone." Allison looked up from the diary and said, "Charles, who is writing this part? This is someone writing in Samantha's diary...who could it be?"

Charles thought to himself, this is strange; however, I do not want to upset her more. "Oh, honey, you know how little girls are, she probably wrote that herself". Allison knew that this had to be written by someone or something, but what or who? Allison continued to read. In the first few pages of the diary, Samantha is talking about hearing voices. She has told her mother and Dad about hearing voices on the stairs, but they do not believe her. Samantha writes, "I am afraid to go upstairs because of the voices. Mother has agreed to let me sleep downstairs and I have not been upstairs for three months now. Who can I trust and whom can I talk with about this?" Allison flips through the pages and finds this passage. "Today, I did ask the voices to talk to me and they did. Now, I wonder if I am losing my mind. I am only eight years old. The main voice is a man's voice and very deep. He told me that I would live forever through others that would move into this house. What could this mean? Am I going to die soon?"

Allison dropped the diary and stared into space. The voice she heard is real. She knows now for sure. This makes her want to stay on and learn what really happen to Samantha. What about the neighbors? Could they have some answers?

The doorbell rang and brought her back to reality. Standing in the door is a very small old black lady. At first Allison was somewhat concerned, but it appeared that she was harmless.

"Good morning". The little lady said with a smile. "My name is Ida. I assume that you are the new owners of this fine old house."

"Yes." Allison said with a warm smile and then said, "My name is Allison Robinson."

"Well, I know all of the history of this old place."

Allison thought to herself, this could be very interesting. "I do have a lot of questions already about this place. Please come in out of the cold air."

Ida came in and slowly looked around the room, her eyes stopping at the staircase.

Allison noticed this and wondered if Ida knew about the voices. "Come in and we will have some coffee." Allison said with a smile.

"Thanks," Ida smiled also. "Not much been done to this old place in years. I seen it all from the early days. My best friend lived here when I was a little girl."

Allison thought this must be Samantha as she asked, "What was your friend's name?" Allison knows the answer before she hears Ida confirms it.

"Sammy. I called her Sammy. Her real name was Samantha. Pretty, she was, and I loved her." Ida looked at the floor and said nothing for a few seconds. Then she looked up at Allison and said, 'You gonna stay here?"

"Why do you ask," Allison asked with a raised eyebrow.

Ida wondered if Allison knew anything about the house and Sammy and said, "Well, you know, sometimes people just don't like a place for some reason or another."

"You know, Ida I have already thought about not staying here. But something happened this morning that changed my mind. Tell me about your friend Sammy."

"That was a long time ago. We were both the same age and went everywhere together. Sammy has an older brother. His name is Bill."

"Is he still around here?" Allison asked.

21

"Yes, Bill is here more than I want him to be."

"Oh, really, and why is that?"

"First, let me tell you more about Sammy. She died you know."

"Yes, I do know." Allison said. "I also think I know how she died. I found a diary in the attic with a lot of interesting information."

"Was it about the voices?" Ida said

"You have heard the voices?"

"Yes," as I was going upstairs last evening, I heard a voice telling me to avoid the stairs."

"And what did they say Allison?"

"They said, slow down and they said I could lose my baby and other things."

"Did you tell your husband?"

"Yes, but he thinks it's just my imagination. Did Sammy die here.... here on those stairs?"

"Yes, but that was just the beginning of Sammy." Ida looked very tired. "I am not sure we should continue this conversation."

Allison frowned and said, "But I need to know all about Sammy."

Ida sighed. "This is enough for today. I am old and very tired. I'll come tomorrow and we can talk more. Please understand, I must have my rest. It's getting late for me."

As Ida left, Allison wondered why early morning is late for her. Maybe she is just confused.

Charles and Allison spent the rest of the day unpacking boxes. Allison could not get Ida and Sammy off of her mind. What was the truth about these two little girls? Was Ida there when Sammy died? She had so many questions that she could hardly wait for Ida to return the next day.

Allison and Charles ordered a pizza that evening, as they were not in the mood to cook. When the delivery boy came with the pizza, he seemed to be afraid as he made the change from a twenty-dollar bill Charles had given him. He quickly ran to his car and drove away squealing his tires. Charles noticed this but said nothing to Allison about his behavior. The second night in the house was more relaxed and Allison was able to fall asleep as soon as her head hit her pillow.

Morning came with a loud banging at the front door. Yes, it was Ida. It was 5:30 A.M. when Charles opened the door and looked at the small lady wondering why she would be up so early.

"Good morning" Ida said with cheerful voice. "Is your sweet wife up and making breakfast?"

"No, we are a little tired this morning, please come in."

Ida went directly into the kitchen and started making coffee. "Got any bacon and eggs?" she called out to the open room.

By this time, Allison was up and getting ready to come down to the kitchen. As she entered the kitchen, Ida said, "You know, you look like Sammy would look, if she had lived.

"Really?" Allison said, "I found a picture of Sammy and she did look like me when I was a child. Isn't that strange, Ida?"

"Child, it's not as strange as you may think. I have always known that you would come here someday."

Allison looked puzzled. "You knew that I would come here?"

"Well, you or someone like you. But you are the one. The one Sammy and I have been waiting for...Waiting for so many years."

As they sat eating their breakfast, Allison's mind was racing with all kinds of thoughts. "Can you stay and talk after we finish?"

Ida smiled and said, "Yes, that's why I'm here today. I have something to tell you that you will find very interesting...."

Allison sat very still and looked deeply into the little old ladies' brown eyes.

Ida began, "Honey, Sammy and I were as close as sisters when we grew up in this house. I made every step that Sammy made. She was sweet and most of all, she was my best friend. Sammy left here when she was a small girl. In fact, she was just nine years old. My Mother and Dad worked for Sammy's parents. My Mother was their maid and my dad was their handyman. We had live-in privileges. Our room was in the basement. Have you been in the basement yet?"

"No," Allison said as she warmed up both coffee cups.

"Well, the basement is divided into three rooms. My parents had one room to sleep in and I also had my own room. We used the other room for sitting. It was like a living room. I was born in this house, as was Sammy. Our birthdays are the same. I think that is why we were so close. Both of our parents thought we should be together as we were born on the same night within minutes of each other.

Sammy had the local doctor with her mother when she was born. My mother was in the basement with my Daddy helping. When we both were old enough to start to school, Sammy went to the local grade school just down the street, and I had to walk to the colored school three miles outside of the city limits. We only had one colored school in the county. This was the first time Sammy and I began to have some differences. She made new friends at her school and naturally, I met some new friends. This was the first time I had played with black kids like me. Living here with Sammy and her family, I never knew that there was any bias about races. I knew we were different and that my parents worked for Sammy's parents. But we were treated very well. We both finished the first grade and had the summer together, every day. We were both eight when we started in the second grade.

That is when Sammy started acting stranger and more distant to me. I thought she had friends at school that she cared for more than me. Sammy spent more time in her room in the afternoons after school. She made excuses not to play with me. I noticed one day that she had a new diary. I ask her about it and she said there were secrets that only she could know about. This is when I first heard about the voices."

Allison had sat there completely mesmerized. She blurted out to Ida, "And you heard them?"

"No, honey. This was when I heard Sammy one evening talking to someone that was not there. She was saying, please let me talk to you. I listen to you, why can't you listen to me? I was just coming up the hallway from the staircase with a load of laundry when I heard her. I stopped and gently pushed open her bedroom door. Are you alright Sammy? I asked her. She looked up from her desk and with tears in her sweet eyes said, "Ida, I need to talk to someone." That was when she told me about the voices. They were telling her things about her and the future of this old house, poor little thing. As I think back, we were both so very scared. I could tell that she was sure she had heard the voices. I told her that she must tell her parents. She was afraid they would not believe her. I left her room after about an hour and the next afternoon, I met her coming in from school and asked her if she had told her parents about the voices. She kicked a small clot of dirt in the yard and looked at me and said she did tell them. They had laughed and said that a lot of little girls her age have big imaginations. She sat on the porch and began to cry. Why don't they believe me, Ida? I put my arm around her and kissed her cheek. I believe you Sammy. We both sat staring out at the street as cars passed by, both wondering what we should do next.

"Sammy looked at me with her pretty blue eyes and said, will you talk to the voices with me, Ida? I was too afraid to answer, but I loved her so much I could not refuse her request. She asked me to come to her room that night, after everyone was asleep. We both agreed that eleven o'clock would be a good time. I crept up the stairs just minutes before the big hallway clock struck eleven. As I opened her door it just finished chiming. Sammy was up and dressed in her best Sunday dress. She asked me to come in and take a chair near her. This was the weirdest thing I had ever heard in my life. Sammy sat there in her fine clothes and asked the voices to please talk with her in my presence. For a minute or so, nothing happened. Then a very low and almost whisper like voice said, who is the black child? Sammy slowly reached across to me and put her hand on my shoulder and8 said, this is my best friend. Her name is Ida. Then more silence. We both sat and waited. "Sammy?" The voice questioned. Then Sammy said, "I'm here." The voice said again very softly. "Ida must be the only one to ever hear us. You must understand."

Sammy said, "I do and she will be the only one. Now, please tell us what this is all about."

The voice said, "You two will experience something that no one else will ever experience and for sure never believe. Sammy, your spirit will live on earth forever. You will take on different bodies, but your spirit will always remain the same. We will talk more about that a little later on. First, we must prepare you for your first life, as you know it...... to end."

Sammy and I looked at each other in disbelief. Sammy said, "Ida, I am going to die."

Before I could answer or comment, the voice said. "This is correct. You will die on your ninth birthday. As you know, this will be on August 10th, just before school starts."

We had just completed the second grade and it was now June 10th. Just two months until the dreadful day. Sammy and I both sat there in shock, not knowing what to say or to ask the voice.

Just then, the hallway clock struck twelve. We both knew that the voice was finished for the night. Sammy asked me to sleep with her. I understood as I was also afraid. We would tell our parents in the morning that we had stayed up late talking and that I fell asleep. After all, we had slept together before.

The next morning, we both awoke and looked at each other and wondered if we had both shared the same dream. Sammy spoke as I was just about to say the same thing. She said, "It was not a dream was it, Ida?"

I shook my head and said, "Sammy, I sure wished it was." We sat up in the bed and hugged for a few moments.

We both used Sammy's bathroom to freshen up, then went down to the kitchen where my mom was preparing breakfast. As we entered the kitchen, my mom, asked, what are you two doing up so early? We looked at the clock and it was only 5:30 A.M. Just couldn't sleep, I guess with a quick glance at mom. You two spend the night together? She knew by us arriving at the same time. We both answered yes in unison.

Well, after all, you are best friends. Come on now and you can help me set the table. Sammy, your mother and Dad will be coming down soon and will want some fresh coffee for sure.

Sammy asked me to join her family at the breakfast table. I had eaten with them on special occasions like birthdays and so, but never just a regular day. Sammy's mom smiled and said it would fine for me to join them. As we enjoyed the fine meal of eggs, biscuits, ham and gravy that my mom had prepared, Sammy and I could not take our eyes off of each other, both of us thinking the same thoughts. This was when I thought I could hear Sammy's voice in my head. I continued to look at her and wonder. Then she said in my mind, Ida I think I can communicate with you without talking. If you can hear what I am thinking now, put your fork in your water glass. I looked at her and slowly lowered my fork in my glass. She had a big smile and said to me in my mind. They are starting to prepare me for my next life. Sammy's Daddy looked over at us and said, you girls are very quiet this morning. I am surprised that you don't have more to talk about. I thought to myself, if he only knew."

Allison again looked directly in Ida's eyes and spoke. "I have heard the voices and you have said that you and Sammy had been waiting for me for a long time. This must mean that Sammy's spirit is in me."

Ida looked back at Allison and said, "Well, not exactly. The voices are trying to keep Sammy's sprit away from you. That is why they have been trying to get you to leave this house. Yes, you are the chosen one, but you will need my help to get Sammy's spirit to come into your body. That is why I am telling you all about how this started out. Now, honey, let me complete the story of Sammy so you will not only understand, but will want to be with Sammy and have her live in your mind and body."

All of this was so very hard for Allison to grasp. "Ida, I want to think all of this is true, but we are living in the twenty first century. It is 2002. These are stories like you read from a Stephen King novel or some Night Gallery episode with Rod Sterling."

"I understand, honey. I know all of this must be impossible to believe. I know, because, I went through this with Sammy when we first heard the voices and the things that actually happened, just like they told us they would. Is it okay to finish my story about Sammy? Or would you rather wait until tomorrow to give you some time to think about what we have talked about today?"

As Allison was about to answer, the phone rang. She excused herself and walked across the kitchen to the phone. It was her mother. Ida heard Allison say, "Well, we are so glad you are here. Okay, see you in fifteen minutes." Allison returned the phone to the cradle. "That was my mother. She and Dad have just arrived in town and are coming here to see our house. In fact, they will be staying a few days. She wants to help me get things set up. You know, a mother's way of giving a little advice without being too bossy."

Ida laughed. "All Mothers are alike. They all mean well. I hope you all enjoy their visit. However, we must continue our talk as soon as they are gone."

Allison held her hands on her face and said, "Oh yeah. Believe me, I can hardly wait. I am sorry this will delay our talk."

Ida left through the back door as she looked over her shoulder with her cute little smile. "Just remember, honey, they want you to leave. You know why now and you must not let them scare you. Okay?"

Allison smiled "I know and you can be sure I will not let that happen. See you soon."

Allison watched Ida as she crossed the back yard to her own little house. She thought, Ida has so much to tell and I need to know all that she has to share. I must now come back to reality and prepare to be with my parents.

Allison had been an only child and her parents had always been very involved in her life. She hoped that they would not cause problems between her and Charles. Charles had come from a very large family, four boys and three girls. His parents were not that involved with him. It made it hard for him to understand why her parents wanted to know so much about her everyday life. Anyway, they would be there in a few minutes and she needed to let Charles know they were coming and would probably stay a few days.

She found Charles in the basement, arranging his tools and work area that he was so very proud of. "Honey, my mother just called and she and Dad are in town and will be here in a few minutes." Charles looked up at his assortment of tools with a frown on his face. "But we are just moving in."

"I know," Allison said as she put an arm around him and gave him a kiss on the cheek. "They will only be here a few days."

"A few days? Allison, I just don't understand why they want to be so involved. Can you imagine my mom and dad coming here and staying a few days?"

"No, Charles. It is different with my parents."

"It sure is," Charles grunted as he pulled away from her embrace. "I think I need some fresh air. When they arrive, tell them I had to go to the market or hardware store." Charles stomped up the steps with each board creaking as he went to the top.

Allison stood there listing as Charles slammed the car door and backed out of the drive.

Just moments later, the doorbell rang. Allison thought, Mom and Dad are here. I must put on a happy face. We have a new place to live and a baby on the way. Why wouldn't I be a happy person right now?

One of the voices answered her mental question. "I can give you a reason or two. It doesn't matter what little old Ida says, we will get you out of here"

Allison looked around the empty room filled with boxes and Charles's tools. "You don't scare me now and you won't scare me later. I believe what Ida is telling me and I know I will get to meet Sammy."

The doorbell rang again. Allison rushed up the steps and skipped to the front door. Her mom and dad were all smiles as she opened the door.

"Our little girl." Her mom said as she held her close to her full body. Allison's Dad reached around her mom to pat her on her head.

"Please come in." Allison said as she hugged her dad. "It is so good to see you two."

"Where is that husband of yours Allison?" Her dad asked as he looked for an ashtray. Allison was never very pleased that her dad had continued to smoke, even after having bypass surgery just three years ago. "Dad, have you tried to stop that nasty habit?"

He laughed as he put out the cigarette in an empty flower pot. "Honey, I have smoked all of my life and I'm not dead yet."

"That's not funny, Daddy. I really worry about you."

"Well, you can rest assured that I will not smoke in your house." "Thanks, Daddy. You know with the baby coming and Charles.... You were asking about him. He had to go to the store. Hardware, I think. He is setting up a work shop in the basement and must need some more hangers or something. Come in the kitchen. I still have some coffee in the pot. One of our neighbors just left. We were having coffee."

"You have already met some neighbors. That's good, honey." Allison's mom said as she looked over the kitchen with an approving look. "I like this kitchen. It is so open and lets a lot of sunshine in." Allison's Dad took a sip of coffee and said, "We want to help you sweetie. Just tell your mom and me what you need us to do and we are here for you just as long as you need us."

Allison thought to herself. I'm glad Charles was not here to listen to that good news. "Well, Mom and Dad, you know, Charles and I have some time to get things set up and we don't want you to come here to work. A visit is fine, and we are both glad you could come to visit so soon."

Allison's parents were named Dick and Ruby, Dick and Ruby Howell. He was a retired insurance agent and had spent 37 years with State Farm. He and Ruby had been high school sweethearts, but only married after dating for over 10 years. He wanted to be financially secure before starting a family. He was twenty-eight and Ruby was twenty-seven when they married. Ten years later, Allison was born. She had been their total life and could not seem to give her the freedom she now needed in her life.

Dick announced that he would get the luggage and take it to their room. Allison showed Ruby the spare upstairs bedroom they would soon set up as a nursery. Ruby was very pleased to see that her little girl was having motherly feelings already.

"Allison, I know you are going to be a wonderful mother, honey."

"Well, I sure plan to be Mom."

Just then Dick came up stairs with a large bag and just behind him, Charles carrying two more. "Look who I found as I was unloading the car." Dick smiled as he nodded toward Charles. Charles came in and set the bags down and went directly to Ruby. "Welcome to our new, old house." They hugged as he looked over her shoulder at Allison and smiled. "This is where our new baby will live, Ruby."

"Yes, I know, Allison and I were just discussing that. It is so good to see you, Charles." Ruby said as she set one of the bags on the bed. "We have a house warming gift here for you two."

Charles and Allison both looked surprised as Ruby pulled out a large candy dish from the bag. "This dish." she explained, "is not for candy. This dish is for money.

Yes, money. This room would be a great place to keep it also. Dick and I want it to become a start for a college fund for the new baby. Piggy banks are so common. Everybody has one. This dish will be easy to use and you can always tell when it is full and take the money to the bank when it is full. Everyone that visits the nursery can drop some change, or bills in for the baby. Pretty neat? Huh?"

Charles and Allison both smiled. "Neat!" They both said in unison.

Allison and Ruby went to the kitchen to put up dishes and other items while Dick joined Charles in the basement to assist him is setting up his work shop. Needless to say, Charles would be much happier with Dick somewhere else. But, to keep peace in the family, he was kind to his father-in-law. Dick told Charles that he and Ruby had planned to take him and Allison out to dinner for the evening meal. It would be their choice. Charles thanked him and they went about setting up the work area.

Meanwhile, up in the kitchen, Ruby was thinking that her little girl was not acting like herself. "Honey, you seem preoccupied. Is there anything wrong?"

"No, Mom. I just have a lot on my mind with the house and the baby coming. I'm sorry if I am not good company."

"Oh, Allison, just being with you makes me happy. I just don't want anything to be wrong with you. Someday, you will understand that mothers have a way of knowing when things are not right with their children."

Allison thought, surely, she can't tell that I am upset about the voices. "Well, Mom, please believe me. I am okay...."

"You're Dad and I have planned to take you two out to dinner tonight. I am sure Dick is telling Charles about now. Where would you like to go? It will be yours to choose."

Allison said, "You all don't have to take us out. We can have something here."

"No, Allison, it's decided, just need to know where."

"Well, let Charles and me talk it over. Thanks, that is so sweet."

"We love you both and the little one in your tummy."

Allison and her mother hugged as Allison thought of her future and what must lay in store for her and her family.

O'Charley's was the final choice. The place was full and they had to take a table in the smoking section or wait for 90 minutes. It wasn't too bad and Dick announced that he would not take advantage and smoke at the table

Charles smiled and said, "Thanks, we appreciate it.'"

They had drinks for everyone except Allison. "No alcohol for me and the baby."

"Good decision, honey," Dick said as he took a sip of his Cutty Sark. Both Charles and Ruby were having Bud Lights. Allison sipped on a glass of water with lemon as she scanned the menu. "We must have at least two drinks to celebrate the new home," Dick said with a raised glass.

"Here, Here." Charles agreed.

Another round with Charles and Ruby changing to Cutty for their second drink. Allison looked at the three and said that she was hungry and it would be a good idea if they order and not consume so much alcohol.

Everyone agreed on the prime rib as it was the special of the evening. Dick and Charles agreed that a good piece of meat needs more scotch. After dinner and five scotches apiece, Charles and Dick were both beginning to talk louder than Allison or Ruby wanted them to. "Well, guys," Ruby said, "it's getting late and some of us may be thinking about going to bed. I sure know that I am."

Allison agreed and started to scoot her chair back as Charles reached for her arm.

"No, honey. This is the first time I have really enjoyed talking with Dick and I am not ready to go yet."

Dick and Ruby could both see that Allison was upset with Charles. Dick said, "Maybe we should go, as Allison needs her rest."

Charles glared at Dick and said, "Yeah, whatever the little girl wants. You two are nuts about her. After all, she is my wife and I should be the one to say when she needs her rest."

"Well, then, Charles," Ruby said with a stern look, "you need to say it."

Charles pushed back his chair knocking over his drink and shifting the table cloth to one side. "You two take your little girl home. I have some drinking to do and I would prefer to do it alone." He left going toward the men's room.

Dick and Ruby adjusted the table cloth as Allison spooned up the ice from Charles's drink. "Allison, I think we have upset Charles," Ruby said with tears in her eyes.

"Oh, Mom, we just need some space. A lot has happened in the last couple of days. I have an extra key to the house. I want you and Dad to go there and I will come later with Charles. We'll get a taxi." "Are you sure Honey?"

"Yes Mom… please."

Dick signed the credit card and kept his copy along with his card and helped Ruby from her seat. "We'll see you at home sweetie." They went to the parking lot.

Allison went and stood outside the Men's room. As Charles came out, she could see that he had been crying. "Let's go in the bar Charles. We need to talk and clear the air."

He put his arms around her and whispered, "I love you."

"I know you do, and I love you too."

In the bar Charles ordered another Cutty. Allison had more water with lemon. "Allison, it's just too soon for company."

"I know, Charles. They are my parents and I love them. I know they get on your nerves. I will ask them to leave tomorrow. Our relationship is more important to me than worrying about their feelings right now."

"Oh, Allison, you don't have to do that. I made a complete ass of myself tonight. I will apologize to both of them tomorrow morning."

"It's okay to apologize, but I *will* ask them to leave tomorrow. Now, let's talk about us and our future."

Charles looked at her lovingly and thought how lucky he was to have found her and to be having a baby with her.

"Charles, I want to talk with you about something and I want you to try to understand."

"Honey, I always try to understand."

"I know you do. But this is different."

"Okay, let's hear it. I promise to listen and try to understand."

"Well, you remember the other day when we moved in?"

"Yes."

"Well, I told you then about hearing some voices? Charles, are you listening?"

Charles took a large gulp from his scotch and raised his glass toward the barmaid. "Yes, I'm listing. I thought you said you were just tired and just thought you heard some voices."

"No, Charles. You said that I must be tired, but I did hear them. They asked me to leave our home, our home where we plan to raise our new baby."

Charles stirred his fresh drink with his index finger. "So, are you telling me that you believe the voices are telling you to leave?"

"Charles, honey, I am telling you that they did tell me to leave. And, you know Ida, the little black lady?"

"Yes, you know that I know her."

"Well, she knows about the voices."

"Now, wait, Allison…. You are saying that you and this little old black lady are hearing voices together. What does she drink or smoke?"

"Charles, you have had a few too many scotches. I think this is the wrong time to make you understand that I am telling the truth. Let's call a cab and go home."

"One more drink."

"No, Charles. Pay the barmaid and let's go."

Charles and Allison returned home to find the lights all out except the front porch light. Allison looked through her purse to locate the extra key. After entering the foyer, Allison heard a faint groan from upstairs. Her dad, she thought. His heart and the extra drinks and probably smoked on the way home. "I am going upstairs, Charles. Please be sure we are locked up before you come up."

"Okay, Allison."

Allison hurried up the stairs to hear Ruby saying, "Dick, it is just indigestion. Now try to go to sleep."

"I can't. I am to upset. I want to go home tomorrow. I don't think we are welcome here…"

Allison listened outside the door until they both were snoring just like they did when she lived at home.

The next morning, Dick and Ruby both seemed to be happy. Ruby had the coffee made when Charles and Allison came down. Black coffee sounded great to Charles. His head was not feeling too good and he still was a little fuzzy.

"Well," Dick said with a big grin, "We sure had some good prime rib last night."

Allison said, "We sure did Dad."

Charles sipped his coffee and wondered if he had prime rib also.

"You okay this morning, Charles?" Ruby asked.

"Oh, yeah, just a little tired and mostly hung over. Listen, folks, I am so sorry for my behavior last night. I am afraid I had too much scotch and for sure had too much to say."

"Hey, that's no problem. We have all been there, done that, Dick said with a grin. Say, Ruby and I are planning to leave today. I just remembered a meeting I had scheduled before we left and I really can't miss it."

"Are you sure, Daddy?" Allison asked. She had wondered how they were going to announce their departure. This was as good as any.

"Well, maybe next visit you can stay longer." Charles said as he poured another cup of coffee.

Soon after breakfast, Dick and Ruby were saying their goodbyes. It seemed strange to Allison that her parents could sense the need to leave at this time. She was, however, going to ask them to leave if they had not said they were going. It was good that she did not have to experience that. Things have a way of working out sometimes.

Allison now needed to work things out with her partner and lover. Charles probably did not remember their conversation in the bar last night. Maybe later this afternoon would be a good time to revisit this conversation.

The phone ringing startled Allison. It was Ida. "Honey, did I see your folks leaving? I'm not nosey, but I did see them loading bags and things."

"Yes, Ida. They decided to cut their visit short. My dad had an appointment he had forgotten."

"Well, that is better for us. Now I can come over and we can continue our conversation about.... "

Allison interrupted, "Ida, I think we need to wait a day or so. After all, you did agree to wait until my parents were gone and that would be a few days. Remember, Ida?"

"Yes, honey. But we must not wait too long."

"Okay. I will call you in the next day or so. Thanks for calling."

"Goodbye, honey."

Allison thought how she must have Charles included in this. It was going to be very hard to get him to listen to such a wild and crazy story. The diary…Sure. Allison had not finished reading it. Maybe it would help to convince her that Ida was telling the truth. She had it next to the night stand in their bedroom. No, it's not there. Where could it be? She could not remember taking it from the bedroom. Then she heard the voice again.

"We have other powers also, Allison. I bet you did not think about us being able to move things. Well, we can," the voice said with a silly giggle.

"So, you have hidden the diary. Is that what you mean?" Allison said with a frown on her face.

Hiding the diary was only a small thing. What Allison did not know was that they had also hidden Charles. And she was about to find out. After calling for him though out the house, Allison thought Charles had probably gone out to walk or just clear his mind from everything that had happened the last 24 hours.

When lunch time came and went, Allison was really worried about Charles. He wouldn't just leave and stay this long. It was then two in the afternoon. Where to look? She thought of Ida. Ida answered the phone on the first ring. "Hello... Ida, this is Allison. I, uh, well; I really don't know how to start..."

"What's the matter honey?" Ida asked with a soft voice.

"It's Charles... He's gone."

"What do you mean gone?"

"I mean he left this morning and I just thought he went for a walk or something, and he hasn't returned and it's two in the afternoon."

"Well, honey, do you remember me telling you that Sammy had a brother?"

"Yes, but what has that got to do with Charles?"

"Well, Billy. He likes to be called Bill, also left one day and never came back."

"Really, When?"

"Oh, it was a few years back now. I am not sure what year. But, honey, I know where he is and he talks to me all the time."

"You mean he moved away?"

"Well, no not exactly.... He's with *them*."

"Ida, what are you trying to tell me? This is getting too weird. I guess you want me to believe that Charles is with them, or whomever you are talking about."

"Well, honey, they can take anything or anybody they want."

"Ida...Who are you talking about?"

"Well, the voices, of course, Honey."

Allison stopped and held her forehead with her hand. Good Lord, she thought. They got the diary. Could they also have taken Charles? Allison's thoughts were interrupted by Ida.

"Allison, Allison, are you still there?"

"Yes... I was just thinking about what you just said. Why would they want Charles?"

"Well, honey, you must know the answer to that. They want to get you out of that house. This is just one way they will try to."

"You mean if I agree to leave, they would bring Charles back?"

"Maybe. They will let you know and probably tonight."

"Ida, could you come over now?"

"Sure, honey. I will be there in a flash."

Allison hung up the phone and placed her hands on her belly. She thought how she must keep her sanity and bring her first child in to this crazy life she was now forced to exist in.

Ida's small frame and big bright smile was standing at the back door looking through the glass. Allison motioned for her to come in.

"Come in, Ida. I will make us some coffee. Maybe a stiff drink would be better."

Ida said she would prefer the coffee. Allison knew she would not drink alcohol with her baby so close.

As they both sipped from their cups, Allison said, "Ida, I'm at your mercy. I have no idea what to do or how to react to this threat from the voices."

"Honey, I'm sure they will contact you tonight with an offer for you."

"You mean leave the house for Charles's safe return?"

"Yes, I'm sure this is what they will offer. But, honey, they won't harm Charles. They can't."

"What do you mean they can't?"

"Well, I guess they could if they wanted to, but they won't harm him. I know. Remember what I told you about Bill?"

"Yeah, Samantha's brother."

"Right. He's been gone for years and I still talk with him, most days."

"Just how do you talk with him?"

"His voice. Just like the voices. I can talk with him. Maybe he would talk to us now and let us know if Charles is with him."

"Ida, this is too bazaar."

"Well, let's try anyway, honey."

Ida sat very still and closed her eyes. She reached across the table for Allison's hand. Allison held Ida's small hand and waited. "Billy...Billy....Billy... I know you are there. You are always there. We have someone now that's with you, we think. His name is Charles Robinson. He and his wife, Allison have bought your old home place. I haven't told you that anyone was living here, really had no reason to. Bill, we really need to hear from you. I have told Allison about our conversations. It's okay to talk."

Just as Allison was about to release her grip from Ida, Bill spoke. "He's here. He's with me. But he can't talk with you now. That will only come later. Ida, you remember how long it was before I could talk to you."

"Yes, Bill, I do." Ida said.

"Oh, Bill, I'm Allison, you don't know me. But I am a nice person and I love my husband. Is he all right?"

Silence for a few seconds, then, "Yes," Bill said.

"Can you tell him that you are talking with me, us?"

"Yes."

Ida and Allison waited for several more seconds before Bill spoke again. "Your husband, Charles is all right. I have told him that I can talk with you. He's not sure about what I am telling him. Tell me something that will prove that I am actually talking with his wife."

Allison thought then said, "tell Charles that the first time we kissed was on my front porch and it was June 21st... 9:30 at night."

After a few seconds, Bill said, "Now we have connected. He knows that I am actually talking with you. I'll try to help him adjust. Don't worry about your husband, Allison. My time is up and I mus..."

"Bill, Bill." Allison was frantic. "Are you there?"

"Allison," Ida held her hand. "I forgot to tell you. Bill can only talk for five minutes per day. It don't matter what time of the day, just five minutes each day. We can contact him again tomorrow."

Ida looked into Allison's frightened eyes. "Well, honey, you know now that Charles is okay and that the voices have him."

Allison was starting to cry as she said, "Well, naturally, I'm glad to know that he's all right, but I am not happy about where he is."

Ida looked at Allison with her dark brown eyes and said, "We must have a plan. I have been around the voices for many years, and I understand how they think. We have until at least midnight before we can talk with Bill again. This would be a good time to tell you the rest of the story about Sammy." Allison thought what else can I do? May as well listen and hope to better understand the truth about Samantha.

Ida poured both cups full and sat down at the kitchen table. "Honey, when we last talked, I was telling you about Sammy's spirit and how it needs to come to you and be a part of you."

"Yes, I remember. I remember, but it is so unreal. Again, this is like a novel you read. Not real life."

"I know, Honey. It seems unreal, but I know it's true and you have had enough things to happen to you in the few days you have been here to start believing also."

Allison knew that Ida was right. How could she not believe? "Well, okay, Ida. Let's continue."

Ida smiled and put a spoon of sugar in her coffee. "The voices continued to talk with Sammy and me. We were both nine years old when they took Sammy. They made it look like she died. The voices were very smart. You know, the first time you heard the voices was on the stairs."

Allison agreed and said that was her first encounter.

"Well, honey, that is where Sammy died."

Allison said, "I thought from the diary that she died from a fall from the stairs."

"Well, that's right. We had both been playing in the attic on a Sunday afternoon. It was her ninth birthday. Sammy had her diary like always. She had made a lot of notes about the voices and what they had said to her. We had both heard the voices in the attic and they were

47

telling Sammy that it was time for her to join them. We were both very afraid. One of the voices said to me, Sammy can't hear us, only you. We let you know about us and now you must never tell anyone about us. Today, we are going to take Sammy with us. After she is gone, if you tell anyone about us, we will kill your mother and Daddy. The voice was very strong and made me repeat what it had said, in my mind. As I sat there with Sammy, I couldn't tell her about the voices saying they would kill my parents. We sat and talked a few minutes more, then, Sammy looked at me and said, I love you Ida and I don't want to leave you. I told her that I loved her too. Just then, we heard Sammy's Mother call us for dinner. It was going to be a birthday dinner; we were both excited. We both jumped up at the sound of her mother's voice. I can remember Sammy leaving her diary on the old sewing table as we both darted out the door toward the stairs. We were both laughing and racing toward the staircase. We knew this was the fatal day, but it seemed like things were going to be okay. But they weren't. As we reached the top step, Sammy stopped and looked at me with a sweet smile. That was the last time I saw her alive."

"She jumped on the banister rail and dove head first to the parlor floor below. She made no sound of any kind. My screams were enough for both of us. Everyone came running from the dining room, her parents, my parents and Bill. I was frozen at the top of the stairs, staring in disbelief, her small body lying in a puddle of blood. She had died instantly. Billy was the first to reach her. He spoke to her in a soft voice and spoke. Yes, I understand.

I didn't know then, but he was hearing one of the voices. I thought, it could not have been Sammy. She was dead. Everyone was crying. Her daddy called the doctor. He came very quickly as they only lived a few doors down the street. Everyone knew it was too late, but the doctor made it official. Her neck was broken and her skull fractured. In those days, many people had the bodies of loved ones at the home. Sammy was laid out in a beautiful pink dress with white ruffles around the neck and cuffs. Her head was covered at the fracture point. She looked like she was asleep. All of the neighbors came. People sat up late that night. My parents made me go to bed at ten."

"Late in the night, I got up and crept upstairs to the parlor where Sammy was laid out. I made sure no one was around. I tip toed over to the casket. A small lamp was left on to give a very low light in the room. I reached into the casket and placed my hand on Sammy's cheek. I love you Sammy, I said to her in a whisper. Just then, Sammy's voice said to me. I know you do Ida and I love you too. It was strange. I was not afraid. It was like I had expected to hear her voice. I thought it was just my mind repeating the many times we had both told each other those words. Then, Sammy's voice said, Ida, it's not your mind playing tricks. I can actually hear you and talk with you. I will always be able to talk with you and only you. The voices have me now and I am trapped here. I must believe that you will someday help me get back to you and my people."

Ida looked up at Allison and said, "I felt that this would be my life's goal and for all of these many years, I have worked to get Sammy back. Bill was my first attempt and they took him and would have killed my parents if they had not already been dead."

Allison was on the edge of her chair staring at Ida. "So, you and Bill tried to get Sammy back."

"That's right, Honey. For years, I would talk with Sammy and Bill. Bill was beginning to learn more of the story and why the voices wanted Sammy. They finally realized that Bill and I were trying to trick them into returning Sammy. We did learn that a chosen person would be the instrument needed to get her back. We just did not know who or when the person would appear."

Allison smiled as she said, "And you think I am that person?"

"Honey, I know you are that person. Others have lived in this house and nothing has happened to them. They stayed a few years and then moved on. You are here a few days and look what has happened. You are the one that will get Sammy, Bill and your Charles back. And, honey, that will be a happy day for all of us."

The phone rang and stopped Ida from continuing. It was Ruby. She and Dick were home. Just wanted to let Allison know they had arrived safely. Ida listened as Allison told them that they were both fine and that she would be sure to say hello to Charles for them.

Things were not fine for the Robinson family. In fact, Allison was thinking about calling someone to report the strange behavior she had experienced in the last few days. But, who would she call, or better yet, who would believe her?

Ida was looking at Allison with a very concerned look on her face. "Allison," she said, "I know you must be having many thoughts now about all that has happened to you. Honey, these next few days are going to be very difficult for both of us. We must not lose control of our thinking. This is truly the first time we have had the opportunity to get Sammy back. Not to mention your Charles and of course, Bill."

Allison sat in silence for most of a minute. Then she looked at Ida and said, "Well, it's for sure, things can't get much worse."

Ida smiled and patted Allison on the arm. "Now, that's the spirit, Honey, we must stick together and work this out as a team. Ida suggested that they both get some rest and get a fresh start in the morning.

Allison agreed. Allison stood at the back door and watched Ida walk across her back yard to her small house. She watched to see the light on the back porch go out and was sure Ida was inside safely. Allison thought, sleeping tonight would not be easy. She was sure the voices would again visit her sometime during the night. She decided that a glass of wine would relax her, knowing the risk with the baby in her tummy. Surely, one glass would not hurt her or the baby. It tasted good and the warm feeling after the first drink made her feel it was okay. Setting in the parlor seemed very comforting to Allison. She knew that this was the house where Samantha had died many years ago. As she slowly sipped the wine, she closed her eyes and tried to think how Samantha and Ida must have had such great times in this old house. The wine was making Allison very relaxed and sleepy. It was just as she was beginning to fall asleep that she heard a very sweet voice. The voice was not like the others she had heard. It seemed to be of her own, but yet different.

"Allison, Oh, Allison. How long I have waited to talk with you. Please do not be afraid. I am, and will always be your closest friend and will love you when no one else will."

Allison sat very still, thinking, could this be Samantha talking to her? She took another sip of the wine. Feeling more relaxed and somewhat bold, she said out loud, "Is that you Samantha?"

The room was silent, only the ticking of the large clock in the hallway. Allison smiled and thought, I am so very tired. I must be thinking I am hearing Samantha. She started to get up from her chair when the voice again said, "Please relax. I will not harm you. I love you and will always protect you. Yes, this is Samantha. I do not want to scare you. I know this has to be so very difficult for you to understand. But, please listen. I have some instructions for you that will help both of us. Do you understand?"

Allison looked around the room, searching for the location of Samantha's voice.

"Allison, you cannot see me. I am in your mind. No one else can hear me just you. I can hear your thoughts. You don't even have to talk to me, just think. Isn't that neat?"

"You do hear my thoughts, Samantha, I know it."

"That's true, sweetie, now let me tell you some things that will help us." Allison sat in silence.

Samantha began, "I have been gone for many years. Ida has told you a lot about my growing up in this old house and the things we shared together. Now, I want to tell you why the things happened and what the voices want from me. Please try to listen to what I am telling you and give me time to explain to you before you start asking questions. Will you do this, Allison?"

Allison smiled and said in her mind to Samantha that she would.

"Okay, honey. Now this is going to be a very bazaar story. As you know, I was born in this house. My being born here is the reason the voices think I belong to them. So, now I have my real first chance to return home to Ida and you. You are my ticket. Your Charles and my brother, Bill will also have this chance. This chance will only come once and with only with one person. Allison, you know now that you are that person. You have the ability to fool the voices. You have the ability to get all three of us back. This is the part that you will not want to hear. Please, please, let me tell you what has to happen and why you must do it. Your baby... Your unborn baby is the key that will open the door to release us."

Allison could not hold her thoughts... "Samantha, I have been through too much since moving into this strange old house. I will not, in any way, consider my baby as a part of this crazy plan."

"But, Allison..."

"No but Allison, Samantha. I am firm on this. So don't ask."

"Well, honey, don't you want to just hear what the child would have to do?"

"No, No, No. A thousand times no."

Samantha then spoke very slowly and softly. "I have the power to talk to your mind as I am doing now, and I am going to tell you. I would feel better though if you would just agree to listen."

"You are right, Samantha. I will have to listen, but I do not have to act." Allison sat with her arms folded and her lower lip sticking out.

"Okay, fine. Now, Allison...Your baby will be born on Saturday, June 21st in this house. This will be exactly 50 years to the day since I was born in this house. The voices have told me that a replacement child could take my place if it came exactly fifty years from my own birth. All they want to hear is a commitment from you that they can have your baby. You tell them that, the moment it comes out of your tummy. They will believe you and it will be their plan to take the child when she is nine years old."

Allison looked around the room with a shocked look. "You said she?"

"Yes, Allison. You will have a girl and she will look like us. But listen... Nine years is a long time and we will have time to change the future. So, you see, all you have to do on June 21st is agree to give them your child. If you do this, we will all be back with you and Ida. Now, Allison, you know this is what must be done. Just think, Charles will be back with you, and your family will be complete. You and I will have the opportunity to know each other and life will be wonderful."

Allison sat there looking at the pale blue wallpapered wall. "Now, Samantha, I do want to talk and I do want to ask questions.... First of all, I have no intentions of giving up my first born for any cause. I love Charles and want him back more that I can tell, or put into words. If I never get Charles, well, I will someday find someone else and go on with my life. I will have my baby...daughter as you say. As for you, my strange invisible friend, I don't know you and really don't want to know you. As for the crazy little lady next door, I'm not sure how I feel about her. She has tried to help me the best she knows how. But, the bottom line for me, Samantha, is you can forget about any of this happening as long as I am in my right mind."

"Allison, your mind will change. It will take some time and you will come to see that you have no other choice. The pressure from the voices has only begun. They will work on you day and night. I am sure you wonder why they are not hearing us now. Well, believe me, if I thought they could hear us, I would not have told you all that I have. I have a safe place, Allison. This is the one freedom they gave me. I can go to my safe place once per day and no one that I don't want to hear can hear."

"Is this true with Charles also?"

"Not yet, Allison. If you remember, Charles had to talk through my brother, Bill."

"Oh yes, I remember. Then, Charles will have a safe place soon and will be able to talk with me?"

"Maybe, maybe not. The voices are going to start talking more to you and will ask about the baby. If you seem to not be at all interested in discussing the future of the child, they could keep Charles from talking to you, forever. I told you, Allison; it will get worse, much worse if the voices think you do not want to cooperate with them. Honey, you have a lot to think about and it is getting late. I think you should go to bed and get some rest. The voices will start early tomorrow. They cannot hear me talk with you, but they are sure we will talk or have been talking."

Silence again filled the parlor. Allison sat alone, thinking, someone or something must be hearing my thoughts right now. "Oh, God, please help me."

Allison awoke with a start. Where was she? Looking around, she could see that she had fallen asleep in the parlor floor. She was sore and tired from lying on the hard floor all night. Moaning, she rose up on one elbow and pushed herself up to a setting position. How could anyone have gotten into this?

"Well," a voice in her head said, "Honey, you can get out of it very easily." It was one of the voices. "Allison, all you have to do is leave this house and never come back. You will have your husband and baby all to yourself."

Allison tried not to think, but it was hard. She knew they could read her thoughts.

"That's right, Allison. And we are reading them as you are thinking. How about sweet little Samantha? Have you been talking to her?" Allison spoke out loud. "NO. No, I haven't talk to her." "Well, if you haven't, it is for sure you will, and we will find out when you do and what you talk about.

Allison slowly rose to her feet and walked slowly toward the bathroom. After relieving herself, she stepped into the shower. As the warm water showered over her face and body, she heard Samantha's voice.

"Allison, I had forgotten about the shower. This is another place the voices cannot hear our thoughts. You can think and talk with me anytime you are in here. They can't see you anyway, so, they never know if you are just not thinking or maybe asleep."

Allison thought, I hope this is true."

Samantha said, "Honey, it is true."

"Do I have to have the water running?" Allison asked.

"No, it is the walls in the bathroom. When it was build, the original owner had lead sheets installed much like x-ray rooms are built. He thought the lead would be sound proof for the bathroom. Maybe it does. Anyway, it works now for you and me."

"I'm so glad I remembered this. Now, let's talk about our future."

"Samantha, I must eat and get some rest before talking any more. I am eating for two, you know. And, I need more rest these days. Last night on that hard floor about did me in."

"I understand, Allison." Samantha's voice was a little curt. "After you have had your rest, let's meet here again in the afternoon. Say, 4:00 PM?"

Allison was finishing her shower as she reached for the towel; she smiled into the empty bath room and said, "Okay, I'll be here."

Allison made a pot of coffee and hoped it would help her dull headache from the wine and lack of sleep. A knock at the back door was her expected visit from Ida.

Ida was smiling as she entered the kitchen. "Honey, let me fix you some breakfast. You look like something the dogs' drug in."

Allison smiled at her comment. "It's just about how I feel also, Ida." Allison wanted to tell Ida about her conversation with Samantha, but knew the voices would hear. Allison made a mistake by thinking about telling Ida. The voices laughed.

"We told you that we would find out when you talked with Samantha." Allison put her face in her hands and sobbed. Ida put an arm around her shoulder and said, "It's okay, honey. You are just too tired and need to get some rest."

Allison looked up at Ida and said, "I am tired, but the voices...."

"I know, child. They are going to be with you from now own."

"Ida, I talked with Samantha."

Ida dropped the glass of orange juice she had just poured for Allison.

"You what?"

"It's true, Ida. Samantha talked with me last night and this morning.... and the voices, they know now. One just told me because I was thinking about telling you and they read my thoughts."

"Allison, this is not good. I am afraid that the voices will be very angry with you." "They didn't know that I can talk with Sammy. It is different with me, Ida. I must have a special connection with Samantha."

"More than you know, Honey. I am sure Samantha will tell you why also."

Allison looked at Ida, "And you know why don't you?" Ida got the broom and dust pan to clean up the broken glass. As she swept up the pieces, she said, "maybe, maybe not. Anyway, Samantha is the one to tell you why your connection is so special."

"I know, Ida, you think I am Samantha's daughter. Well, I am not so sure about that. If Samantha is real and I do get to meet her, there are test, you know, like DNA to prove or disprove who the real parent is." Allison was finishing her breakfast and starting to take her plate to the sink.

One of the voices said in a very slow and low tone. "Allison, it is true, we are not happy with you talking with Samantha. However, now that you know what we want from you, it makes it easier to reach an agreement with you. At first, we were trying to get you to leave the house so your baby would not be born here. It's too late for you to leave now...Now that you have talked with Samantha, and you know what we want with your baby. You can stay and not have any problems with us."

Allison stared into space and thought, "You mean I can get Charles back and we can live here in peace?"

The voice sighed, "Well, yes. But it will take some time and a lot of commitment from you."

"You mean me agreeing to give you, my baby?"

"That's it, Allison. Now, it will be easy for you to agree with us. We know that you could lie to us. So, there will have to be conditions that you must meet."

"In other words," Allison said, "you want a guarantee?"

"Now, we are beginning to understand each other."

So, Allison thought, "if I do agree to these conditions, you will return Charles today?" The voice slowly began to hum as if it were thinking to itself. "I will have to discuss this with others and let you know later today."

Allison thought, "What others?"

"Oh, Allison, you must realize that there are others."

She had no private thoughts. It was so hard to remember this. Allison could feel her body shaking. It was Ida tugging on her arm.

"Allison, Allison, snap out of it, honey."

Allison looked at Ida with glazed eyes. "Oh, Ida, I have been with the voices."

"I know, Honey," Ida said as she handed Allison a new glass of orange juice. "Let's set down and discuss this Honey."

Allison looked at Ida and said, "Could we talk in the bathroom?"

Ida looked puzzled and said, "Well, I guess so." After closing the bathroom door, Allison sat on the commode and explained to Ida what Samantha had told her about the security of the bathroom.

It was time for Samantha to again enter the conversation. "Oh, this is so wonderful," Samantha said in an audible voice.

Allison looked at Ida and said, "Did she speak out loud?"

Ida smiled and said, "Yes, Honey. She can do this when she wants or needs to."

Samantha said, "It will be much easier to talk with each other this way. The voices still cannot hear."

Allison's head was spinning. Voices reading my mind, Samantha reading my mind. Now Samantha talking out loud.

"Well, Allison," Samantha started, "What did they say to you this morning?"

"They read my mind when I was thinking about telling Ida about you. So, I told Ida out loud and the voices then talked with me about my baby." Allison was running her fingers through her hair as she told Samantha these things.

"Allison, you must relax. We are very private here. Only you, Ida and I can hear what is being said."

Allison then continued, "They will talk with me again later today. I asked them if they would return Charles today if I agreed to their request."

Samantha's voice was stronger than Allison could imagine. "You only ask for the return of Charles? What about me? What about Bill?"

"Oh, Samantha, I just didn't think."

"Well, Allison, you must think. If you do not ask for my return and Bill's, they will have your baby and both of us also."

"They want a guarantee, Samantha." Allison said with her voice breaking with sobs.

"Of course, they do. How can they know that you will keep your word? Allison, I am the only one that can help you." Samantha said. "I have the power and knowledge."

Allison hesitated then said, "Somehow I get the feeling that all of this is just to get you back here and really you have no concern for me or my family."

"Allison, we all have to work together. Each person involved must be included in the switch."

Allison was wiping tears from her cheeks as she said, "you mean switch my baby for all of this?"

"Yes." Samantha said firmly. "That is the simple truth. Three lives for the promise of one baby. Allison, I told you in the parlor last night that you would not like this arrangement. But we can make it work. We must have a plan. Remember, they would not actually take the baby until she is nine years old."

Ida broke her silence. "Now, ladies, I have met and known both of you. Sammy, you know how much I love you and want you back. Allison, we have only just met, but I have grown to love you also. You two have not met. It is very interesting how much you are alike. Not only in looks, but your personality also. You are both head strong and stubborn. Ida placed her small foot on the edge of the bath tub and continued, "If we are to work this out for all of us, we must trust each other and not end up slugging it out."

Allison thought to herself, I would like to slug Samantha.

Samantha spoke out loud and said, "Maybe you will get the opportunity."

Allison said, "It is still hard to remember that you can hear all of my thoughts. Well, since you have all the knowledge and power, what do you think they will ask me to do as a guarantee?"

"I do know what they will want. I have one also. It is like a monitor. They will want to place a device in the baby that will allow them to track it anywhere in the world. So, if you and Charles should decide to move from this house, they will be able to find the baby when she is nine and becomes a part of them. The device will be removed from me when I am returned and placed in your baby while she is still in your womb. This has been happening for many years. My mother had the device placed in her and she never knew it. It is placed in some women when they are not pregnant. When they become pregnant. it attaches to the womb and baby."

Allison and Ida both stood looking at each other in total disbelief. Ida spoke, "Well, Allison, this sure has to be your decision. I can understand how you would not want to lose your first and only child."

Allison was staring at the floor as she slowly looked up at Ida. "Ida, a lot of things can happen in nine years. The voices also know that I will be trying to think of something over the next nine years."

It was Samantha speaking now, "Allison, that's the attitude you must take if your Charles, Bill and I are to be freed."

Allison was silent for several moments, then, "Samantha, do you think I could talk with the voices now, I mean, tonight and try to make a deal with them. Would they return you three if I agreed to have the devise implanted in me now?"

More silence. Then Samantha's voice was very slow and soft. "First of all, they are very smart and as you know can read your mind. So, if you try to lie to them, they will know. You must, always remember that. They know what you really think."

Allison thought before speaking again. "So, you are saying that if I am honest now, and tell them they can have the baby, they won't have any way to know how I may think or feel next week, next year or nine years from now."

Ida was watching Allison as she talked with Samantha. "Honey, I think you have a plan. I told you we must have a plan, remember?"

"Yes, Ida, I remember. So, what do you two ladies think? Will it work?"

Samantha spoke with much authority, "I know these voices and have been with them for forty-one years, or will be on the night you little girl is born. They would prefer to have new blood and a younger little girl. I told you that you have the ability to fool them and you must try to make it happen and tonight if possible."

Allison and Ida left the bathroom and returned to the kitchen.

"I'll make some more coffee for us, Allison." Ida said as she filled the pot at the sink.

Allison sat at the table and tried to gain control of her thoughts. She was thinking.... thinking.... thinking. Then, she heard them.

"Well, Allison seems you have been out of service. I guess you took a little nap. But you are awake now and

I can read your thoughts, seems like you are trying to convince yourself of something."

Ida could tell that Allison was being contacted by the voices, but made no comment. She put the coffee pot on the stove and left the room. Allison sat and waited. Then she had a strong thought for the voices. "You know how much I want my husband to return."

Then after several seconds, "Sure, we know, and we are sure that Samantha and Bill have asked you for their release also." Allison knew she had no other choice but to agree.

"You can read my thoughts and you know that is true. So, what can we do to bring all three back to this house?"

The voice laughed and then made a low moaning sound.

"You know what we want, and if we don't get what we want, then you can forget about seeing any of these three."

Allison decided to talk aloud. "Well, I want to tell you what I will do and I will say it out loud. My unborn child...."

The voice stopped her with, "Your unborn daughter!"

Allison continued. "Yes, my unborn daughter is the key to getting Charles, Bill and Samantha. I am telling you here tonight that I will agree to promise her to you, but you must wait until she is nine years old."

The voice was silent. Allison waited.

Ida came back into the room. The coffee was done and she went to the stove and brought two cups to the table. Allison was setting with her eyes closed. "Coffee? Honey."

She opened her eyes. "Yes, please." They both sat in silence and sipped their coffee.

Allison went to the kitchen cabinet and picked up a pad and pen. She wrote a note and slid it to Ida. It read, "Let's go to the bathroom."

Once in the bathroom Allison took a deep breath. "Oh, Ida, I offered by unborn daughter to them and they did not respond. What does this mean?"

Ida looked as surprised as Allison was feeling. Then she spoke. "Allison, don't be concerned. They want you to sweat. They will contact you tomorrow and will either agree or ask for more guarantees. They will contact you for sure. I must go as I have been out of their range too much today."

After Ida left Allison decided to take a nap and went upstairs to their bedroom. She was totally exhausted and hoped some rest would help her.

Allison had a hard time waking up. She could hear Charles's voice, but couldn't think straight. She opened her eyes and saw Charles standing over her and smiling. She rubbed her eyes and then looked around the room. She then sat up and opened her arms and said, "Oh, Charles you're here, you're here."

He sat down on the bed and took her in his arms and said, "Honey, sure I'm here. You have been sleeping for at least 12 hours. Did you have one of your dreams?"

She knew she had, but it all seemed so real. Then she knew it could not have been real. Charles was with her. She was so relieved. She kissed him and said, "Yes I did have a dream."

Charles smiled at her and said, "Maybe you could write a book about some of your dreams. The ones you have told me about were so real. Was this one like real life?"

"Well, it was different, but maybe someday I could write it down and maybe read it to our daughter."

"So, you think we are going to have a little girl?"

She smiled again and said, "Yes, I really believe it, Charles and I think I know what her name should be."

Charles smiled again and asked. "So, are you going to tell me what her name should be?"

She kissed him again and said, Samantha, her name should be Samantha."

Charles looked surprised as he said, "That's so strange, honey."

"Strange? Why do you think Samantha is a strange name?"

He smiled at her and said, "While you were sleeping our next-door neighbor came over to welcome us to the neighbor hood and her name is Samantha.

Big Brother

2020

They had been married since 1982 and no one knew their secret. Ronnie Jackson is the same age as his wife, Jennifer. They married after graduating from college. They had been high school sweethearts since the tenth grade. They both had applied to several universities and had been accepted by the same school. They were very pleased to be in the same college and continue their relationship. They had both agreed that they would marry someday, but wanted to have their educations behind them. In their second year of college, they moved into an apartment and lived together. They were living like a married couple and had used protection, but one time forgot. It only took this one time and they found themselves expecting a baby. They had many long discussions and finally agreed it was too soon for them to have a baby. When Jennifer started to show her baby bump, she took time off from school. Neither of their parents were planning to visit before next summer and this would give them enough time to have the baby and place it in an adoption clinic. It was all arranged and no one in either family knew of the birth. They never saw the baby, but Jennifer did ask about the sex and was told it was a boy and he was born on March 3, 1980. Jennifer went back to school and soon made up for her lost time.

Two years later, Ronnie and Jennifer graduated and like they had agreed, got married. They went back to their hometown and had a nice wedding with family from both sides attending. Jennifer's father gave the bride away and it was a beautiful ceremony. Ronnie had majored in chemistry and found a job working as a lab tech in the same city they had gone to school. Jennifer had gotten a nursing degree and was a register nurse working in the same hospital with Ronnie. They were very happy to be back in their old college town. After four years, it seemed like home to them.

Now, it was time to think about a baby. They both had thoughts about what they had done over three years ago, but remembered it had been their decision and must go on with their lives. Jennifer was pregnant again and this time looking forward to being a mother and Ronnie was just as happy knowing he would be a dad. It was a girl and they named her Jenny Anne. It was close to Jennifer's name, but still different. Jennifer took six months off from her job to spend this special time with their little girl. They also moved during her time off and was happy to have a family with a little boy next door. They were very nice people. Bill and Carol Simpson and their son William, Jr. Bill was an elementary school teacher and Carol was a stay-at-home mom. She was very dedicated to their little boy and wanted what was best for their only child.

Jennifer and Ronnie both felt very comfortable with Carol and decided to ask her to babysit their little girl, Jenny. Carol was pleased that they trusted her with their baby and did agree to take care of her after Jennifer went back to work. So, it was agreed and after little Jenny was six months old, she stayed with Carol during the day. Jennifer was lucky to continue with a day shift at the hospital and everything worked out fine for both families.

For the next ten years, both families had become very close. They had many meals together and had gone on vacations together. William was now thirteen and Jenny was ten. They had grown up together and were very close. Both families felt like the two were more like brother and sister than just neighbors. William was very protective of Jenny and was like a big brother to her.

After another five years, William was getting ready to graduate from high school and Jenny was in the tenth grade. William was very popular and a star basketball player. He had many girls wanting to date him, but he only had interest in Jenny, even though she was three years younger. He had even taken her to the senior prom. Some of his team mates had kidded him, saying he was robbing the cradle. He just laughed at them and said they had no idea about what true friendship meant. William received a full basketball scholarship at the local college. Jenny was so proud of her "Big Brother" as she sometime called him.

Jenny was now in the eleventh grade and had boys wanting to date her. She was sixteen and most girls started dating at that age. She had many requests for dates and refused them all. Like William, she knew who she wanted to be with. William's birthday was March 3rd and Jenny's was February 10th. Just a little over a month apart. Over the years, they had celebrated their birthdays together always between the two birthdates. On William's nineteenth birthday and Jenny's sixteenth birthday celebration, William took Jenny to dinner at one of the nicer local restaurants. They had always enjoyed talking with each other. On this night, they discussed how they had become so close over the years. They grew up in the same house with William's mom helping raise Jenny as well as her own son. They shared a love that no one could understand. Just like siblings. They were both an only child in their families and this made them feel even closer.

After the dinner, William ordered the house special for dessert, homemade banana pudding. They both loved banana pudding. As they enjoyed the dessert, Jenny asked William a question that he had really not thought about. She knew from talking with her mom, Jennifer, the nurse that she had been born in the same hospital where her mom worked. She had never asked William about his birth place.

After finishing her pudding, she said, "you know, William my mom has always told me about being born in the same hospital where she works." She smiled and then continued, "As much as we know about each other, I have never asked where you were born."

William smiled and pushed his empty dessert plate aside and said, "I really don't know where I was born." He had always kidded her and made jokes.

She thought this was another joke and said, "I know you were too young to remember... Right?"

William was not smiling then and said, "No, I'm not teasing you. I really don't know where I was born."

Jenny frowned and said, "How could you not know? Surely your mom and dad told you."

"Well, Jenny, they have never told me."

She thought he must be kidding. Everyone had been told where they were born. She started laughing and said, "William Simpson. You've had your fun, now tell me smarty pants."

"I was adopted here; I do know that."

Jenny sat with her mouth agape and staring at William. "You are serious, aren't you?"

"I am very serious, Jenny. My mom and dad told me when I was about seven years old. They didn't want me to find out from someone else. I don't feel different by being adopted. My parents could not love me more if I was their own child. My love for them could not be stronger in any way." He sat looking deeply into her pretty blue eyes. I hope that doesn't change the way you feel about me, Jenny."

Jenny's eyes were moist as she said, "William, there is nothing that could ever change the feelings I have for you. You know I love you and want to be with you. You

73

are my big brother, my protector and most of all my very best friend."

William reached across the table and took her hand and smiled. "You know I feel the same about you. But there is one thing you left out."

She had never felt the love she was having for him at that moment. Her eyes were filled with tears as she said, "And what did I leave out?"

"You could have said that you want to marry me some day."

They sat in silence for a long moment and continued to hold each other's hands and smile.

Jennifer had learned just a few months after they moved next to the Simpsons that William's birthday was the same month day and year, she and Ronnie had given up their baby boy for adoption and thought how ironic that was. She had always thought William was their natural born child and had no idea he had been adopted.

That was before Jenny came home from her birthday celebration dinner with William. It was just after eight that night and Ronnie and Jennifer were watching TV. Ronnie had an early morning the next day and after asking Jenny about her dinner, excused himself and went to bed.

Jenny sat on the couch next to her mom and kissed her on the cheek. Jennifer knew Jenny was happy and said, "You always have a fun time with your big brother, as you call him."

"Oh, mom I sure did. I learned something tonight that I knew nothing about. Maybe you did."

"And what was that Honey?"

Jenny frowned and said, "did you know William was adopted?"

Jennifer tried to not show her shock. She had always thought how ironic it was that William was born on the same day, month and year as her first-born baby boy she and Ronnie had placed in the adopting agency. Could William actually be their child? She sat in complete silence and stared at the coffee table in front of them.

Jenny couldn't imagine why her mom acted so strange. "Mom, what is it? It is a surprise to me too, but a lot of people are adopted."

Jennifer cleared her throat and looked at Jenny and said, "well, I guess I am just surprised like you were. Why did he tell you?

"We were just talking about growing up together and I told him how you had told me about being born where you now work."

Jennifer had to ask the next question but hoped the answer would not be what she suspected. "Did William know where he was adopted? Was it here in this town?"

Jenny smiled and said, "Yes, he said he was adopted here, but did not know if he was born here." She smiled and looked at her mother and then said, "It doesn't matter where he was born. I am so lucky to have him in my life. He is truly like a big brother to me."

Jennifer looked at her and thought he could really be her big brother.

Jennifer and Ronnie had always had many discussions on issues that involved both of them. They were very honest and open with each other and always reached an agreement. Jennifer thought of their discussion over nineteen years ago when they decided to give up their first child and wait to have a family after graduation. Now, she wondered if they had made the right decision, knowing what she knew now.

Jennifer waited until the next afternoon when they were home alone. Jenny had gone to a friend's house to spend the night. This was a perfect time to tell Ronnie what she had learned the night before. They had a simple dinner of soup and half sandwiches with water. They always had a light dinner.

After clearing the table, Ronnie started to go to the den to watch the news and she called to him. "Honey, wait a minute. We need to talk."

Ronnie turned and said, "Talk? We just talked during dinner."

She smiled and said, "I know, but this is important, okay?"

He pulled out the chair he had just been sitting in a minute ago. "Okay, you look so serious now. You were just smiling before."

After they both sat for a few seconds Jennifer said, "I don't know where to start." She closed her eyes and when she opened them, they were very wet with tears. "Ronnie, I just learned last night that we may know where our son is." She waited as he stared at her.

His voice was just a whisper. "Our son? What in the world are you saying, Jennifer?"

She covered her face with both hands and sobbed.

He moved around to her and put his arm around her shoulder as she continued to cry.

She took a napkin from the table and wiped her eyes and said in a choked voice, "I think it could be William."

Before she could continue, he said, "Oh, Honey, we know he has the same date of birth, but he's Bill and Carol's son. Why could you think this?"

He was still standing next to her as she looked up at him and said, "He was adopted."

"Oh, Jennifer, how do you know? Did Bill or Carol tell you?"

"Jenny told me last night...William told her during their birthday celebration dinner."

Ronnie moved back to his chair and sat down. "You know how he likes to kid and joke with Jenny. He must be just having fun with her. He will probably tell the truth today."

Jennifer had not thought about that. William was a joker and maybe, just maybe he was kidding Jenny. She finally smiled and said, "Honey, I had never thought about it being a joke. You may be right.

"I'm sure I'm right, so please put this out of your mind. We both agreed over nineteen years ago and made the decision. I am sure we will never know where he is and I think that is the way it needs to be. It needs to remain our special secret.

She knew he was right and they both stood up and embraced. She said, "I'm sorry to upset you. I just thought..."

"It's okay, Honey. I'm sorry you were so upset. Now, let's relax and watch some TV."

They walked arm and arm to the den and relaxed in their recliners and watched a movie on Netflix.

No one had mentioned William's reported adoption since their last discussion and Jennifer had tried to put it out of her mind. She really wanted to know for sure and had a plan. She knew that DNA would confirm someone's true relationship with a relative. She felt like Ronnie did not believe William was adopted, but she needed proof. There are many ways to get a DNA sample and she wanted to get a good one. Most were gotten by a swab inside the mouth. There were others, like an item that was touched by the person in question. She thought, being a nurse, she could surely think of some reason to get a swab from William's mouth. Maybe she could tell him it was a new test for the flu or other viruses and also check Jenny just to make it more believable. She would think about it. They had never thought they would know the identity of their son until recently. There was no hurry. She must put her plan together and hopefully make it work.

Jenny had thought about what William had said to her at their birthday dinner and wondered if he really wanted to marry her someday. She had no doubt about her love for him, but really had not thought about marriage. She was now 16 and three more years of high school before graduation. She, like William, wanted to have a degree from college. She might want to be a nurse like her mom, but wasn't sure just yet. Where would William go after college? He would graduate from college the same time she graduated from high school. Did he expect her to go with him? She was sitting at her desk in her bedroom supposed to be studding for a history test the next day. She closed her eyes and tried to clear her mind of William and hopefully get her studies done.

William had also thought about their dinner and his almost proposal to Jenny. He smiled as he sat in his room and looked at his computer. He was also studding but Jenny kept coming back in his mind. He had always loved her, just like a big brother, as she had always called him. But now, it was different. His love had changed from being a brother to a lover. He knew he was truly in love with her, but wanted to make sure they did not move to fast toward marriage. He really didn't know if she wanted to marry him now, but he was planning to help her understand why they need to be together. He went back to his studies also.

Late in the night William awoke suddenly and could not get the question out of his mind about where he was born. Jenny has asked him and then said, "surely your mom and dad told you where you were born." He sat up and sat on his bed and rubbed his face with both hands. Why had he never asked his parents where he was born? He really had not thought about it, but now Jenny had made him wonder, want to know. He went to the bathroom and then back to bed. As he went back to sleep, he knew he was going to ask his mom in the morning.

He wasn't up as early as usual after being up during the night and did not have time to talk with his mom. He would have time in the afternoon.

It was just after 4 when he came home and found his mom in the kitchen. They hugged and she asked about his day. She was always happy to be with him and so very proud of her son.

He sat at the table and then asked if she had coffee made. She always had a pot warming. After filling his cup, he asked his mom to sit with him.

He looked at his mom over the cup of coffee and said, "I need to ask you a question about me."

She frowned. "A question about you?"

William laughed and said, "Well that sounded strange, I know." He paused and then continued. "You know, you and dad told me that you adopted me here in the city, but you never told me where I was actually born."

"William, I am surprised that you would bring this up now. You haven't asked before, why now?"

"It's Jenny."

"What do you mean, Jenny?"

He took a sip of his coffee and sat down his cup on the table. "She asked me at dinner the other night and I told her I didn't know. Will you tell me?"

She smiled and said, "Honey, it's no secret. You were born here in the General Hospital where Jenny's mom and dad work."

William sat in silence and then said, "Well, I haven't really wondered until Jenny asked me. Now, I do know and I can tell her."

"So, you must have told her about being adopted."

"Well, yes. That is okay with you, right Mom."

"It has never been a secret and you should feel free to tell anyone you want to tell. I know Jenny is very special to you as you are to her."

William thought if you only knew how much we mean to each other.

William now knew where he had been born and wanted to tell Jenny, but he also had another thought. He had heard about family members locating siblings and other members they never knew they had. Some of these people had searched on Facebook and others had used DNA to locate family members. Maybe, he could actually learn who his biological mother is, or was. He did not want his parents to know he was considering this. He knew they would not agree with his desire to find his real mother.

Then, he thought about Jennifer, Jenny's mom. She had been at the General hospital for many years and might have some knowledge of past births or could find records of births. He was going to ask her, but must have her agreement not to tell his parents. The big question was, how could he have a private discussion with Jennifer?

William knew how he could have some private time with Jennifer. He had just not thought about her running. She did run most evenings after dinner. Ronnie was not a runner and she was usually alone. She had encouraged him a few times, but had given up as he really did not like to run. William had joined her a few times and this would be a great way to be with her alone. He knew she usually took a short break at a city park a couple of miles from their home.

He wanted to be sure she would allow him to join her, so he called and she answered the phone. He hesitated and then said, "Miss Jennifer, it's William, uh I just wondered if I could join you in your run this evening."

She paused and wondered why he had called. He had joined her in the past as she passed their house. She cleared her throat and thought about him being adopted, if it was really true. "Sure, William. I was just getting my running shoes on. Are you ready now?"

William was so pleased. He smiled and said, "Yes mam, I'm ready. I'll be in the front yard."

They were soon jogging side by side and enjoying the evening breeze. After several minutes they arrived at the city park. There were water fountains and many picnic tables with benches. They both had a sip of water and then sat at one of the tables.

They were both a little out of breath, William more so than Jennifer. He looked into her pretty blue eyes and thought how much Jenny looked like her. He wanted to be careful and be sure he asks his question the right way. He looked away and then back at Jennifer and said, "I really need your advice."

"My advice?"

"Well, yes. I am sure Jenny has told you about me being adopted, right?"

Jennifer had not expected him to discuss this and looked shocked.

He noticed her expression and said, "She did tell you, didn't she?"

"Oh, yeah she did tell me, but Ronnie and I thought you must be kidding her."

He knew how everyone was aware of his kidding and having fun with everyone. "Miss Jennifer, I was not kidding. You can ask my mom and dad. They will confirm it. Jenny had asked where I was born and I had never known. Yesterday, mom told me that I was actually born in General Hospital."

Jennifer could not continue to look at him. She looked away and finally said, "Well, we had no idea. Your mom or dad had never mentioned it and we had just thought you were their natural born child."

"Well, now you know and I hope you believe me. Now, this brings me to my question for you." He paused again and looked into her eyes.

This was too much for her, but she had to know what on earth he could be wanting to ask her.

"First of all, I need you to promise not to tell my parents about my question for you."

"Well, I guess I'll have to know what the question is first. William, what on earth are you getting to?"

"I need to know if you think it is proper to try to find my biological mother. I have read about people finding siblings, cousins and even children and parents they had no idea they had. Some used Facebook and others used DNA and hospital records."

"So, you think I might have access to this information because I work at a hospital? Is that what you want to ask me?"

William smiled and said, "Well, yes. It took me a while to get there, but yes that is what I want to ask you." He paused and then held up a finger and said, "But I need your promise not to tell my parents."

Jennifer did understand why he would want to fine his birth mother, but she also knew she could be that birth mother. It had to be true now. Ronnie thought William was kidding, but he wasn't. He had been adopted. William was very serious and he had also told her that his parents would verify his adoption. Now he was waiting for her answer.

She reached for his hand and held it with a firm grip. "William, as you know, I have known you since you were three years old and you have been like a family member to us. You and Jenny are like brother and sister. I love you like you were my own, the same way you mom and dad love Jenny. Our families are so blessed to have this kind of relationship. So, to answer your question, I do understand that you could want to know who your birth mother is." She paused and released his hand and then continued. "However, there are many people who have no desire to learn who their biological parents are. I've known some who said they wanted to find out and after thinking about how it could affect their adoptive parents, decided against it. So, my advice to you is to wait. Bill and Carol love you just like real parents and even more than some real parents. You all are so blessed to have each other. You have gone all of these years without knowing. My advice to you is to wait, give it some thought and most of all time. I really believe your desire will go away with time." She looked away and then back at him and said, "And you have my word, my promise to never mention this to your parents."

They both stood up and William walked around the table with open arms and they held each other as he said, "Thank you, Miss Jennifer. You have given me so much relief. I really appreciate you taking time to explain this to me."

As they stood back, still look looking into each other's eyes Jennifer said, "I love you, William. You are like a big brother to Jenny and real son to me."

They continued the run and were soon back home. Both had dreams that night about the discussion, with William feeling at peace and Jennifer awoke from her dreams during the night knowing in her mind that William had to be her first-born child.

Jennifer had been with the hospital for over seventeen years and knew everyone there, but most of all the ones that were there when she first started. It had now been nineteen years since she gave birth there and there were four nurses who had been there over twenty years. They were all four there when she gave birth. She had always wondered if they had any idea that she had given birth there. She was only there one night and it wasn't likely that they would remember anyone that long ago and just overnight.

Mary Stevens was the oldest nurse at the hospital and she and Jennifer had become friends soon aster Jennifer started. Jennifer had learned so much from Mary and considered her to be her best friend at the hospital. They had discussed many patients and surgeries they had both been involved in. Mary had many stories about her early days and some were strange stories and some were funny.

It has been a few days since Jennifer's discussion with William and she could not get it out of her mind. She decided to very carefully ask Mary about birth records from the past. Mary had worked in records for a few years, but came back to the medical side. She really wanted to help people and not sit behind a desk all day recording files and history about patients.

So, at lunch Jennifer broached the subject about history records. Mary was surprised that she wanted to know about a patient's history. "Well, Jennifer, there are tons of records, and I'm sure some on everyone who was admitted here." She took a sip of her water and then asked, "Do you have a name? I can look up someone for you. They have no problem with me looking. After all I worked in there for a few years."

Jennifer wanted to ask, but wasn't sure how to without giving up her secret. She finally said, "Well, is there a way to check by date?"

"By date? What do you mean?"

Jennifer was more nervous than she could ever remember. Mary was her best and closest friend and she had never felt uneasy with her, until now. She cleared her throat and looked around the room and said, "Can you look up a date of births on a single day?"

"Jennifer, you look so concerned. Are you okay?"

She smiled and said, "Oh, yeah I'm okay. It's just…"

Mary was sure she wasn't okay, but didn't want to embarrass her. "Jennifer, we've been close friends ever since you started here. Fifteen or sixteen years ago."

"It's seventeen years, Mary."

"Okay, now you can ask me anything or tell me anything. You know that."…

Jennifer thought she could ask without involving herself by telling a little lie. "Well Mary, I have a friend who is trying to find out where her adopted son was born." She then looked at Mary and waited.

Mary smiled and said, "You would tell me if there is something wrong, right?"

Jennifer tried to control her expression and cleared her throat again and spoke. "Mary, you know I would."

"Okay, I believe you, Jennifer. Now, do you have a date of birth?"

Jennifer felt relieved for the first time since their conversation started. She smiled and said, "Yes, it's March 3, 1980."

"And you said it was a male?"

"Yes, a little boy. Can you find out without getting in trouble?"

"Jennifer, they never ask me what I'm looking for. I'm not scheduled for anything after lunch. I'll see what I can find and let you know."

Jennifer had no idea she would find out this soon. She didn't want to overreact but did give Mary a big smile and said, "Thanks, Mary, I appreciate this."

They both took their empty trays to the cafeteria window and left the room.

Jennifer went back to her station and was soon busy with a new patient and getting the patient ready for surgery.

Mary was in the records office and soon looking at birth dates on a computer. In 1980 all records were on paper and kept in file folders. Many had been transferred to the computer files, but March 3, 1980 had not been.

Her only choice was to go the file folders that were in file cabinets in the basement of the hospital. She hesitated and then asked the office manager if she could have access to the basement. She had no problem with Mary looking and gave her a key to the file room.

It was cold and dark after opening the door. She switched on the light and it was soon bright with florescent lighting. The files were in metal cabinets with dates marked on the front. She finally found 1980 cabinet and pulled open the drawer. The folders were marked with the month on the tab. She pulled out the March folder and then moved to the only desk in the room and opened the file.

There were more than births recorded. Some were surgeries and illness that required hospital stays. Then she found births. Births on March 3, 1980. They were all listed on one sheet of paper, neatly typed with name, weight and parents' names. There were two boys and one girl. All but one had names of parents. One male baby had been assigned to the local adoption agency. The birth mother had requested to remain anonymous. It was noted that the baby was taken by the adoptive parents the next morning after it was born the night before. She thought this must be the one Jennifer's friend was looking for.

As she started to place the form back in the folder, she noticed another small index card in the folder. She took the index card out and saw a man and woman's name with phone number. It was only first names, Bill and Carol. Then, she looked at the writing on the index card. It was her own handwriting. She closed her eyes and remembered. She had only been with the hospital for two years. She had started in 1978 and this baby boy was born in 1980. She had been given the first names and phone number of the adoptive parents and asked to call them. She had made that call as she was working that night. How could she have forgotten this. It had been nineteen years ago and she had seen many births during her career.

Then she thought about the young lady who had given birth. She only saw her for a few minutes and told her she had given birth to a boy. Anyway, she felt like this was the information Jennifer's friend needed.

It was usually after seven when they both left the hospital. All nurses worked 12-hour shifts, but only worked three days per week and were credited with 40 hours.

Jennifer saw her friend coming down the hall just before seven. They both smiled and both looked tired as they did most days. Mary had gone back to her station after her visit to the basement and Jennifer had gone to surgery with a patient and they were both ready to go home.

Jennifer looked up and down the hall and then asked, "Did you get a chance to look at the records?" She could tell by Mary's expression that she had.

"Well, yes I did and I have some names for you. Can you look now?"

"Oh, yeah I have already done my transfer with the night nurse. What did you find?"

Mary handed Jennifer the note with the two babies parents' names. Two boys sand a girl, but one boy had no parents' name.

Jennifer studied the names an did not recognize any. "So, these are the only two parents' names. The other boy had no parent name?"

Mary had made a separate note from the index card. She looked at her note and said, "No, but I think I may have found the one your friend is looking for, but it does not show the birth mother's name. In fact, she had requested to remain anonymous."

"So, is that all it says about the boy who was adopted?"

"Well, he was adopted and the birth mother was only here over night. The baby had already been assigned to the local adoption agency."

Jennifer could feel her pulse racing. This had to be her baby. "Is that all it said about him?"

"Well, it did mention the adoptive parent by first names only."

"Well, can you tell me the names?"

"Well, I can and I will, but first I need to share something with you."

Jennifer was getting more anxious as she stared at Mary. "Share something. You mean about the baby boy?"

Mary smiled and giggled softly. "The information I found about the names was in my own handwriting and I am the one who called the adoptive parents. I had forgotten all about that until I saw the names in my handwriting. Isn't that interesting?"

Jennifer could not wait any longer. "Mary, please tell me the names."

"Well, I'm going to tell you. I just thought it was strange that I was actually involved in the birth."

Jennifer knew she had no idea how this was affecting her. "It is strange, Mary." She frowned at her and waited.

Mary looked at the note she had made from the index card and said, "Their names are Bill and Carol."

Jennifer finally knew. This was the proof. William was her son. She had to get away for a moment. She thanked Mary and then said, "I'm sorry but I must go to the restroom." She walked very quickly down the hall to the lady's restroom.

Mary stood at the nurse station and wondered what was affecting Jennifer. She wanted this for a friend. Why did she seem so upset?"

Mary had waited long enough. It had been fifteen minutes. She went to the restroom and slowly opened the door. She could hear Jennifer softly sobbing. She was sitting on a toilet in an enclosed area.

After a few minutes Jennifer came out and went to the sink and filled her hands with water and tried to clear up her makeup she had smeared with her tears. She turned to Mary and said, "I'm sorry Mary."

Mary knew there had to be more to this than a friend's request to find out the birth mother of her adopted son. "Jennifer, we've been friends for many years and we know each other well. Now, I know there is more to this than you are telling me."

"You said you called the adoptive parents. Did you meet them?"

"No, they came the next morning and I was on the night shift then." She paused and then said, "I did see the birth mother for a few minutes and told her she had given birth to a boy. She wasn't concerned, but did want to know the sex."

Jennifer remembered being told she had given birth to a little boy, but she had been so heavily sedated could not remember who the nurse was. Now, she knew. She again stared at Mary and asked, "Was she a young girl? Do you remember what she looked like?"

Mary studied Jennifer's face and then said, it has been nineteen years, but she actually looked a little like you. Same hair color and pretty face and blue eyes. Isn't that strange?"

"Yes, it's strange. Is that all you remember about her. Her name or anything else?"

"No, Jennifer. That's it. Now you have avoided my question. What is so upsetting about this birth. I love you and want to help you. I know something is wrong. No one is better friends than us, right?"

Jennifer knew that was right. She loved Mary also. She waited for several seconds and finally said in a soft voice, "Mary, I would never have thought I would tell anyone this, but I am going to share something with you and I need your promise to never tell anyone." She waited and looked deeply into Mary's eyes.

"Honey, you know you can trust me. Now, I think we need to go somewhere private and talk. Do you agree?"

They both called their husbands and told a little lie, saying they were going to have to work some into the night shift. This had happened in the past and both husbands understood.

Jennifer and Mary left together and went to the Holiday Inn lounge and both ordered a glass of wine. After the waitress brought the wine, they both took a drink and seemed to relax for the first time today.

Mary sat her glass down and said, "Jennifer, before you say anything, I want you to know that I do understand why this has upset you."

"Jennifer took another, larger drink and said, "Oh, really?"

"Yes, I told you that the young mother looked a lot like you, remember?"

Jennifer only smiled and remained silent.

"Jennifer, most of all, I want you to know that what you did was the right thing to do at the time."

"You really think I am the mother you told me about having the baby boy."

"Oh, Honey you were going to tell me. What else could you be so upset about?"

Jennifer cried and covered her face with both hands. After a few seconds she moved her hands and looked at Mary with tear filled eyes. "Mary, there is no one I could ever trust as much as I trust you."

"Are there any other people who know about your baby boy?"

"Only my husband. We agreed to never let anyone know about our secret."

Mary took another drink and said, "I think we could use another glass." She held up her glass and the waitress gave her a thumbs up.

As they waited for the second glass of wine Mary continued. "So, are you sorry that I know?"

"Oh no, Mary, I know my secret is safe with you. It may seem strange to you, but I feel better after telling you."

Mary laughed and said, "So, you told me?" She was trying to get Jennifer to laugh and hopefully help her get through this.

She did laugh and said, "Well, not in so many words, but my actions told you."

The waitress brough the wine and asked if they needed anything else. They looked at each other and Mary said, "Could you bring us a menu?"

They both ordered a house salad and were soon eating and both had water after two glasses of wine.

Jennifer wanted Mary's advice and hoped she would help her do the right thing. "So, Mary, I do need your advice. I'm not sure what is the best thing for me to do. I'm sure this young man, William is my son. He has to be, right?"

Mary was silent too long.

Jennifer broke the silence and said, "What is it? You look so serious, Mary."

"Well, Jennifer. You have shared a secret with me and I do have a secret also. And it is about the same little baby boy."

Jennifer sat with her mouth open. "Mary, what do you mean?"

"Jennifer, I also have never told anyone about my secret, and I never would. But I must tell you. You need to know that there is a possibility that this young man, William is not your son."

"But you called Bill and Carol and you saw the baby."

"Jennifer, oh this is so bad. I have promised you and now I need you to promise you will never tell anyone what I'm about to tell you."

Jennifer sat and waited.

Mary looked for the waitress and said, "I need to have one more glass of wine." Jennifer declined.

Mary took a long drink of the third glass and then set it on the table. "Jennifer, the night you gave birth we had a power failure." She took another swallow. "We had just received two baby boys in the nursery and they had not had their name tags placed on their arms. They were side by side when the lights went out. The generator soon restored the lights, but I wasn't sure which one was your baby or the other family's baby. I may have gotten it right, but I have thought about it over the years and have felt guilty, not knowing for sure."

Jennifer could not believe what she was hearing. "So, there is a possibility that William is not by son, right?"

Mary finished her wine and frowned at Jennifer and shook her head. "There is only one way to find out."

Jennifer knew that and also knew it would have to be DNA to learn if the babies had been switched.

It was now 9:00 and they both were exhausted from their conversation. Mary was feeling a little light headed from three glasses of wine. Jennifer had only had two glasses but really didn't feel safe to drive. She knew Mary shouldn't drive. She smiled at Mary and said, "Mary, I don't think either of us should drive."

Mary frowned and said, "Really, I think I'm fine."

"Mary, making that statement shows you should not drive."

"And, why is that, Jennifer?"

"Because if you could think straight, you'd agree with me."

Mary had always loved and respected Jennifer and knew she was right. "So, what do we do, call a cab?"

"I'll call Ronnie. He will come and get us and we can leave our cars in the parking lot. Okay?"

Mary only smiled and nodded.

Jennifer took out her cell phone and called Ronnie. His first words were, "Are you on your way home, Jennifer?"

She hesitated and then said, "Well, I really need you to pick me up."

There was silence on the phone and then Ronnie said, "I don't understand. Is there something wrong with your car?"

She knew this was strange for her. "Ronnie, uh, Mary and I went to the Holiday Inn after we got off and had some wine and we really don't need to drive." She waited.

She heard him exhale into the phone. "I can't believe you would do this. You are not a drinker. You hardly ever drink. What's going on?"

She had to think of something that he would understand. "Well, Mary and I had a very stressful evening with a patient and we just…"

"Is it the Holiday Inn that is close to the hospital?"

"Yes, can you come now?"

"I'm on my way." The phone went silent.

They were both standing at the front entrance when Ronnie drove up. It had taken longer than they thought. Then they found out why. Jenny was in the front seat with her dad and Mary's husband, Charles was in the back seat. With little conversation, Jenny got in her mom's car and Charles took Mary's arm and led her to her car. Everyone would be safely home with their own cars.

Jennifer was embarrassed and told Ronnie and Jenny she was sorry when they arrived at home. They both thought she had had a bad experience at the hospital and said very little to her.

They were soon all three in their beds.

Mary had some of the same reactions when she got home.

Jennifer was late getting up the next morning. The stress of not knowing now that William could be her son. That and the wine kept her from sleeping well. Ronnie had not slept well either, but was up and drinking coffee when Jennifer entered the kitchen. "Good morning, honey. You feeling better?"

Jennifer smiled at ham and said, "Yes and I want to tell you how sorry I am for last night." She poured herself a cup of coffee and then sat down across from Ronnie.

He knew she was sorry as he said, "Honey, please forget about that. I am sure you and Mary had a stressful time with a patient. I understand. So, let's forget about it and have some breakfast."

They both had scrambled eggs with bacon and more coffee. After clearing the table and placing the dishes in the dishwasher, Jennifer turned and said, "Ronnie, I need to tell you about last night."

"Honey, please don't feel like you have to explain the problem you and Mary had with a patient. I told you it is okay."

"Ronnie, it's not about a patient."

Ronnie frowned. "It's not? Then what can it be?"

"It's about William."

"I can't imagine, but I'm sure you're going to tell me."

And she did. First, she told him about William asking her about trying to find his birth mother. She had thought she would not tell Ronnie, but with all she had found out the day before, he had to be told. She then told him about Mary and the birth records she had found and the possibility that they babies could have been switched. She didn't tell him about Mary seeing her after the baby was born. She might later, but not now.

After listening for half an hour Ronnie finally said, "So, I thought this thing about William was over. So, now you know by his own admission that he was adopted and born in our hospital?"

"Ronnie, I was in agreement with you to let this go, but after William telling me, well, I just had to try to find out." She hesitated and then continued. "Ronnie, there is a good chance that William and Jenny could marry someday. He could be her real big brother."

Ronnie closed his eyes and was silent for a long moment. He then shook his head and said, "Well, I do understand your concern after learning about William. But there is a chance that he could not be our son, right?"

"That's why we must find out, Ronnie. We have to know for sure."

"And how do we do that?"

"Well, I know that you know about DNA."

"Well sure, so how do you get William's DNA? You can't ask him. You would have to have a reason."

"Well, I've thought about that and do have a plan."

"I want to get Mary's thoughts on this and hope to meet with her again in the next day or two."

Ronnie frowned and said, "I hope it's not at the Holiday Inn."

Jennifer smiled and said, "No, I've learned my lesson."

Mary agreed to meet with Jennifer a few days later. They met at the local mall just before noon and had lunch at one of the fast-food restaurants. It was on Saturday, a normal day off as they both only worked a three-day week.

It was a perfect place to talk and Jennifer couldn't wait to get her advice. "Mary, you know that I am wanting to find out about the baby I gave birth to nineteen years ago."

"Well, I guess I know that better than anyone. So, what are you thinking?"

"I know a person can order a DNA kit and take the samples at home. Right?"

"Yeah, people do that all the time now. Do you want to do that?"

"Well, I think so. Just wanted to know if you see any problem with that?"

Mary smiled and said, "Well, first of all, it's really none of my business. But to answer your question, I really think you should go with it. You don't need to live with this on your mind for the rest of your life."

"So, you're saying to go for it, right?"

"Exactly. Now, is there anything I can do to help?"

"No, not really. I just need your agreement and support and you have given me that. I really appreciate your love and concern for me."

They then actually did some shopping and finally left for home at four that afternoon.

A week later Jennifer had put a plan together to get the test from William. It was another little white lie, as people say. She was going to tell her family and William and his family that a new virus was in some foreign countries and the swab would let them know it they may have it. She would tell them it was little chance of it even being in the United States, but she wanted to protect both families.

She had already ordered the DNA kits and had them in her dressing table drawer. She invited William, Bill and Carol to dinner the next night and they had accepted her invitation. It was a common occurrence for them to have meals together.

After the dinner, she told them about the virus and was pleased that everyone agreed to have the test done. She took each sample and did one for herself in their presence, using a cotton swab inside the mouth.

After their company left and Jenny went with William to a movie, Ronnie smiled at Jennifer and said, "That's a great plan. You told me you had a plan." He placed his index finger on her nose and said, "There's not a virus, right?"

She grabbed his finger and laughed. "Well, if there is one, we'll be ahead of the curve." They both laughed and kissed each other.

Jennifer was able to send the samples, just hers and Williams by Fed Ex and should have the results before the week end.

They did arrive before the week end. The results came by Fed Ex. It was a letter with a lot of medical numbers and more information than she needed. The answer she wanted was at the bottom. "No connection between these two samples."

Jennifer reread the final statement over again. That was it. William was not her son. Now, they were where they had been before learning that William was adopted. Now, her son was somewhere out there. She really needed to let it be. She had naturally worried about William and

Jenny marring someday. Now, if they did decide to, it would be okay. She now knew that she and Ronnie would agree.

They went to their favorite restaurant and after ordering their meal, Jennifer was so pleased to have this moment and reached for his hand and told him about the test results. "Honey, I've thought about this and I do agree with you. We are exactly where we were before the thought of William being our son. So, I'm okay with this and want us to go on with our lives."

Ronnie held her hand firmly and said, "I'm so glad. I love you so much."

The waitress was soon there with their meal. It was a very special night for Ronnie and Jennifer. They were both relieved.

Five years later, William and Jenny did marry. It was such a special occasion for both families. They had grown up just like family, like brother and sister. Not many people have this kind of love. They both felt that their relationship was meant to be. They both had degrees with William having a law degree and Jenny, like her mom was a registered nurse. They had moved across the country and were living 500 miles from their families. William had achieved a partnership with a firm and Jenny was in one of the hospitals in the city. They both were very dedicated to their professions, but really wanted to be back close to their parents.

Ronnie and Jennifer and Bill and Carol continued their relationships and had many times together, mostly at dinner and sometimes movies. They were all four excited as they were planning their first trip to visit with William and Jenny. They would leave in a week and both families planned to stay a full week with William and Jenny.

After arriving at William and Jenny's home the four parents were pleased to see they had enough room for all of them to stay there. It was a very large four-bedroom house with two guest rooms that included private bathrooms.

They were soon unpacked and everyone met in their large family room. William took drink orders and Jenny kept her seat with their guest. After serving everyone except Jenny William said, "I am sure you all have noticed Jenny not drinking anything."

Everyone turned to look at Jenny. She was smiling with her eyes sparkling.

Jennifer was the first one to respond to William's comment. "Are you two going to make us grandparents?"

Jenny could not wait any longer. She jumped up and said, "Yes! William and I are so happy and so please to be able to share this wonderful news with the four of you at the same time."

Jennifer's thoughts went back to their concern years ago about William and was so grateful they knew the truth about his birth. She looked at Ronnie and smiled. She was sure he was having the same thoughts.

After congratulations and finishing their drinks, the conversation soon turned to their future and their plans. Would they move back closer before the baby came? Both parents hoped they would agree to come back closer or even back home.

William and Jenny shared a look and then William said, "Well, we've talked about that and we would really like to be back with you all."

"Then, are you thinking about coming back?" Bill asked.

William frowned before speaking. "I've got a very special friend here and he has made me a partner in his law firm. He and his wife have become very special friends to us." He looked again at Jenny and then continued. "It is amazing how he and I found each other after all these years."

Everyone looked surprised as Jennifer said, "After all these years? Did you go to college together?"

Jenny laughed and said, "William, quit playing games with them."

Everyone laughed and remembered how he love to play jokes and tell stories to everyone from the time he was a little boy.

William looked at his watch and then said, "Well, it's such a special relationship. I want to let Joe to be present when we share this with you all. They are having us over for dinner tonight and we can tell you then."

Everyone smiled and were looking forward to meeting his new friend and his wife.

They arrived at the Johnson home at six that evening. Joe and Beverly were very nice and gave a warm welcome to William and Jenny's parents. They were soon sitting in the din and Joe was taking drink orders.

William laughed and said, "A few more drinks and we won't need dinner."

Everyone laughed thinking about just having drinks at William and Jenny's home.

After everyone had received their drinks, William looked at Joe and said, "well, I have told them that we would tell them how we met."

Joe smiles and said, "Oh, I am so glad you waited so we can see their reaction."

William laughed and said, "We don't remember, but we saw each other when we were born."

Jennifer had been staring at William and now her mouth was open as she remained silent, thinking she knew what he was going to say next.

William smiled and said, "I just thought it was strange and have been looking forward to telling you all that Joe, my partner, and I were both born in the General hospital back home, and on the same day. Isn't that strange? He and I have laughed about that and both thought it seemed that we were meant to be together later in life."

Bill and Carol thought it was special how they had both been born at the same time and were now friends. They had both laughed and agreed with William. Jennifer and Ronnie did manage to smile, but it wasn't easy for them.

Jennifer kept looking at Joe and trying to see some resemblance to Ronnie or her. He did look a little like Ronnie, but not enough for anyone to notice. She was so impressed with his manor and kindness. She could see how he and William had become friends. She could not understand her feelings. He had to be her son and he would never know. Only Ronnie and she would know. Should he ever be told? What about his parents?

She decided to ask. "So, joe do your parents live near here?"

He looked down at the table and then back at Jennifer and said, "Well, no, uh, my grandparents raised me."

Jennifer blushed and said, "I'm sorry I don't mean to be nosey."

"It's okay, you see like we just told you I was born in the same hospital you and Ronnie work in." He paused again and then continued. "We did not live in your town. We were traveling through when my mom went into early labor and my dad took her to your hospital. We were there for a few days until the doctor thought it was okay for us to make the 500-mile trip. We came home, here where we are now. My dad was a lawyer and had been very successful." He looked around the room and smiled. "This was their house." When I was just two years old, my parents were killed in a plane crash. My mom had gone with my dad to see a client. It was a private plane and from what I've been told should not have flown in the bad weather of that day."

Jennifer was so touched by his story of losing his parents. She looked at him and the others and said, "Oh, Joe I know we are all so sorry. Please don't feel that you have to tell us all of this."

Joe looked around the room and said, "Well, except for Beverly, I've never told anyone about my life. I really want you all to know."

Everyone sat in silence and waited for him to continue.

"After my parents died, my grandparents took ownership of this house and moved here. They raised me and were just like parents to me. They both died a year apart. It's been over five years now. When they died, I inherited this house." He smiled and then said, "So, that's my story and I do feel better after telling you."

Jennifer sat hoping her expression didn't show her feelings at that moment. They had just met Joe and his wife. But the amazing thing about meeting Joe was, he had to be their son and Jenny's brother. The big brother she had never known. Jenny had always looked at William as her big brother until they fell in love and married.

Now, Jenny was sitting in the same room with her real big brother. Jennifer's feelings were so mixed. She felt good knowing their son was such a nice person and a very successful lawyer. She felt so proud of him. That was all good, but should Joe ever know his real parents and should Jenny ever know that she has a real Big Brother?

Beverly and Charlie

September 23, 2010

The five o'clock news was always the first sound before the alarm went off. She never heard the news. It was always the buzzing alarm five minutes later that awakened her.

. Beverly was dreaming she was lying in the woods, nude. The weather was cold and it seemed strange that anyone would be out lying on the cold ground. She could feel the stings and itching from lying nude on the forest floor. Slowly, she moved her head from side to side. She sat up and looked in every direction and saw bare trees as far as the eye could see. She was nude, but why? Why had she awakened in a forest, nude and cold? Where was she and most of all, how had she gotten there?

Beverly James awoke for real from the buzzing sound of her clock-radio. It was five-o-five a.m. Monday morning. It was time to get up and start a new week at her job with the local police department. Beverly couldn't get the dream out of her mind. She couldn't imagine why she had such a crazy dream.

Beverly worked with the special victim's unit of the Memphis Police Department. She had a college degree and had majored in business with a minor in physical education. She was physically fit and could out run most of her male co-workers at the Police Department. Beverly had a quick mind and was always one of the first to be at the crime scene. Her partner was a guy she really liked. He was married and had three small children, all girls, five, seven and nine. Charlie Baker was married to his high school sweetheart, Angie. They had the perfect family…. anyway, it seemed so to Beverly.

Beverly and Charlie had been teamed up for five years and the only partner Beverly had ever had. They were a good team. Charlie Baker had a lot more time with the department. He was starting his fifteenth year with the Memphis Police Department. Charlie had started as a rookie, walking the beat in downtown Memphis, moved up to a cruiser and finally to his present position with the special victim's unit. His experience had been a lot of help for Beverly. She had learned so much from Charlie.

Now she was fully awake. The dream, what does it mean? She wanted to tell someone, but whom. She thought about Charlie, but decided against it. It was too silly and personal…being nude in the dream.

Beverly had never married and dated rarely. She was twenty-eight and thought she had plenty of time for romance later. Her job was her life. She could hardly wait for the weekend to be over so she could get back to her job. She even rode with some officers on Saturdays and Sundays when they could make room for her. Charlie thought she was nuts. "Get a man in your life before you get shot and end up wounded with no one to take care of you." She recalled Charlie telling her something like that each time he found out about her "moonlighting" on the weekends.

So, it was Monday, her favorite day of the week. She jumped out of the bed and went to the bathroom. Before showering, she always did one hundred push-ups and fifty sit ups. After showering, she had orange juice and a banana with cereal and skim milk. She was a health nut and it showed. She was firm and stronger than most men.

Charlie was drinking his second cup of coffee since he had arrived at the office. He looked up as Beverly came bouncing in.

"Caffeine will make you nervous, Charlie."

Charlie smiled and gave her a grunt. "Beverly, if I had a dollar for every time, you told me that, I could retire."

Beverly gave him a pat on the shoulder as she said, "If you retire, then you wouldn't see me every day."

They enjoyed small talk and started most days with jokes back and forth until Charlie would say, "Okay, Wonder Woman, Let's see what the captain has for his Super Heroes today."

Beverly would always agree. "I'm with you, Superman."

Sammy Willis was in his late fifties and had been with the department for most of his adult life. In fact, he would soon celebrate his thirty-first year with the force. He was promoted to captain when he was in his late forties and was very happy to remain in that job until he retired. Charlie and Beverly loved having him as their boss. He

111

was smart, kind and strict. He had a good attitude and expected positive feedback from his troops.

The special victim's unit had a total of twelve people in the department, including Sammy Willis. There were four two-person teams. Beverly had been the one to change this from "two-man team" to "two-person team." Sammy thought it was politically correct and had no problem using that term. The ladies that joined the force after Beverly were grateful for that distinction. The other three personnel were office clerks and a secretary. It was a very tight family type group. Sammy had held a department picnic every Labor Day and most attended with their families. It did a lot for the morale to include the families.

It was the usual Monday morning briefing and Sammy Willis was at his favorite position, at the flip chart, pointer in hand. He always had assignments written on the chart and after discussing these with the teams, gave each team a chance to volunteer. No volunteer, he volunteered them. The day was like any other with new cases and some old cases they continued to work.

Beverly almost stood up when Sammy Willis described a report that had been received over the weekend. A nude lady had been found in the woods just north of the city. Two hunters had found her and thought she might be dead, but learned that she was not. When they approached her, she simply walked away, saying nothing to them. That was strange enough, but the next day, two other hunters told the same story to the state game warden. It sounded like the same lady.

Beverly did stand up then and said, "Captain, I would like to have this assignment, uh, of course with Charlie."

Charlie looked up at her with a frown. Sammy Willis was surprised that Beverly, of all people, would want a human-interest story. After all, there didn't seem to be any crime committed with this one. He smiled at Beverly, "Sure, Beverly. It's only a report, but we do need to check it out and get it resolved. Let me know what you and Charlie find out."

Charlie and Beverly were on their way to the wooded area where the nude lady was reported to have been seen by two sets of hunters on two different days. Charlie was gripping the steering wheel as he glanced over at Beverly. "Why in the world do you want to investigate a simple report like this?"

Beverly knew why. It was her dream. It sounded just like her dream, but she wasn't ready to share this information with her partner. "Charlie, sometimes, you have followed a case or a lead because you had a gut feeling, right?"

Charlie smiled and nodded with agreement. "So, you have a gut feeling about a nude lady in the woods in the winter time?"

Beverly hesitated, and then said. "Well, yeah. Humor me, okay?"

"I'm your partner, Wonder Woman," Charlie said as he turned the car into the parking lot of a small grocery store.

The store clerk was old, maybe seventy-five or older. He was stooped and looked like he had worked hard all of his life. He wore a white apron that looked like it hadn't been washed in weeks. He was balding and his eyes set deep in his head. They were brown and seemed to penetrate as he looked at Beverly and Charlie.

As Beverly and Charlie walked up to the counter, he looked them up and down with his piercing eyes.

"You two lost?" He asked.

Beverly laughed and said, "Do we look lost, sir?"

The old man looked outside at their car and said, "I don't reckon I've seen that car around here…pretty plain, kind of like a plain police car."

Charlie put his mind at ease. "It is, Sir. We are with the special victim's unit out of Memphis."

The old man again looked at Beverly and then back at Charlie, eyes again penetrating. "Well, I hope you ain't looking for me," he said with a chuckle.

"No sir," Beverly said. "We are looking for information though. Maybe you can help us."

"I'll sure try. I always want to help the law, for sure."

Charlie extended his hand and said, "I'm Sergeant Charlie Baker and this is my partner, Sergeant Beverly James."

"I'm Lawrence McBride, owner of this old place, been here for over forty years. I know most everyone around here, so maybe I can help. What is it you want to know?"

Charlie turned to Beverly. Beverly smiled and thought to herself, He wants me to run the rabbit on this part. "Well, Mr. McBride," she said. "Have you heard anything about a lady being seen in the woods around here…and was reported to be nude?"

McBride looked shocked. He looked at Beverly and put both hands on the counter between them. "Well, just where did you hear that?" He looked wild out of his deep brown eyes.

Beverly looked shocked as she said, "Actually we got a report from The Game Warden. Some hunters reported it to him and then he reported the incident to our department."

McBride looked angrier now. "Well, some state boy then. I was sure no one here talked about her." He paused then said, "I never thought it would get to the police. It would be best for everyone to just forget about her."

"And why is that, Mr. McBride?" Beverly asked.

McBride looked around as if to not let anyone hear what he was about to say, even though they were alone in the store. "Well, it ain't nobody's business. That's why and anyway; she means no harm to anyone."

Charlie and Beverly exchanged glances. Then Charlie said, "Sounds like you know her."

McBride smiled and then slowly frowned. "Well, what if I do...you going to arrest me?"

Beverly was getting more excited now. This was someone he must know. She didn't want to alarm him as she asked, "You think if you tell us who she is that we will arrest you, or her?"

He was still frowning. "Well, will you?"

Beverly could see that McBride was getting more upset. "Now, Mr. McBride, we don't just go around arresting someone until we know that there is a good reason to do so."

McBride became very quiet. In fact, he quit talking all together. Beverly and Charlie waited. Charlie's cell phone rang and he excused himself and went outside.

Beverly waited a few more seconds before saying, "Mr. McBride, do you know this woman?"

He only nodded.

"We just need to talk with her and be sure that she is all right. People just don't lie on the frozen ground, nude. Maybe we can help her."

McBride looked into Beverly's eyes. "Young lady, you would never understand this lady. She started doing this about six months ago. Sometimes she is out there for five or six nights in a row. Then she might not be seen for a week. It's so strange. She thinks she is having a dream that this is happening to her."

Beverly couldn't speak for several seconds. Then she asked with an almost whisper, "She thinks it's a dream?"

McBride smiled and spoke. "Yeah, she has told me that her dreams started about six months ago."

"Can you at least tell me how old she is or anything about her appearance?"

"Well, I would say she looks a lot like you, Miss. I'd say she would be in her twenties. Very pretty, like you."

"And she lives around here?" Beverly asked.

"Yeah, she lives just down the road in the woods."

Charlie came charging in the door. "Let's go Wonder Woman. I just got a call from the captain. They need us in down-town Memphis."

Beverly knew it was urgent and that duty called. She was torn between talking with McBride and going with

Charlie. She handed McBride her business card and asked him to call her on her cell phone that night. He took the card and said nothing. Beverly followed Charlie out and they drove away.

```
```

Lawrence McBride watched them drive out of sight. He then picked up is phone on the counter and called a cell number.

The phone was answered on the second ring. "Hello."

"Some police were here and they are looking for you."

He waited then she said. "Did you tell them anything?"

McBride paused and looked at the phone as if to give her a stern look. "You know I'm not going to say anything. We've talked about this ever since you came."

Her voice was slow and smooth as always. "Lawrence, you're the only person I know and trust. You know that. I've told you why I came here and chose this place. You're the only one who knows who I really am."

And he *was* the only person who knew about her and who she was. He had promised her he would never tell, and would abide by her wishes.

It had been six months ago when this pretty young lady had arrived at his store. She had come to his store after they had corresponded for many months. She was from out west and wanted to move close to Memphis, but not live in the city. She had asked about a house in the woods. She wanted it deep in the woods and having a road to the house was not important. Lawrence had remembered an old trapper's cabin that had been vacant for many years. He had agreed to take her there and did,

117

after closing his store on the day of her arrival. She loved it and had asked how she could buy it. No one really knew who owned it, so he told her to move in and if anyone asked to tell them that he had told her she could live there. That was six months ago now, and she was getting out too far from the cabin. Others had seen her and now, the police were asking questions. Lawrence had to see her and make sure the police didn't find her first.

"Lawrence, are you still there?"

McBride came back from his thoughts about that first day. "Oh, yeah, honey. I was just thinking. You know, I really need to see you tonight. It's very important."

He waited. Then she said, "Must come alone, like always."

McBride closed his store at six and drove out to the cabin in the woods. There was an old dirt road that led up to within fifty yards of the cabin. It was very cold and a light snow was falling. McBride brought a flashlight and used it to expose the small cabin from the darkness. There was no electricity or utilities of any kind in the cabin. He made his way to the door and knocked. No answer. He then called out, "You in there? It's Lawrence. Let me in." No response. He slowly pushed open the door and shown the light into the cabin. It was only one room furnished with a small bed supporting a dirty straw filled mattress. The rest of the cabin was empty, except for a pair of jeans, t-shirt and panties lying on the floor. It was just as cold in the cabin as it was outside. He knew then what she was doing, but where? Somewhere in the woods, she was lying on her back, completely nude. He must find her before

118

the police did. McBride had found her before and had taken her back to the cabin. She had not awakened the two times he had found her. He had placed her in her bed and left before she had awakened. On other visits, she had confided in him about her "dream ... her dream of being nude in the woods. He didn't have the heart to tell her it wasn't a dream. She was sick and only had a few months to live. He knew that when she came and had agreed to let her live out her remaining time as she wished. Now, he couldn't find her and was afraid of what must have happened.

Beverly and Charlie had been called to a domestic fight between a man and his common-law wife. It had taken them most of the afternoon to get them booked and placed in jail. Beverly was exhausted. She could never understand how couples could be so cruel to each other. It seemed to be happening more every year. More crime and fights within the same families.

She got home at eight. She still had not heard from McBride. She wanted McBride to call her, but knew that it was not likely. She sat down and replayed the discussion in her mind she had had with McBride. "Six months ago, she started sleeping out in the cold.... nude," McBride had told her. She had to find out who this lady was and what part McBride played in this arrangement.

Beverly made a peanut butter and cracker sandwich and drank a small glass of skim milk. She then took a shower and got ready for bed.

That same night, Lawrence McBride *was* talking with the nude lady. "Wake up. You are too far from the cabin. I told you to stay close to the cabin. Now, I am afraid the police are going to find you...get up...get up now! We agreed that you would not venture out from the cabin." Lawrence was getting upset with her now. Why wouldn't she wake up? He squatted down and shined the flashlight in her face. No response. He touched her face. It was as cold as the ground beneath her. She appeared to be dead. There was no pulse and he could not see any signs of breathing. McBride stood up and turned off the flashlight. What would he do now? She had come to him six months ago, looking for a place to live and have her space and be alone and die in private. She had been diagnosed with a brain tumor and only given months to live. He had agreed to grant her wish. Now she was alone.... alone and dead. He must do something with her body, but what?

It was cold in the old trapper's cabin. McBride had dragged her body through the leaves and freshly fallen snow covering the frozen ground and was now sitting on the straw mattress covered bed, looking at the dead naked body of his friend. He switched off the flashlight and sat in the darkness, wondering what his next move should be. He had to dispose of the body. No one around the community knew who she was. Lawrence was the only one that knew her and talked with her. He had tried to protect her from the public and give her the privacy she wanted. Now, she was dead. He now had to protect himself. It was worse now, now that the police were involved. He knew they would be back, asking more questions about the naked lady in the woods.

Later the next morning, Beverly James woke up for the second time. The first time, she was awakened from her dream. Now, she was in the shower, trying to get her thoughts together. The warm water took the chill off and made her feel more like herself.

She had no time for breakfast or her exercise that morning. She would have just enough time to make it to the police station at seven a.m., her regular starting time.

Charlie Baker was at his desk, like always, drinking his cup of coffee. "Good morning, Wonder Woman.... running a little close, aren't you?"

Beverly smiled and sat down across from her partner and best friend. "Good morning to you, Charlie." She looked tired and haggard.

He couldn't remember seeing her looking like this. "Hey, partner, you look a little washed out this morning.... you all right?"

Beverly hesitated before saying, "Well, I am tired, had a bad night...dreams and stuff.... kept me from resting."

Charlie took a sip of his coffee. "Want to talk about it?"

Beverly reached for his cup of coffee and took a sip. Charlie's eyes widened. He had never seen her use caffeine of any kind.

"Yeah, Charlie....I do want to talk.... I need to tell someone, and I think it should be you."

Charlie Baker sat, looking at his partner, wondering what she was going to tell him.

Charlie usually droves, but today, Beverly had asked if she might do the driving. Charlie didn't care; in fact, he liked the idea of being chauffeured around. They had no specific assignment for the day, but Charlie was sure where Beverly was heading. "You want to call it in, Wonder Woman?"

She nodded and punched the number on her cell. She advised dispatch that they were on the way to the wooded area, north of the city, where the nude lady had been reported.

Charlie smiled and said, "So, we are still going to look for the nut-case in the woods, I presume."

Beverly looked over at him. "Yes, Charlie, this is very important to me....and I need you to work with me and try to understand."

Charlie had never seen a tear in Beverly's eyes before. This morning, they started running down her face.

It took twenty minutes to reach the old store, and Beverly drove in total silence for those twenty minutes. As they drove up to the front of the store, they saw a small sign on the front door. Beverly jumped out and sprinted up the steps. She stood looking at the note with her hands on her hips. "Closed?" She said and then turned to look back at Charlie. "The store is closed. This is Tuesday morning. Why would they be closed on Tuesday?" She was fuming and getting angry.

Charlie gave her time to cool off then said, "Look, Beverly, I know this is important to you, but don't get so upset. We'll find out what's going on......just calm down."

Beverly cupped her hands on the door glass and tried to see inside. There were no lights on and she saw no one inside.

Charlie placed his hand on her shoulder. "Come on, Wonder Woman. Maybe we can ask around and find out why Mr. What's-his-name...."

"McBride, his name is Lawrence McBride, Charlie."

Charlie had never seen her so upset about anything and to him; this was nothing to get upset about. After all, they were investigating a woman that was reported to be nude in the woods, a nut-case in his mind.

Beverly went back to the car and got under the wheel. Charlie got in and closed the door. She beat her hands on the steering wheel. "Charlie, I must find Lawrence McBride." Then she did cry. Not just a tear like Charlie had seen earlier. This time she sobbed and cried. Charlie sat and waited, not knowing what to do or say.

She turned and looked at Charlie. "I'm sorry, Charlie. I know you think I'm nuts."

Charlie laughed and said, "Well, maybe a little Looney?"

She smiled, with tears still in her eyes. "Charlie, I told you earlier that I wanted to tell you what this is all about."

"Yes, you did. So, shoot. I'm a good listener."

She studied his face for a long moment then said, "It may take a while to explain. Would you be willing to listen to me...off duty?"

"Sure Beverly. I am beginning to worry about you, kid."

"So, can we meet someplace after our shift?"

Charlie Baker and Beverly James had never met after work, alone. They had, however, been together socially with Charlie's wife and kids many times. When Beverly had been assigned to Charlie, he took her home to meet his wife and kids. That was five years ago. Angie Baker liked Beverly when they first met and the Baker kids loved her. Kimberly was four, Jodie was two and Becky was just two months old. Beverly had been so impressed with the family and the love that they had for each other. When Charlie introduced Kimberly to Beverly, she looked up at her and said, "You look like Wonder Woman."

Beverly had knelt down and took Kimberly in her arms and had said how sweet that was. Kimberly was only four at the time and had watched Wonder Woman on TV just a few days before Beverly's visit. The next day at work, Charlie started calling Beverly "Wonder Woman" and it stuck. She had to get back at him, so she called him "Superman". Their working relationship was strictly professional, but Beverly was close to Charlie and his family.

Charlie hesitated before saying, "Angie and the girls are visiting her sister and her sister's husband in New York, and so I really am open tonight. Maybe we could have dinner and talk." He looked at her and winked. "You can buy, of course." He laughed and touched her arm. "I'm sorry, just kidding. Tell me where and I'll meet you and we can talk. I do want to help if I can."

They decided on the Peabody Hotel in downtown Memphis. It was old, but the food was always good there. Beverly picked up Charlie at his home at seven. They arrived at the restaurant at seven-thirty. Beverly was dressed very nice with a blue pant suit. She wore small diamond earrings and a small gold necklace. She looked very pretty. Charlie wore a suit and tie, much like the kind he worked in every day. They made an attractive couple. Charlie was older, but not that much. He was thirty-seven, the same age as his wife. They had both married at twenty-two and had spent the last fifteen years as husband and wife. Beverly at twenty-eight didn't look much younger than her partner.

The waiter suggested an appetizer with their drink. They both ordered shrimp cocktails. Beverly was having red wine and Charlie ordered a light beer. They were both having a hard time starting the conversation. Charlie was waiting for her to broach the subject and Beverly was not sure how to tell him about the dreams, and how it matched the real nude lady in the woods. She took her second sip of wine and smiled at Charlie. "I want to thank you for agreeing to listen to me. I know you had rather be home in your recliner, watching TV."

Charlie laughed and said, "Well, I wouldn't do this just for anyone, but for a Wonder Woman, well, that makes a difference." He looked at her pretty face and thought; *"I hope she's not pregnant. But then, how would she get pregnant? Maybe one of the cops she rides with on the week-ends. She never talks about dating anyone."*

She took him away from his thoughts. "It's my dreams, Charlie. I want to talk with you about my dreams."

"Dreams?" Charlie took a shrimp and poked it in his mouth.

"Yeah, I have been having the same dream for the last couple of nights." She paused and sampled her shrimp cocktail. "Oh, this is very good shrimp."

Charlie took a big gulp of beer and washed down his shrimp. "Yeah, it's good. What about the dreams...a whole week and no new titles?"

Beverly lay her fork down and looked into her wine glass. "No, it's the same.... always the same, and it's not a week, just a couple of nights...so far. I first had the dream Sunday and again last night."

Charlie was about to finish his shrimp and trying to not look like a slob. Angie had always told him to slow down, indigestion.... heartburn and the like. He let his last shrimp rest for another moment. "So, what do you dream about? Is its scary stuff, ghosts, monsters...? aliens?"

Beverly blushed and said, "It's about me. Me in the woods....in the woods like the report of the lady we went to check out." She paused and waited for Charlie's reaction.

He ate his last shrimp and took another big gulp of his beer. "You mean in the woods.... like she was reported to be...."

Beverly looked straight at him and said, "Nude, just like the report. Now, you know why I wanted to take this case."

The waiter came back and asked about drinks and dinner. Beverly passed on more wine. Charlie said he would have one more, since Beverly was driving. She smiled. She had never known him to drink more than one beer and drive. Charlie Baker was a good cop and a good man.

Charlie knew also, how Beverly felt about driving and drinking. It was really the reason she chose to be a cop.

She respected him and considered him her best friend. Beverly ordered salmon with steamed vegetables. Charlie, of course, ordered a steak, rare, with baked potato.

After the waiter left, Charlie smiled and said, "I'm sitting here and trying to imagine you lying in the woods, nude. What on earth would make you dream that?'

"Charlie, I wished I knew. You know, the dreams are weird enough, but when we got the report of that woman.... well, I just about lost it." She paused then said, "There's more."

Charlie's eye brows rose. He started to speak, but the waiter sat his beer down in front of him. He thanked him and took a big gulp. Beverly waited. "So, you said there is more?"

"Yes. The dream last night, I was awakened in my dream by none other than, Mr. Lawrence McBride."

"McBride in your dream.... well, dreams are like that sometimes. You know, you see or do something during the day, and then you dream about it, happens to me all the time."

"Well, that could be, but it still doesn't explain the dreams. I know we saw him and he told us he knew the woman, so I guess it could cause me to dream about him. But there is still more."

Charlie moved back as the waiter returned with their food. After they were served and the waiter had gone, Charlie asked, "Still more?"

Beverly cut a piece of her salmon and took a small bite. Chewing slowly, she said, "Yes." She took a sip of water and looked down at her plate. "Charlie, I woke up during the night. It was around three this morning. I had dreamed again about being nude in the woods. I was wet with sweat and shaking. It seemed so real to me."

Charlie just stared at her, saying nothing. They both ate for a few moments in silence.

Charlie finally spoke. "So, is that it?"

"Yeah, that's it. It has troubled me since the first dream, but for the first time...I'm afraid."

"You afraid? I've known you for five years and afraid doesn't seem to be part of your make up." He paused then said, "But, today.... today when you got upset...."

"It's okay to say it," she said. "I cried."

He could see the tears building in her lower lids as she spoke. He stopped eating and put his napkin on the table. "I've upset you. I do believe you.... that you are afraid... And, I want to help, I'm sorry."

Beverly excused herself and left the table. Charlie sat and tried to think of what he could do or say to help his best friend. She needed his support and understanding, and he knew it.

She was back in a few minutes. He could tell she had been crying and felt so helpless and sorry for her. She sat down, then stood and said, "I would really like to go, if you don't mind."

Charlie stood up, and then sat back down. "Please sat down until we get our check and then we can go, okay?"

She sat.

They had parked on the street, just a block from the Peabody. They walked in silence to the car. As they drove, Beverly began to cry again. She was trying to suppress it but not doing very good job of it. Charlie was silent. When they pulled into his driveway, Charlie reached over and put his hand on her cheek. It was wet from tears.

"Beverly, I'm not sure what to do, but I do want to listen...sometimes, listening helps.

She was sobbing softly. Charlie spoke very quietly, almost like a father would to his child. "I don't want you to go home in this condition. Come in with me and we can talk...talk this out, together, just like we talk out some of the cases we have."

Beverly followed Charlie into his house, without speaking. She was in a state of fear and really didn't worry about what anyone would think seeing her going in his house without his family being there.

Beverly sat on the couch in the family room. She had been there many times and knew the house as well as she knew her own apartment. It felt safe and good just being there. There, with Charlie Baker. He would protect her. She needed to be protected. Then she thought about going to her apartment alone, and having the dream again. Charlie had gone to the kitchen.

She heard Charlie on the kitchen phone talking to Angie and the girls. They were so lucky to have a daddy and husband like Charlie. He loved them more than life. She heard him say goodbye to all three girls and that he loved them. After a few moments, Charlie appeared in the doorway from the kitchen. He had two wine glasses and a bottle of chilled wine.

He sat next to her and poured both glasses full. He held up his glass and said, "Here's to whipping your bad dreams."

They clicked glasses and both sipped their wine. She was shocked when Charlie said, "I want you to stay here tonight."

She had stayed with the kids when Charlie and Angie had anniversary dinners and on other occasions. Sometimes, on week-ends and when they got home late, she had spent the night. But tonight, well, that was different.

"Oh, Charlie, I don't know. This is not right with your family gone.... It just wouldn't be right."

Charlie finished his glass of wine and said, "Want me to call Angie and have her ask you to stay?"

She looked at him and thought how lucky she was to have found him and have him for her partner. "No, I know what she would say, so okay, I will stay over."

"Good, then it's settled. And tomorrow, you will call in one of the many sick days you've never used."

"Charlie, I'm not......"

"Listen, Wonder Woman, I'm pulling rank on you, so button it up. You need some rest and rest is what you are going to get."

Beverly finished her glass and sat it on the coffee table. "Yes sir, Mr. Boss Man. I will obey your orders."

Charlie laughed and said, "Okay, that's more like it." He stood up and looked down at her. "Well, that doesn't mean I can call in sick too. So, I'm going to turn in. You know where the guest room is, and everything else, so sleep well, and if you have dreams.... I hope they are pleasant." He looked at the wine bottle and said, "And the rest of the wine is yours, by the way."

Beverly waved as he left the room. She sat there with the bottle of wine and stared into space. They hadn't talked any more, but really, what could they say. She had said it all, and Charlie, well Charlie had no magic bullet to kill her dreams. Maybe being there, the dream wouldn't find her. She closed her eyes and said a silent prayer, giving thanks for being safe with Charlie.

Lawrence McBride was in a panic. He had gone home now and was sitting in his little house thinking. Thinking about his dead friend, who was still in the old trapper's cabin deep in the woods. He had dragged her there. Maybe he should have left her in the woods. There would be evidence of his dragging her. But he thought why would they suspect him? Only one person knew about his knowledge of her, and his old friend wouldn't tell. Then it hit him like a ton of bricks. The two police sergeants, he had told them. He could hear himself saying, "What if I do know her?" And then telling the pretty lady cop, "She lives just down the road in the woods." Oh, God. He did have a problem. The police or somebody would surely find her, and then they would be calling on him. He had to hide the body. That was the only answer. No body, no crime. For all they would know, she just moved away.... just like she moved in. Yes, here for a while and then moved away. He could tell them that. He sat and smiled. Now, he felt like he could go to bed and sleep.

Tomorrow, he would take care of that problem and his life would go on with no worries.

Beverly was still sitting in the family room of the Baker's home. She had drunk two more glasses of wine and thought she would just finish the bottle.

She had had a simple life. She had grown up in Memphis, the child of a single parent. Her father had run off with a waitress when she was just two years old. She really never knew him. Her mom had to work to put food on the table and keep a roof over their heads. It was hard for Betty James. She had no skills or formal education. She had; in fact, gotten pregnant and had quit school in the tenth grade. Frank James was older and had swept Betty off her feet when she was only sixteen. Frank was twenty-five and very handsome. He worked at the local phone company and made good money. They seemed happy and things were fine with the new marriage. Betty's mom and dad were not pleased about her pregnancy, but it seemed all right since they had married. They accepted Frank as their new son-in-law. Just eight months after they married, Beverly Ann James was born. It was the happiest day of Betty's life. She had her own little girl. Frank seemed happy too, but had admitted that he had expected a boy.

Betty had become suspicious of Frank. It wasn't long before he was keeping late hours...having a few beers with his buddies. Betty wanted to believe him, but there were a lot of things that made her realize that he was seeing someone else. The main concern was his lack of wanting to have sex with her. Said he was tired or, his back was acting up.... lots of excuses. She tried to make it work, then after their second wedding anniversary, she asked him to leave.

Frank made no big deal of it. He confessed that he had another woman and an opportunity to move to California for a better job. So, that was the end of Betty's dream marriage. Now, she was alone with a little girl whom she adored. Beverly Ann was her entire life, and Betty promised herself that Beverly would have a better life than she had. She started saving for a college fund the very next year. It was hard with the limited income. She worked in a small clothing manufacturing plant in Memphis. The good part was, the company had a retirement plan, very much like a 401K. They would match what she put into the plan and in twenty years she could withdraw the total balance. This was Beverly's college fund, and it worked. Beverly went to college and got her education, thanks to her mother. Sadly, Betty James didn't live to see her daughter graduate. She was killed in a car wreck by a drunken driver when Beverly was in her senior year. Her mother's death was a turning point in her life. After graduation, she enrolled in the Police Academy and graduated at the top of her class. From there, she got her first job with the Memphis Police Department. After a year, she was assigned as Charlie Baker's partner.

Beverly had a very bad opinion of men in general. After seeing what her mom had to go through, she wanted to be very sure about any man. She was not sure at that time in her life, if she would ever marry.

But now here she sat, twenty-eight years old.... She finished the bottle and sat it on the coffee table. There was only a couple of swallows in the glass. She drank that and took the glass and bottle to the kitchen. It was midnight, actually twelve twenty-five. She was very quiet as she didn't want to wake Charlie. She turned off the lights and walked softly down the carpeted hallway to the guest bedroom. The bed was a double, like hers. She liked plenty of room when she slept. She went across the hall to the guest bathroom. There she found a new tooth brush and wash cloths. Angie always kept the guest bath stocked. She was very thoughtful and kind. Beverly was very close to her. She couldn't help but wonder what Angie would think about her spending the night without the family being there. Charlie would probably tell her about it. He and Angie were that close and trusted each other completely.

When she got up the next morning, Charlie was already gone. Her prayer had been answered, no dream, no naked lady in the woods."

She had some orange juice and a piece of dry toast. She then showered and drove to her apartment. She intended to rest and put all of these silly dreams behind her. But there was still the real lady in the woods.

There was a package on her front steps when she arrived at her apartment. It was in a plain brown package, with heavy packing tape. It was addressed to her, with a UPS tag. She picked it up and went into her apartment. She had an attached garage, but seldom used it. She went to her phone to check her messages, laying the package on the kitchen table. She had two. The first one was from her hair dresser. She wanted to change her appointment on Saturday from two to three in the afternoon, if that would be all right. And to please let her know.

The second one was Charlie. She listened to his voice. "Hi, Wonder Woman....just wanted to say hello and hope you had a good night. Guess you were still sleeping when I left this morning. Well, that's good for you. I tried my number at home, so I guess you are on your way to your apartment. Have a good rest today.... I'll call you this evening.... Bye..."

There was no return address on the package, but it did have a UPS label. So, it had been delivered today, probably this morning. She cut the tape and pulled the brown wrapping paper away, exposing a box. It looked the size of a shoebox, but a little longer than normal. She removed the top and looked inside. It was filled with dried leaves. They were damp and had a smell of mold. She began to remove the leaves, placing them in the floor. After the third hand full of leaves, she screamed.

There was a picture in the bottom of the box, a picture of a nude lady lying in the woods. She took it out and studied it closely. It could be her. It was not a close up, but did have the same hair and body. There was another picture in the box. This one was more alarming. The nude lady was lying on a wooden floor. It appeared to be a small room. There was no furniture in view, except for a bed with a straw mattress. She could see straw sticking out of the ragged mattress. The lady did look like her, as this one showed her closer. It was not her, however. Beverly had seen enough dead people to tell that this lady was one of those...a dead person. Why had she gotten this, and who had sent it? The dream...she had only told Charlie about the dream. No one else knew. What connection did she have with the actual lady that was seen in the woods? Lawrence McBride, she had given him her home phone number. Could he have used the internet to locate her address from her phone? That was her best guess. It almost had to be him, but why? He had told her that he knew the lady, but she could tell he didn't want to talk about her. She put both pictures on her table and looked at them for several minutes.

Beverly stayed home the rest of that day. She had a lot to think about. Her most important issue was, of course, her partner. What did he think about his "Wonder Woman" now?

She thought about Lawrence McBride. She needed to see him. He had to be the one to send the pictures. Maybe, tomorrow, but then maybe Charlie would not want to follow up on this. She had not had the dream last night. Would it come again? She was not looking forward to going to bed that night.

Charlie came home about six, his usual time to get home unless they had a case that kept them later. The house was quiet and lonesome. He missed Angie and the girls.

Dinner for Charlie was a frozen meal with roast beef, potatoes, peas and a crunchy biscuit. He nuked it for the recommended time. It wasn't very good, but did fill his empty stomach. He had not had breakfast and his lunch was a greasy hamburger. This frozen dinner wasn't any better and it didn't set too well with him. After finishing his last bite, he called Beverly's home phone. She answered on the third ring. "Beverly?"

She smiled. Hearing his voice was always comforting to her.

"Hi, Charlie, how was your day?"

He paused then said, "Well, it was okay, I guess. It's been different and strange. I missed you."

They both sat in silence for a long moment. Then he said, "I just wanted to call and tell you that, I mean, I hope you don't have one of those dreams...I know they have upset you." He could hear her softly sobbing.

Charlie felt like crying himself, if it would help anything.

"I'm ashamed of myself, Charlie....I'm acting like a baby. You'll be looking for a new partner, someone stronger than me." Her voice broke as she spoke.

"Beverly, my dear friend, I love you so much. I'm so proud of you and so proud to get to work with you every day. I look forward to seeing you each morning. You make my work a real pleasure. I don't want to think about us not working together."

Beverly was wiping tears from her cheeks as she spoke softly, "Oh, Charlie, that's what I want too. You are my hero and I admire you so much. Thank you for being who you are."

"Okay now, Wonder Woman, what about tonight.... what about those dreams? Are you still afraid the dream will come to visit you?"

She paused then said, "Well, I had none last night and hope they are gone for good, but I got a package today.... and, well, I can tell you tomorrow......"

"No, you're not going to tell me tomorrow. What kind of package?"

"It's pictures.... I think it's the lady in the woods."

Charlie sighed, and then said, "Well, that's it. Get your stuff together; I'll be there in twenty minutes."

"Charlie...."

"No, I'm coming to get you and you are staying with me until we find out what's going on...understood?

The line went dead.

Beverly looked at the phone and thought, what am I doing? He wants to protect me. I know that's all. I must remember that.

He arrived at seven thirty. She was packed with pajamas and a night gown, plus her work clothes for the next day. They rode in silence to Charlie's home. Beverly went directly to the guest room and put her things in the dresser and closet. She could hear Charlie talking on the phone. After a few minutes, he came to her door with the cordless phone. "It's Angie. She wants to talk with you, Beverly."

Beverly's mouth was open; her heart was pounding as she looked at Charlie in disbelief. He held his hand over the receiver and said, "It's okay.... talk with her."

Beverly took the phone and said, "Hi, Angie." She wondered what Angie was going to say and what she thought about her being there with Charlie.

She was surprised as she heard Angie say, "Beverly, Charlie has told me about the problems you are having with the dreams and now, the weirdo that sent you those awful pictures. I'm so sorry you are experiencing this, honey. I just want you to know that I want you to be there just as much as Charlie does. He told me that you were concerned about being there with him, alone. We both love you and any way we can help you we will. You know that, right?"

Beverly had to swallow twice before speaking. "Yes, Angie....you are both like family to me." She swallowed again and said, "I feel so bad to unload my problems on Charlie, and now you. You are both so kind and sweet to me."

"Now, Beverly, I want you to take good care of Charlie. He needs some TLC while the girls and I are away, so you can make him some dinner and breakfast. You know he can't cook, so be sure you do the cooking. Also, you have my permission to make him clean up and not leave his clothes in the floor. So, you see, your stay at the Baker house has some responsibilities attached."

Beverly felt better hearing Angie talk to her like she was a relative. She also felt guilty. She knew that Angie nor Charlie didn't need additional problems in their lives. They had a young family and this alone took a lot of their time. Beverly thanked her again, and they said their goodbyes and hung up.

Charlie and Beverly spent the next hour talking and looking at the pictures she had received earlier that day. They both went to bed just after the ten o'clock news. They both slept soundly, in separate bedrooms....and Beverly's dream did not come to visit her.

Lawrence McBride was not feeling very well that night. He had done his deed early that morning. He had disposed of the body and thought all of his worries were over. He took the body of his friend to his store and prepared her for her final resting place. No one would ever know what he had done with her. It would be his secret.

But, when the UPS delivery came by later in the day, he became very upset. His package was identical to Beverly's. It also had damp leaves, covering two pictures of his lady friend. There was one difference; McBride's box had a note enclosed. It was in box letters and it read, "I know what you did...You will hear from me soon."

He was so upset he had already vomited three times. The last time, only green bile came up and burned in his throat. He couldn't sleep and even had thoughts of killing himself.

Wednesday morning, Charlie was up before Beverly. He did know how to make coffee and had it going when she came in the kitchen at five a.m.

"Hey, I got orders from your boss Charlie to do the cooking around here."

He pointed at the coffee maker and said, "That's my limit, from here on, it's your baby."

She smiled and looked at him strangely. She thought should I be here like this? He smiled back at her. Both were wondering what the other was thinking. They both felt a little uncomfortable.

"Bacon and eggs?" She asked as she opened the fridge.

Charlie smiled and said, "Yes, over easy on the eggs, if you don't mind."

They enjoyed breakfast and left the house at six thirty, headed for the station.

No one noticed them arriving together. Sometimes they would ride together as they were only twenty minutes apart and most times one of them had the cruiser, usually Charlie.

After a few reports were filed, they started their day. Charlie was driving. He looked over at her and said, "Well, it's back to see your friend, Lawrence McBride."

"Not sure I would call him my friend," she said, as she looked out the window.

The store was open that day. They saw customers coming out and three cars parked outside. McBride was busy with a customer, showing a man a used chain saw. He sold a little of everything and took things in on trade. It was one of the last of the general stores, soup to nails as they say. The man thought the chain saw was priced too high for its condition and left the store.

McBride saw Charlie and Beverly looking at some hardware items. "Well, I see you two are back." He seemed very unsettled and nervous. "How can I help you?"

Beverly spoke. "Well, we are still looking for the lady... you know the one we asked you about on Monday."

"She's gone," McBride said, as he looked down at the floor.

"Gone? Gone where?" Beverly asked as she tried to make eye contact with him.

141

"Yeah. She, uh.... called me, uh, yesterday.... said she was moving.... didn't say where. You know she moved in and now she's moved somewhere else." McBride tried to force a smile, but his face quivered as he made the attempt.

Beverly knew he was lying. He wouldn't make eye contact and was talking too fast. His facial expressions were all wrong for someone telling the truth. She looked at Charlie, hoping he had seen what she had. Charlie rolled his eyes, but said nothing. She turned and looked back at McBride. "So, that's it.... she's gone?"

McBride looked away again and said, "Yeah, she's gone.... that's all I know to tell you. Is there anything else, officers?"

"No, I guess that's all we need to know for now, Mr. McBride." Beverly was fuming inside.

Charlie and Beverly left.

Going out the front door, Beverly noticed a large dumpster next to the store. "Wait a minute, Charlie." She went over and looked inside. She saw brown wrapping paper and a box. A box the same size as the one she had received. She took it out and held it up for Charlie to see. "It's the same. It's the same wrapping and box that the pictures came in."

Charlie looked around to be sure McBride wasn't watching. "Beverly, you know we can't take that without a warrant. If we try to, a judge will throw it out. Please put it back.... we'll have to think of something else."

Beverly knew he was right. She tossed the evidence back in the dumpster and frowned at Charlie.

"I want to go back inside and question him some more, Charlie."

"Now, Wonder Woman, you know we are out of questions. It's time to plan some strategy, remember how it works.".

"I do," she said.

They drove back to Memphis and went to the station and started looking up information on Mr. Lawrence McBride. He had no arrest and only a few speeding tickets and parking violations over the years. This gave them nothing to go on. It appeared that Mr. McBride was a law-abiding citizen, but there was still something strange about his behavior. It was obvious that he knew more than he was telling them about the lady in the woods. They had to talk with him and try to get some straight answers.

Lawrence McBride was restless again that night. He had some real problems and didn't know how to handle them. The note in the box…. He could see the boxed letters in his mind, "I know what you did……" Oh, how he wished he had never met her. And now the two police detectives. He knew the pretty lady detective doubted him. He knew he had been nervous, and he was sure it showed, to her anyway. Maybe not the guy, he didn't seem very interested…. didn't say much anyway.

Charlie and Beverly got home at around six, Charlie's home. As they got out of the car, Charlie said, "So, what's for dinner, partner?"

She turned and looked at him with a crooked smile. "Charlie, are you sure coffee is the only thing you can make?"

Charlie held up his right hand, as if taking an oath. "I swear it's the truth."

She followed him inside and said, "And you are always telling me that I should get a man in my life. Well, sounds like more work to have one of those."

"Wonder Woman, if you ever do get a man, I am sure you will train him to do what you want."

"You got that right.... Maybe I should give Angie some ideas."

"Now lady, you are overstepping your position. I know all I really want to know about cooking and stuff." They both were laughing as they entered the family room.

Charlie noticed two calls on his answering machine. The first one was someone trying to sell replacement windows. The second one was for both of them.

"I saw you both at the store, talking with McBride. I also saw you looking in the dumpster. I know what McBride did. I just don't know what he did with her body."

There was a long pause. Charlie thought that was the end of the message. Then, it continued, "But I will find out, and when I do.... maybe we can make a deal."

Charlie replayed the recording three more times. He and Beverly listened for any background sounds. They thought they could hear some type of engine, but couldn't really tell for sure. Could be a truck, but it sounded like a larger engine.

Charlie recorded the message on his portable recorder. They would take it to the lab the next morning and see if they could enhance it to better hear the background sounds. They both sat in silence, and then Charlie said, "Let's go out and eat. I know you don't want to cook after listening to this."

Beverly agreed.

They went to a small Italian restaurant. It was quiet and very clean. They both had veal and pasta. It was prepared very well. During dinner, Beverly suggested that they have McBride's phone tapped. Charlie thought that sounded good, but how could they get a judge to agree? "Beverly, it would be great to hear who he is talking with, but I really don't think we can make it happen."

She knew his knowledge was very good when it came to the law. After all, he had been doing this a lot longer than she had. "So, what is our next move, Charlie?"

"Let's sleep on it and give it more work tomorrow. Maybe the new guy in the lab can help."

They were both back at Charlie's house and asleep by eleven.

Beverly made Charlie a big breakfast the next morning, eggs, over easy, of course, with bacon, toast and jelly. He was smiling from ear to ear. She watched him eat and thought what a great person he was. She knew that she loved him, but worried how she was beginning to love him. Was she going over the line?

They were out the door at six thirty.

The department had an excellent lab. They had a new sound man who had just joined the force. He was anxious for new challenges and this was one for him. His name was Jimmy Swift. Charlie thought to himself, I hope you can be swift, Jimmy and give us something to work with.

Jimmy wanted some time, naturally. He asked them to check back with him around four in the afternoon.

Now, they wanted to talk again with McBride. The phone message indicated that someone had been killed. Everything they had seen and heard made them think the victim could be the lady in the woods. They wondered if the voice on the answering machine could be McBride's voice. Jimmy Swift was going to compare that later today. All he needed was to call McBride and try to get him to talk. Maybe do some type of survey, he had told them. He knew a lot of ways to get people talking. It was part of his job.

Strangely enough, when Charlie and Beverly arrived, McBride was on the phone. There were no customers in the store. They walked in and heard him saying, "Well, I don't know anything about global warming and anyway, why do you care about my opinion?" He slammed down the phone and turned and glared at Charlie and Beverly. He looked like he hadn't slept for a week. His eyes had dark circles under them and it appeared he hadn't shaved for a least a day or two.

"Hello, Mr. McBride." Beverly was smiling as she greeted him. He didn't smile. He looked like he could kill from his expression.

"You two back again?" He placed both hands on the counter next to the cash register. "Look, I have told you all I know.... this continuing to come back could be considered harassment."

Charlie leaned over the counter and glared back at him. "You think so, Mr. McBride....well, let me tell you something. Withholding evidence is a crime. Did you know that?"

McBride looked more worried than scared. He placed his hand on his forehead and then said, "What makes you think I'm withholding evidence?"

Charlie was in the attack mode. Beverly loved it. "We got a phone call about you, buddy......and it wasn't from one of your fans."

McBride stuttered and said, "A phone call.... about me? No one called you about me. Why, that's just crazy. I want you two out of here.... and now." His voice was cracking as he spoke. It was obvious he knew something and that *something* wasn't good.

Charlie waited for a long moment then said, "Okay, we are going to leave, but before we go, I want to tell you something." Charlie was in his face. "We know that you know something about the lady we discussed, and the longer you wait to tell us, the more trouble you are going to have from us. Don't think we can't get a warrant to take this place apart. So, it's up to you."

McBride and Charlie's eyes were locked. McBride blinked. Charlie smiled, turned and walked out. Beverly followed him, smiling with pride.

McBride was snarling when they left his store. He glared at them through the window as they drove away.

"Boy, Charlie. I've never seen you so fierce. I thought you were going to attack him for a minute there."

Charlie smiled and looked ahead, as he drove. "We're starting to get some clues now, Wonder Woman."

They headed back to talk with Jimmy Swift....See what he knew about global warming.

"The voice on the recording isn't McBride's," Jimmy told them when they walk into the lab. Beverly was somewhat surprised, but Charlie, didn't really expect it to be him. "The background sounds," Jimmy continued, "are from some type industrial plant. It breaks down as some continuous rhythm, unlike a combustion engine found in a truck or piece of construction equipment."

"So," Charlie said, "We're looking for someone, maybe working in an industrial plant?"

"Exactly," Jimmy said. "And, there is more, another sound that confirms that." Beverly and Charlie looked at each other, and then back at Jimmy.

"Yeah, it's a break whistle, you know, so the employees can take a break. But it's not easy to hear because of the sound of the motor or compressor type unit drowning it out. The phone must be close to this equipment."

It wasn't much, but it was a lead, and they had to investigate. It could be a plant of many types. From small manufacturing to repair shop, or any type of plant that would have need for continuous air, assuming it is an air compressor.

They started with the yellow pages. There were at least twenty businesses within the city that could be possible suspects. They started with a small repair shop, just five minutes from the office. They had no break whistle, so they were eliminated from the list. By late afternoon, they had visited ten locations. None had both continuous sounds from a unit running and a break whistle. They knew it wouldn't be easy, and maybe even impossible to find the exact location the phone call came from.

Charlie and Beverly had been staying in the same house now for a week. They had both talked with Angie every night. She was interested in knowing how Beverly was doing with all the stress, and to reassure her that she was still all right with her being there alone with her husband. It still seemed strange to Beverly, but the security meant so much to her. She and Charlie had good times in the evening and were beginning to have more meals at the Baker house.

It was Sunday night and the start of another week would begin the next morning. Beverly had not done any moonlighting on the weekends since she had been staying with Charlie. He had insisted that she stay in his sight most of the time. She was beginning to say "Yes, Daddy" every time he reminded her about not going anywhere without him. It did give her a more secure feeling, though. She had not had any more dreams. She was pleased and was beginning to sleep more soundly.

It was ten-thirty and the nightly news had just gone off. Charlie stood up and looked over at Beverly. She was almost asleep on the couch. He walked over to her and said, "Well, one more week and this house will be full of noise with Angie and the kids back here."

She smiled and stood up, stretched and yawned. "I know you will be glad to have them home, Charlie."

Charlie smiled and looked at her as she was stretching. It was plain to see with her body pressed against her sweat shirt that she was not wearing a bra. "Yeah, I have missed them." He was still looking at her firm breast. "I really miss being with Angie." He hesitated then said, "You know, at night....in bed."

Beverly was shocked by his comment and blushed. "Well, never being married, I guess, it's hard for me to understand."

Charlie smiled and walked to her, putting both hands on her shoulders. "Beverly, you are so pretty and as I have always said, so very smart. I just can't understand why you haven't got you a feller."

"Oh, Charlie, you worry a lot more about my love life than I do. You know, I am just fine.... I mean I just don't need a man in my life. Why can't you understand that?"

He put his arms around her and held her up close, then put his nose against hers. They were looking eye to eye. "You want to know why I wonder so much about you're.... you're sex life."

She could feel the warmth and moister from his breath. It smelled a little like coffee and some other odor she could not identify, but she liked it. "Yeah, Charlie...I want to know."

When he kissed her, she made no effort to stop him. It was a long and wet kiss. She put her arms around him and returned his kiss. After the kiss, they stood in the middle of the floor holding each other.

She looked into his eyes and then kissed him again, then said, "Do you want this to happen, Charlie?"

He paused then said, "I think we should do what we each feel is right."

"You mean what is right, or what seems right.... now?"

Charlie stood back from her and said, "I miss having sex with my wife, and I know this is not the way to satisfy my wants and needs."

"Oh, Charlie, I shouldn't be here with you like this. It's not right and I think it will be best for us if I move back to my apartment tomorrow." She started to cry. "I have caused you and your family enough problems.... I hope no one will ever know about tonight. I was getting carried away, and that scares me, Charlie."

Charlie hugged her again. "I let my lust get in the way of my better judgment. You are so very desirable and when I looked at you, well, I just let my feelings control my actions.... I'm sorry, Beverly. I hope you believe me.... I will never touch you again.... please forgive me."

She stood looking into his eyes. "You know, Charlie, I have always looked at you as a father figure or older brother."

"I know, Beverly....I know." She kissed him on the cheek and said, "And I want to continue to love you the same way.... let's promise each other that this won't change our relationship.... I need you so much."

Charlie was on the verge of tears as he said, "You are so right.... everything you have said is right on. So, as you said, let's put this behind us and start a new week tomorrow. Okay, Wonder Woman?"

"You got it, Superman."

They were having breakfast the next morning when the phone rang. Charlie thought it might be Angie as she hadn't called the night before. "Must me Angie, excuse me." Before he could say hello, someone was talking.

Beverly watched as he frowned and said nothing. It was the caller again. As Charlie listened the voice said, "Well, Mr. Detective, did you enjoy having sex with your partner last night? I got some pretty good photos that should be of interest to your wife." Charlie made no comment. The bastard must have been peeking in the window, he thought.

The caller continued. "I didn't know that I could get a double header out of this, but between McBride and you, I should be able to collect some big bucks. Well, you and your little sweetie have fun at work today, and by the way, try not to smooch too much on the job."

The line went dead.

Beverly was clearing the dishes as Charlie replaced the phone. "It wasn't Angie, was it?"

Charlie was still frowning. "No, it was, uh, the caller, the one on the answering machine. He saw us last night."

Beverly sat the two plates back on the table. "Saw us? What do you mean, saw us?"

"Said he had photos of us, you know, kissing."

Beverly sat down hard in the kitchen chair. "Oh, God....pictures. Who is this guy...? what does he want?"

"Money, Beverly. He wants money. He said he was going to get money from me, and McBride." Charlie looked at the dishes and said, "Leave them. We need to get to the office. We can do dishes tonight."

Beverly looked at Charlie and said, "I won't be here tonight. I have decided to go back to my apartment where I belong."

Charlie frowned but said nothing. He really understood her feelings and knew it was the best for both of them.

McBride's phone call came a little later that morning. It was nine thirty when he picked up the ringing phone. He was in a very bad mood these days and every noise caused him to jump. "McBride's General Store," he barked in the phone. There was no sound, only silence, silence to cause a nervous person like McBride to grit his teeth. "Hello....anyone there?" He looked wild out of his blood shot eyes. "Hello!"

"Well, Mr. McBride. I'll bet you thought I'd never get around to calling." Then the caller laughed. "How've, you been, you old fart? Have you dragged any more naked dead women through the woods lately?"

McBride's heart was beating so hard he could hear it in his ears. His eyes were glaring and his expression was one of a crazy person. Sweat was forming around his bald head just above his arched eyebrows. "Listen, you son-of-a-bitch....I... I, don't know who you are but you, you, you...."

The caller was laughing so hard and loud that McBride stopped talking. Then he stopped laughing and said, "Now, you just shut up and listen. First of all, calling me names isn't going to help you. In fact, the only person that can help you is me. So, I think you had better just listen and hope I don't turn you in to the police. I have the pictures and I saw you dragging that poor naked lady through the leaves. I have pictures of her in the cabin. But," he laughed again, and then continued, "You

153

know that. I forgot...you have your own copies." He then laughed for another fifteen seconds.

All McBride could do was to listen. He knew he had to listen and he did.

"Okay, McBride, here's the deal; I don't care about your naked lady. She doesn't mean anything to me, but she sure does to you. She does because you will be the one accused of killing her. You still with me?"

McBride grunted a very soft, "Yes."

So, it's money I want...not a lot, just fifty thousand, in cash of course. So, that's all I want to tell you for now. Now, you gather up the money, all in twenties and I'll call you back in a few days and tell you how to get it to me." The line went dead.

McBride could feel the bile coming up from his stomach. He hadn't slept much in the past week and for sure hadn't eaten much. When he had eaten, most of it came back up within minutes after it hit his churning stomach. He was a sick man.

Charlie and Beverly were starting their second full week on the investigation of the naked lady in the woods. Nothing new had happened, and they had very few good leads to work with. McBride was still their most important person, a person of interest, as they called suspects. He really had done nothing to cause more questions and they had no right to arrest him. The lady was missing, but no one other than McBride knew anything about her, and he wasn't talking now. They wanted to visit him again in hopes of learning about the missing lady. Charlie told Beverly that he would be the good cop on this visit. She smiled and said, "You want me to be the bad cop, then?" Charlie didn't answer. He was thinking about the photos and wondering when they would show up.

It was ten fifteen when they arrived at the general store. It was quiet. No customers in view. No cars outside. Charlie and Beverly walked in and looked around. It was totally quiet. Then Charlie called out, "Mr. McBride.... Hello." No response.

"Could be in the restroom," Beverly offered. Charlie nodded, and began to walk around the rows of bins. In the third isle he found McBride. He was lying face down with his head turned to his left. Both arms were raised above his head, like he could have fallen forward and tried to catch himself. Charlie knelt down and felt for a pulse on his neck. It was there, but very faint. His breathing was very slow and his body felt cool to the touch.

"Is he alive?" Beverly's eyes were wide with fear.

"Just barely.... We need to call 911....I don't think we should try to move him." Beverly punched in the number on her cell.

The Paramedics arrived in about twenty minutes. Beverly had covered his body with a blanket she found in the stock room. She had also placed an old jacket under his head. Charlie removed the key ring from McBride's belt, as he knew the store must be locked when they left.

Charlie pulled the front door closed and locked it with McBride's key, after placing the closed sign in the window. He and Beverly followed the ambulance to the hospital. The same one, Beverly thought that Elvis had been taken to, except he was already dead when they took him. She hoped McBride wasn't in the same condition when they arrived. They went directly to emergency. McBride was already being examined by the doctor on duty. Charlie and Beverly waited outside for their findings.

The young resident was a fellow from India and was very hard to understand. Charlie thought why do they have so many people with foreign languages in positions like this? They listened as the resident, Dr. Amiri Singh, explained to them. "He is very sick man.... low blood pressure...looks like malnourished, and close to being in coma. Your father, maybe?" He looked at Beverly.

"No, actually, we are with the Memphis Police Department....Special Victims...."

Dr. Singh looked at Charlie and said, "You too?"

Charlie thought, but didn't say, No, I'm her father, you idiot. He did say, however, "Yeah, I'm with the police too. What can you tell us about his prognosis, doc?"

Singh looked at his watch. "I have a lot of patients, uh, waiting for me. Maybe you come back later.... say in an hour. I will know more by then anyway."

Charlie remembered telling Beverly about being the good cop and held his comment. "Okay, we'll be back at noon."

Singh smiled, turned and walked back into the emergency room.

On their way out a nurse stopped them. "We need some information on the patient. I heard you tell Dr. Singh that you are with the police, can you give me any information?"

Beverly looked at Charlie. He nodded. Beverly smiled at the nurse. "About all we really know is his name.... its Lawrence McBride and he owns and operates a general store north of Memphis....maybe his wallet?"

The nurse thanked them and they left.

Their next stop was to see their boss. Sammy Willis was in his office on the phone when they arrived. He waived them in. They both sat as he finished a call with one of the other detectives. "Well, I missed you two this morning. Are you late or just forgot our Monday morning sessions?"

They had both forgotten. Charlie spoke up. "It's my fault, Captain. We were both focused on a suspect and just forgot. I'll take the blame."

Sammy looked at both of them and then said, "Then, I won't have to remind you to not let this happen again, right?" They both said in unison, "No Sir."

"Okay, now, what's going on with the naked lady investigation? Any more leads, developments?"

Beverly spoke up. "Yeah, we have a development, but no more leads. She explained about finding McBride and him now being in the hospital.

"We need a warrant, Captain," Charlie said.

"A warrant?" Sammy looked surprised.

"Yes, Beverly and I believe there may be evidence in the store, you know, about the missing, uh, naked lady."

"You mean the phone call on Charlie's answering machine."

They both looked at Sammy and nodded. He paused then said, "Okay. Let me make a call to one of the judges.... shouldn't be a problem.... I'll call you when it is signed."

They stood up and Charlie extended his hand. "Thanks, Sammy. We'll wait until we hear from you."

"You better," Sammy said as he waived them goodbye.

They were back at the hospital when Charlie's cell rang. It was the captain.

"You got it. Do you need any help or back up...? someone from the lab, perhaps?"

Charlie thought for a second and said, "Not just yet.... We'll call if we need more help.... thanks, Captain."

Beverly overheard Charlie and knew the warrant was signed.

Young Dr. Singh came in with his scrubs on. He pulled off his cap and ran his fingers through his coal black hair. He looked tired. Beverly thought, these guys work entirely too many hours. I hope they can make the right decisions when needed.

"Well, I do have some news for you. Mr. McBride has slipped into a coma." He paused then said, "That can sometimes be bad news, but not always. All we can do now is wait and hope he comes out."

"So, what do you think?" Charlie asked.

"You mean about coming out of the coma?"

"Yeah, how long....a day, a week...?"

"Oh, really no one knows. It could be anytime." Then he hesitated and said, "Or in the worst case, he could never come out.... he could die, unfortunately."

Charlie and Beverly looked at each other then back at Singh.

"So, we should just keep in touch...call or come by?" Beverly asked with a concerned look.

Dr. Singh placed his hand on her shoulder and said, "Just call. That would be best. If he's better, then you could come."

They thanked Singh and left.

There was an old Chevrolet pickup parked in front of the store when they arrived. The man under the wheel looked as old as McBride. He got out when Charlie and Beverly drove up. "Good morning," the older man said. "I seen you all here the other day.... cops, right?"

"Yes sir, my name is Beverly James and this is my partner, Charlie Baker." They shook hands.

"I seen the closed sign in the wender and wondered about Lawrence. You all know anything about this, is he gone some place?"

"He's in the hospital, sir...your name?"

"Oh, I'm sorry lady." He looked down then back at Beverly. "I'm an old friend of Lawrence McBride's. Yeah, him and me, we go way back.... knowed him for more than forty years.... I'm Nat Bernard...sorry I didn't introduce myself."

"That's okay, Mr. Bernard." Beverly could tell he was upset hearing that his friend was in the hospital. "We just came from the hospital," Beverly continued. "He's pretty sick, in fact he's in a coma and not doing very well, I'm sorry."

"Oh, me I sure hate to hear that. How'd he gets to the hospital...you take him?"

Charlie put his arm around Bernard's shoulder and said, "The paramedics, they took him, you know, in an ambulance."

"Oh, I see." Bernard looked very sad. Beverly felt so sorry for him.

"Can we do anything for you, Mr. Bernard?" Beverly asked.

"No thanks. Think I'll just go home and rest a spell."

Beverly took out her notepad and pen. "Mr. Bernard, could we have your phone number? We will call you when we get information about your friend."

He smiled and looked a little brighter. "Oh, sure, that would be nice." He gave her his number and got in his old Chevy truck and drove away. They watched as he drove out of sight.

"Think he knows something, Charlie?" Beverly asked as she watched the old truck fade into the distance.

"He might, but today isn't the time to ask."

Beverly agreed.

They let themselves in with McBride's key. The old store seemed so dim and dirty. It must have been years since it had a good cleaning. Some of the inventory looked as old as the store itself. Charlie locked the door behind them and followed Beverly to the back room. They both thought, if the body was there, that was the most likely spot. They were not disappointed.

You would have to know it was there to find it, a walk-in freezer. It was neatly hidden behind two rolls of crates. Charlie had noticed marks on the wooden floor near the crates, like they had been moved recently. Dust covered other parts of the floor and crates. Moving the empty crates exposed the door. The freezer was old, but still in working order. It must have been at least zero inside. It must not have been used in years, but it was in use now, and for one occupant.

She was wrapped in a wool blanket from head to toe. Only the top of her head was exposed. Her hair was the color of Beverly's....light brown. Beverly felt a chill when she saw her lying there, and it wasn't from the frigid cold in the freezer. Charlie took out his cell and called Sammy Willis.

"We need some lab people.... We found the nude lady's body."

After the lab techs arrived Charlie and Beverly drove in silence back to their office. Now, more reports must be filed and information recorded while it was fresh on their minds. They both wrote up their own versions, then compared notes for their final report to Sammy. It was six-thirty when they finished the final version and placed it on Sammy's desk.

Sammy looked at the report briefly and said, "Well, nothing's going to happen tonight. I'll go over this in the morning. We can discuss our next move then. See you two here at seven sharp."

As they drove away from the station, Beverly looked over at Charlie and said, "Don't forget, I'm going back to my apartment.

He nodded and said nothing. Her car was still at Charlie's place. They both went in without talking. She went to the guest bedroom and started gathering up her clothes and personal articles. She could hear Charlie on the phone. She knew he must be talking with Angie. She knew he was worried about the photos and how it would impact his marriage, if they got out. She stood there, staring out the bedroom window. Who could know about McBride and her and Charlie? It would look like they had slept together from the pictures. She regretted it so much, but that would get her nowhere, regretting the past. She must think why this was happening. She would have some quiet time at her apartment tonight. Maybe she could come up with someone or something to get to the bottom of this mess.

Charlie was suddenly in the doorway of the bedroom.

"Looks like you are moving out," he said.

She looked at him, thinking about what almost happened.

"Yeah Charlie, we both know its best, and I am going to be all right, now. How are Angie and the girls?"

He put his hand on the door facing and leaned against it.

"Oh, okay, I guess.... Angie's met up with one of her old college friend of some years ago." He looked down at the floor.

"One of her girlfriends, I'm sure they will have a lot to talk about," Beverly said.

Charlie looked back up and into Beverly's eyes.

"Oh, they will have a lot to talk about all right, but not girl stuff.... her old friend is a guy.... the guy she knew before we married."

"But I thought you married your high school sweetheart."

"I did, but that was after she got out of college. We dated in high school, and then she went to NYU for four years. She came back to Memphis and we got together again." He hesitated then said, "She spent four years with this guy.... Arnold, Arnold Stephenson."

Beverly was sure, from what Charlie was saying that this guy, Arnold had something more than a platonic relationship with Angie. Also, he looked angry as he mentioned his name.

"Oh, I didn't know that Angie had a degree."

"She never talks about it and really has never used it," he said as he frowned again. "I guess she don't talk much about it because I only have a high school education."

Beverly wanted to comfort him, but knew better. Instead, she said, "Oh, I know Angie is proud of you, Charlie and loves you very much. She knows she is lucky to have you for her husband and daddy to your girls."

Charlie smiled and blushed. "Aw, shucks, lady...you shore know how to make a feller feel better," he said in his best impression of John Wayne.

Charlie helped her take her things to her car. As she started the engine, she looked at him.

"Charlie, I can never tell you how much you have helped me. I really do appreciate what you did for me."

163

He smiled and said, "The spare bedroom is always available to you.... all you have to do is come over." He watched her until she was gone through the last intersection, before turning onto the freeway.

Charlie was the one that didn't sleep well that night. His thoughts were about Angie and Arnold. She had confessed to him, after they married, that she and Arnold had been lovers during college and had talked seriously about marriage. Arnold's family and opportunities were in New York. He wanted to be a stock broker. He had wanted that life since high school and wouldn't consider living or working anywhere else.

So, their last year of college, they decided that moving was not an option for either, and the relationship ended. They had remained friends and sent Christmas cards and pictures of their families to each other, over the years. Angie never made any comments about the Christmas cards and when Charlie had the opportunity, he threw them in the trash. His mind was filled with thoughts of Angie being with Arnold. Could she really let something happen between her and her old lover?

Then Charlie thought, I almost did...I almost did, with Beverly.... Could she really? Sleep finally overtook his thoughts and he had a fitful night of dreams with interrupted sleep.

Beverly was able to sleep and her returning dream still failed to make its scheduled visit. She did have thoughts before falling to sleep.... thoughts about Charlie. How sad he had looked when he told her about Angie's friend in college.... She must have had an affair with this guy, this

Arnold...something. Beverly slept soundly and awakened refreshed.

Charlie wasn't there at seven sharp. Beverly was sitting in Sammy Willis' office at ten after, looking at her watch and casting a nervous eye at Sammy.

"Have you heard from him this morning?" Sammy asked as he poured another cup of coffee from his Mr. Coffee maker the staff had given him a year ago as a Christmas present. Before she could answer, Charlie came bouncing in the door.

"Sorry, boss.... there was a pile up on west Jefferson.... had to take a longer route around it."

He looked sleepy and tired. Beverly was sure he must have overslept. That would be unlike Charlie, but she knew he was worried, worried about more than the photos now.

Sammy looked over their report and asked some obvious questions, like finger prints and any signs of trauma to the victim. The report included all they really knew at that point. They told him about meeting Mr. Nat Bernard. Sammy agreed that he should be questioned. He instructed them to find him that day and glean what information he could provide about his old friend. As they left, Charlie looked back over his shoulder and said, "Sorry about being late, boss."

Sammy held up his open palm and said, "Go out and save the world, you two."

Charlie and Beverly made their first visit to see Nathan Bernard. He wanted them to know about him and Lawrence McBride. They were glad to hear his story.

165

Nathan Bernard was eighty-one. He had met Lawrence McBride when he was forty-one, forty years ago this week, he told Beverly and Charlie. Nat had moved to Memphis with the railroad. He had worked as a conductor early on, and then transferred to the freight department. This allowed him to be home with his wife Nelly. He worked five days a week and had the week-ends to be home and putter around with his garden and help Nelly with her antique hunting. They traveled all around Memphis, sometimes as far as Nashville.

That was how he had met Lawrence McBride, McBride's old store. Nelly and Nat found it one afternoon, forty years ago, this week. McBride had a lot of junk for sale, but Nat took a liking to him right off. They were both forty-one and had a lot of the same interest. They both liked to hunt, mostly rabbits. So, they became fast friends and had remained friends since then.

They both had lost their wives in the last few years. Nat's Nelly died five years ago, and McBride lost his Mary Jo, just six weeks after Nelly's death. These events brought them even closer. Nat had found an old farm house for sale a year after Nelly died and now lived in the same neighborhood with his old buddy, Lawrence McBride.

Beverly and Charlie enjoyed hearing Mr. Bernard relate his story of his friendship with McBride. Beverly had taken most of his comments down in short hand. This was a real benefit for an officer of the law and made for good reporting later on. Charlie always had his pen and pad out, but doodled mostly. He knew the real meat of the interview would be in Beverly's shorthand.

They did appreciate knowing about how they met, but they really needed to know what Bernard knew about McBride and the naked lady. Beverly took her shot. "Mr. Bernard, we really appreciate you telling us about how you and Mr. McBride met, but we do have some questions, if you don't mind."

"Well, sure, but first, you haven't said anything about Lawrence's condition. I know you said you would call, but...."

"Well, sir, there is nothing to tell you. He is still in a coma, but he isn't any worse," Beverly said, hoping to console him somewhat.

Bernard looked worried as he said in a low voice, "I'm so worried that he may not make it. He's been so sick lately....and worried too...." He looked away from them and stared into space. After a long moment he said, "He got a package.... I told him to call the police, you all, I guess. He wouldn't...Said it was a private matter."

Beverly leaned closer to him. "Did he tell you what was in the package, Mr. Bernard?"

"Made me promise not to tell." He looked at Beverly. "But you are the police and I think I should tell...when someone's in danger, you know."

"You think Mr. McBride is in danger?" Beverly was trying to go slow and easy.

Bernard rubbed the stubble on his chin with his wrinkled old hand and said, "Guess it don't matter now. He's safe there in the hospital.... he can't bother him there."

Beverly was patient. "Who, who won't bother him, Mr. Bernard?"

"The man that sent the package with the pictures and note." He paused and then said, "Now, I've said it.... I promised I wouldn't tell. He's going to be mad at me.... I don't want him to be mad at me.... He's my only friend."

Charlie and Beverly waited in silence. Finally, Beverly said, "You do believe that we are trying to help your friend, don't you?"

He nodded and looked from her to Charlie. "Yes, I do, but he was afraid to call the law, said they could find out other things that would cause him trouble.... big trouble," he said.

"And do you know what that might be?" Beverly asked.

He shook his head and exhaled. "No, but I sure wished I did know.... If I did, then maybe I could help him."

Beverly wasn't sure if she should come right out and tell him about the body. They were not reporting it to the press yet, but they would soon have to. It would only be fair to Mr. Bernard to know before he read it in the newspaper or saw it reported on local TV. She looked at Charlie and said, "I want to tell Mr. Bernard about the freezer. Do you agree?"

Charlie looked at the sad face of Bernard and then back to Beverly. "Yes, I think now is the best time."

Bernard looked puzzled. "The freezer, what freezer? I know about the freezer in the back of the store. Lawrence hasn't used it in years. He used to let some of his friends use it to hang deer in there for slaughter, but that got to be too much, so he quit it. Quit it more than ten years ago."

"Well, Mr. Bernard, someone used the freezer this week." Beverly hesitated then said, "Charlie and I found a dead nude lady in the freezer yesterday."

The shock on Bernard's face was hard to read. Did it mean he really had no knowledge of the dead woman, or was he shocked that they had found her. The freezer was, after all, hidden. Charlie had just been lucky to see the scuff marks on the floor.

They waited for the shock to subside in Bernard. Then Beverly said, "So, you know nothing about the dead woman, is that correct?"

Bernard was not listening, or it seemed like he was not. He looked like he was having chest pains as he bent over and placed his hand on his chest. Beverly was alarmed.

"Are you all right, Mr. Bernard?"

He looked up, still holding his hand on his chest. "NO!" Then he said, "My pills…. on the night stand next to my bed…. nitro…have to have it now."

Charlie found the bottle. It was nitroglycerin for heart angina. Charlie remembered his grandmother having them, carried them with her everywhere. Beverly opened the bottle and got out one pill. Bernard opened his mouth and held up his tongue. Beverly placed the pill gently under his tongue.

Bernard closed his eyes and sat very still. In a few moments, he opened his eyes. "Have a weak heart…. Doc Simmons says someday it will quit on me…. I thought that day had come."

Beverly was so upset she could hardly control herself. She was shaking and her voice was broken as she said,

"I am so sorry to upset you.... I had no idea. Maybe we should take you to the hospital and let them check you over."

He closed his eyes again and said nothing. Charlie knelt down by his chair. "Let us take you to the hospital, Mr. Bernard. It's the least we can do, I agree with Beverly. Will you let us take you?"

Bernard was feeling better now and it showed.

"Well, I guess it wouldn't hurt, and who knows, maybe I'll get to see Lawrence."

Beverly rode in the back with Mr. Bernard and patted him on the shoulder every few seconds. He smiled as he looked into her pretty eyes.

"I'm sure I'm not the first to tell you how lovely you are, young lady."

Beverly smiled and took his hand. He held her hand tight the rest of the way to the hospital.

Now the two old friends were in the same hospital. Both in intensive care, but Bernard was unable to visit his old buddy. He had been placed on a heart monitor and given an I.V. Charlie and Beverly were both allowed a five-minute visit before the nurse asked them to leave. Beverly promised to visit him again the next day.

As they left the hospital Beverly turned to Charlie and said, "If he dies, I don't know what I'll do." She was crying. He put his arm around her as they headed for the car. In the shrubs a camera clicked. The telescopic photo lens brought their faces in clear view.

It was a bad night for both detectives. Charlie was still having thoughts about his wife and Mr. Arnold

Stephenson. She sure sounded happy on the phone to let him know she had run into her old buddy, "Arnie." Well after his call to her sister's house that night, he was pretty sure something was going on. It seemed that Angie had gone to dinner with an old college friend.... Might be late when she got home. He told his sister-in-law to not have Angie call back as he had an early call in the morning and would be turning in early.

When his phone rang at ten, he felt it would be Angie for sure. It was Beverly.

"Hope I haven't called you too late, Charlie." Charlie smiled and felt warm, just listening to his partner's voice.

"Oh...No Beverly. I was just, uh, just," He laughed and said, "really doing nothing." He paused and said, "You feeling better, I mean, about Mr. Bernard?"

"Well, maybe a little, but it still makes me feel so bad. The poor man could have died."

"Well, that's part of the job, Wonder Wom...." He stopped himself and said, "You know, I think I am going to stop calling you that."

"Really...Why?"

"Well, as you know, it started out as kind of a joke; with Kimberly calling you Wonder Woman...I don't want to keep it up. I don't want to do anything to sound condescending to you. You are a very professional lady and, sometimes, well, I just think you deserve better."

Beverly felt a sudden twinge in her chest. He was paying her a compliment, and he was sincere.

"Charlie, that is so nice of you to say. You are going to make me cry, again."

171

They sat in silence for a long moment. Then Charlie said, "I miss you."

She didn't respond.

"Beverly, you still with me?"

"Yeah, I'm here; just don't say that.... we agreed."

"I know, I guess you get tired of me saying I'm sorry.... but I am. I'm sorry I said that, but I'm not sorry I miss you."

"Charlie, we'll be together all day tomorrow, and we must go see about both the elderly gentlemen."

"I know, and we will."

"Oh, Charlie, I almost forgot, how is Angie and the girls?"

He hesitated. "The girls are fine.... Angie is having dinner with her old buddy, Arnold."

"Oh," Beverly said, in a very soft voice. "Well, see you at seven, okay Charlie?"

"I'll be there.... good night, Beverly."

"Night, Charlie."

They were both early. Charlie was sitting with his favorite cup of steaming coffee. Beverly came in, whistling.

"Morning, Mr. Baker."

He smiled and gave her a small salute. "Morning to you, Miss James." They both laughed.

"We are going to have a great day, Charlie; I can feel it."

"Hope you're right, partner. You ready to ride?"

"Take me to your carriage, sir."

It was great for both of them to be kidding and having fun.... just like old times.

Dr. Singh advised them that McBride had no change. His vital signs were improving, however. The IV was improving his overall nutritional needs and his color was better. Charlie and Beverly were allowed to look in on him, but just for a minute or two. From there, they went down the hall to see Mr. Bernard. He was sitting up and drinking juice through a straw. His I.V. had been removed and he was able to eat solid food. He smiled when he saw them.

"Well, you did come back, and you brought your partner, too."

Charlie smiled and said, "I'm not as pretty as she is, but I do care also."

"I know you do," Bernard said. "The doctor told me I might be able to go home in a few days, if I continue to improve."

Beverly patted his arm and said, "Great news. I am so happy for you. We are going to get out of here and let you rest, but one more thing, Mr. Bernard."

"Yeah, what's that, young lady?"

"You tell all those pretty nurses that you already have a girlfriend, okay?"

He smiled and said, "I will and I'll tell them that she the prettiest cop in town." He waved and smiled as they left his room.

"You don't want to ask him any more questions, do you, Beverly."

She walked with Charlie down the hall a few more feet before answering.

"He'll have to get a lot better, and even then, I'm not sure. In fact, I'm not sure anyone should ask him."

They took the elevator to the lobby. A young man with a camera strung around his neck was standing at the front door as they went out. They both looked at him. He smiled and went inside.

They finally got some good news, at least good news for Lawrence McBride. The Medical Examiner determined that the cause of death was from cancer. The naked lady had a large tumor in her brain. She must have had it for a few years. There was no way she could have lived with a tumor of that size. The pressure from the tumor had finally taken her life. Even though she had been in the freezer for a period of time, it was determined that she had died before being put in there. Now, the question was, why did McBride have her body in his freezer.

Had he found her, Beverly thought, perhaps in the woods...dead? Maybe, but why not call the police? Why the freezer? Hopefully, he would recover and answer this important question. It was certain that he had not killed her. Beverly knew Charlie must be having the same questions.

It was mid-week and Angie and the girls would be home in a couple of days. They would be flying in Friday afternoon. Charlie was excited, and reminded Beverly that he would need to take off at noon on Friday to pick up his family at the airport.

Friday morning, they made their visit to the hospital. No change in McBride, but Bernard was scheduled to go home on Monday. He was now in a step-down room and was being walked down the hall twice a day. They met him on his morning walk. A young nurse was assisting him. As they approached, Bernard said, "I told her, she knows about you."

Beverly smiled and took his other arm and walked with them back to his room. After a short visit, Beverly told Bernard that she would call him at home on Monday. He said he would be looking forward to the call.

Beverly went to the office to finish up their reports for the week. Charlie went home to change clothes. He was going to be casual, in his jeans and boots when he picked up his family.

Their flight was on time and Charlie was waiting just outside the gate. All three girls came running, screaming, "Daddy, Daddy, Daddy...."

He had his arms stretched out to reach around them. It was a happy reunion. When he looked up, Angie was standing there smiling.

"Do you have a hug for me too, Angie?" He took her in his arms, but the feeling was different. He felt cold and aloof. Was it just his feelings, or did she feel the same? Now was not the time to discuss that. They would have their private time later. The girls talked constantly on the way home. They told him about all the sights in Manhattan. It sounded like they took all them in. It was so great to have them home.

When they walked in, Angie looked surprised. "Well, this place looks great. What did you do, hire a maid?"

He smiled and said, "Beverly was here for a week."

She frowned and said, "Just a week? She went back to her apartment then?"

"Yeah, she got to feeling all right and seems to be doing fine now."

Angie took a small bag to the bedroom and started to unpack it.

"I wanted us to go out for dinner, Angie. Let's unpack tomorrow."

She put the bag on the bed. "Sounds good to me, where are we going?"

"Well, you all have traveled with casual clothes, as I thought you would, so how about burgers and fries?"

The girls heard and started jumping up and down with joy.

That night, after the girls were in bed and the TV had been turned off, he turned and looked at his wife and said, "I sure missed you, Angie."

She touched his arm and said, "me too."

He waited, and then leaned over to kiss her. She turned her cheek to him.

"Lip stick. I know how you hate to get it on your lips, Charlie."

They had been sitting on the couch for several minutes and this was the first time he had tried to kiss her. He got up and stood over her.

"Angie, is there anything you want to tell me about your trip to New York?"

Angie raised her eye brows. "What do you mean, Charlie?"

"You know what I mean. I mean...Arnold."

"Are you crazy? I told you that I had run into Arnie....
and well, you knew that. What are you saying?"

"Did your sister tell you that I called when you were
out with ARNIE?"

She looked away and closed her eyes.

He thought how McBride had looked away when they
were questioning him about the naked lady.

"It was just dinner. My God, Charlie, you make it
sound like I went to bed with him."

Charlie was glaring at her now. "Well, did you?"

"Don't raise your voice like that. The girls will
hear you."

"Do they know you went out with your old lover?"

She stood up. "I'm going to bed, Charlie. You can stay
in here and shout all night if you want to, but I am not
going to listen to this crap."

He stood up and put his finger in her face. "It is
crap all right and you caused it to be crap for us, for our
family."

She closed her eyes again. This time tears came
flowing from under her lids. She turned and walked to
the bedroom, leaving him standing in the family room.

Later, they lay in bed without speaking. He knew she
had cheated. She couldn't hide it.

He hated her for doing this to him and to the girls.
How could she betray him?

She turned to him and cried softly. "I'm sorry, Charlie.
It was wrong. I don't want to hurt you. It just happened."

"So, you admit it, and so easily. My God, Angie, do
you still love him."

"I don't know," she said through her sobs.

"You don't know?"

Charlie got up and walked around to her side of the bed and sat down.

"Fifteen years," he shouted. "We have been married fifteen years. Does that not mean anything to you?"

She turned her back and put the pillow over her head. He sat and looked at his wife, and the mother of their sweet little girls. How could they go on with this hanging over their heads? She had readily admitted having sex with her old lover, and she wasn't sure if she loved him or not. He knew this would be the end of their marriage. He sat and stared at the wall for a long time. Then to his surprise, he heard Angie snoring. She had fallen asleep after this discussion about the future of their marriage.

"God help me," he said as he got up and went to the guest bedroom. He lay there in the bed, thinking about Beverly. She had been in that same bed for a week. He wanted her. He felt like Angie was pushing him toward Beverly. He felt so confused, hurt and so lonely.

Saturday was a very sad day in the Baker house. Charlie was up early and made coffee, his only cooking skill. The three girls were up by nine, looking for cereal and milk. He could help with that, and did. They sat and talked while eating cereal together. The girls laughed and told more stories of their adventures in the Big Apple.

Angie slept until eleven. She came in the kitchen and picked up the coffee pot. It had been warmed over and smelled rank. She poured it out and started to make a fresh pot. Charlie heard her and came in from the family room. He had been watching cartoons with the girls. They looked at each other. Neither one smiled.

"Did the girls have breakfast?" She asked as she filled the pot.

"They had cereal with me. There are fine, for now."

She turned to face him and asked, "For now?"

"Yeah, fine until you tell them what you did and how you are going to destroy our family."

She turned back to finish her task of making coffee. Charlie went back to the girls.

Charlie took the girls to the movies in the afternoon. Angie begged off claiming a headache. They had a fun-filled afternoon. After the movie, they went to an amusement park and rode every ride at least twice. Charlie had a ball being with his three girls. While they were together, he forgot about Angie and the climax that was yet to come.

Charlie and Angie made it through the week-end without fighting, at least not in front of the girls. He was glad to see Monday come around, probably as happy as Beverly was about Mondays, on this Monday, for sure.

A certified letter came to the precinct, addressed to Mr. Charles A. Baker. He had to sign for it. It was in a large brown envelope. The mail carrier left and Charlie looked across his desk at Beverly. They both thought about the promised photos.

There were four prints, two with then kissing in Charlie's home and two of them walking out of the hospital. Charlie had his arm around her and she was crying with her head on his shoulder. He passed them over to her. She stared at them and then looked over the top of them at Charlie.

He was smiling.

"My God, why are you smiling, Charlie?" She asked in a whisper.

"I'll tell you over lunch."

She looked shocked as she tried to smile.

They had lunch at a small Mexican restaurant. Charlie chose a table in the very back corner. It was actually a booth with sides that almost concealed the occupants. It was very private. The waiter came and asked about drinks. They both asked for water. He left the menus and went to get the water.

"Well, you have been very quiet all morning, Charlie."

The waiter was back with the water.

"Have you decided, Sir?"

Charlie looked at Beverly then said, "We'll both have the chili and a burrito."

Beverly smiled. The waiter left again.

"Hope that's okay, I mean, ordering for you," Charlie said.

"Sure, it's okay, now talk. Why were you smiling when you saw the photos this morning?"

He took a sip of his water and said, "Well, you had better hold on for this."

She frowned again.

"It's Angie," he said.

"Angie? What's that mean?"

"She's having an affair."

Beverly had started to take a drink from her glass. She sat it down, spilling some water on the table.

"An affair? I can't believe it. Are you sure?"

Beverly was staring at Charlie with her mouth open.

"Well, Wonder Woman, oh, habit, sorry.... you had better believe it. She admitted it to me Friday night." He took another drink of water and said, "And, it's her old lover, yes lover. The guy I told you about, they lived together during college."

Beverly was shaking her head. "This can't be true. Not Angie. I know Angie. I love Angie. What about the girls? This is awful." She looked away then back to face Charlie. "Oh, Charlie, I am so sorry for you."

The chili and burrito came. They were both hot with heat and chili powder. The waiter brought more water, and not too soon. They both ate in silence for a while.

"So, the photos," Beverly said.

"Yeah, I just thought how funny it is now. The guy said he would show them to my wife, if I didn't follow his instructions, looks like he just lost his leverage."

"I guess we'll be hearing from our Peeking Tom soon, huh, Charlie?"

"Oh, yeah, I expect to hear anytime, maybe tonight."

Beverly looked up from her chili bowl. "You'll call me if he calls, right?"

Charlie smiled and said, "Yep, as they say, you'll be the first to know."

Their next call was to Mr. Nat Bernard. He had gotten home earlier in the day. He answered the phone and was glad to hear Beverly's voice.

"Well, hello, pretty lady. It's good to hear from you."

"And it's really good to hear you sounding so good, Mr. Bernard. Been home long?"

"Got here about ten this morning, are you coming out to visit?"

Beverly looked over at Charlie.

"Yes, in fact we are on our way, if that's okay with you."

Bernard laughed and said, "Those cell phones, never know where someone is when they call you.... sure, you come on. I'll be looking for you."

Mr. Bernard came to the door almost before they could ring the doorbell.

"Oh, I see you brought your sidekick with you."

Charlie smiled and said, "Yes, sir...It's my job to drive her around."

They all laughed.

"Come in. Hope you have had lunch, because I have not got much here."

"Yes, we just finished and came on out to see you," Beverly said.

They sat in his living room again and Beverly immediately thought of his angina attack at their last meeting.

"Mr. Bernard, we do want to talk some more about your friend and the lady that was found in his freezer. But, we won't if you feel too uncomfortable."

He looked at them and then down at his old wrinkled hands. He rubbed them on his pant legs and then said, "I'm sure that Lawrence put her body in the freezer, but I'm also sure he didn't kill her." He sat and waited for their reaction. They showed none. He then said, "You both act like you already know that."

Charlie said, "Well, Mr. Bernard, we kind of do. You see, the medical examiner told us that she was terminally ill. It was cancer. The ME is sure she was dead long before she was put in the freezer, so we agree with you."

Bernard was nodding and smiling. "Oh, I'm so glad to know that. Now, I can tell you that Lawrence did tell me about finding her, and she was dead. He was afraid he would be accused of killing her, so he put her in there for safe keeping." He paused for a long moment. Then said, "First of all, I'm pretty sure Lawrence is not going to wake up. You see, one of the nurses told me they did an MRI on his head and he has had a stroke." He looked down again and when he looked up at them, a single tear rolled down his old wrinkled cheek. He allowed it to stop and lay in a crease in his face. "So, I know.... I know that my old friend won't ever know that I'm telling you this."

Beverly was worried that Bernard would become more upset. "Mr. Bernard, you don't have to continue if this too stressful for you."

Bernard laced his fingers together and looked at his hands for a long moment. "Lawrence was trying to help that lady. She confided in him. You see, when she came here, she knew she was dying and she only told Lawrence. Only he knew."

Beverly and Charlie waited as he seemed to be thinking and trying to recall the rest of his story for them.

"Well, it was after he found her in the woods....it was then that he told me about her. He told me she had a brain tumor and wanted to die in private. That's why she wanted the cabin in the woods. She wanted to die alone." Bernard sat and looked at them. He seemed like a little boy that had finally told the truth to his mother and was waiting for her approval.

"So, you really didn't know about her until after she was dead," Charlie said as he took out his note pad and pretended to make notes.

"That's right.... I asked him why he hadn't called the police when he found her."

"And what did Mr. McBride say, Mr. Bernard?" Beverly asked.

"Well, he seemed a little mad at me for asking."

"He seemed mad?"

"Yes ma'am. He looked at me and said that she was dying and he had tried to help her. Then he remembered you two asking about her and he thought he would be in trouble with the law." Bernard sat for a few moments and then said, "I guess, I should have called the police, uh, you all."

Charlie and Beverly exchanged glances, but said nothing. Beverly felt they had asked enough questions and said, "Well, Mr. Bernard, we have kept you long enough. Again, we are so glad you are feeling better and are able to be back at home."

He smiled and stood up. "Thank you, and thank you for checking on me. I really have no one now that Lawrence is gone." He looked down at the floor and then back at Beverly. "He is gone, you know. His mind is dead.... they said brain dead at the hospital."

Beverly hugged him and said, "I'm sorry you have lost your friend.... I'll call you in a few days, and if you need us, you be sure to call us." Beverly had a sad feeling that they may never speak again.

It was going on five when they left Bernard's house. Charlie drove and was quiet for the first five minutes. Then he said, "Beverly, let's grab a bite when we get back to Memphis, okay?"

She looked over at him. He seemed to be in deep thought. She knew he wanted to talk and she was the obvious one to listen.

They stopped at a small family restaurant on the north side of Memphis. It was soul food, as Charlie liked to call it. Everything fried and soaked in butter. They got a table in the back corner. Charlie ordered coffee. Beverly had water with lemon. He looked across the table at her and smiled. "Well, looks like I'm going to be single soon.... sounds crazy don't it."

As she looked at him, he looked so old and tired. His spirits were very low. She knew he was sad, and he had reason to be. His wife of fifteen years had taken up with an old lover. She couldn't believe it.

"Oh, Charlie....It just seems so unreal. I just wish I could make it go away for you." Then she said, "I know you don't really have anyone to talk with about this, so I want you to know that I am here for you.... You are my best friend and I love you, and care what happens to you."

The server came and asked if they were ready to order. Charlie looked at Beverly, "You ready?" She ordered a house salad and half a tuna sandwich. Charlie wanted more than a skimpy salad and only half a sandwich. He ordered the grease and butter food. Fried chicken, mashed potatoes, with gravy, white beans, peas, and cornbread.

After the server left the table, he reached across and took her hand. "You know that I love you too, Beverly. But you have had some issues lately and I'm not the only one who needs someone to listen."

She squeezed his hand and said, "You know, after the second night, I haven't had another dream."

"Really?"

"Yeah, and I have figured it out, Charlie. "She continued to hold his hand. "Charlie, it was my clock-radio."

Charlie looked shocked as he said, "Your clock-radio?"

"Yeah, I set it for five a.m. and the radio comes on for five minutes before the actual alarm sounds. The report of the naked lady was on the news, I called the radio station and they confirmed it." She was beaming and sounding more excited than she had in the last few days. "I must have heard the news as I was still in a semi-conscience state."

"You mean not awake and it caused you to dream about it?"

"Exactly, I know this is what happened. I was beginning to think I was a psychic or a psycho or something."

She released his hand and sat back. "I do appreciate you thinking about me, but I'm really fine now, so, let's talk about you and the kids.... what about the kids?"

Charlie slowly sipped his coffee. "Well, I'm sure there will be joint custody. Most times, the judge will let the kids live with their mother and the dad has visitation rights.... maybe week-ends and holidays."

"So, would you be all right with seeing them just on the week-ends?"

"Well, no, but I may not have a choice."

It seemed like she was talking with a stranger. He was so aloof and distant. She knew he was sad and upset.

"So, are you staying home with Angie, now, I mean like tonight?"

He looked up from his coffee and a slow smile moved across his lips. "I guess so, unless.... you invite me to stay with you tonight."

Beverly could feel her face warming up as she blushed. "I thought we had settled that, Charlie."

Now, he looked embarrassed again, like he had the night he had kissed her. They were now looking into each other's eyes, saying nothing.

Beverly spoke just above a whisper. "Charlie, you were there for me when I needed security and compassion. If you really want to stay with me tonight, it's okay with me."

He raised his eye brows. "You serious?"

"I'm serious," she said without blinking.

The food came and they started to eat. Charlie seemed to be more relaxed. She wondered if it was the food or her invitation. It was both. He was happy to have the meal and happier to not go home and face Angie.

After the meal, he said, "If you're sure, I'll call Angie and tell her I won't be home tonight." He looked into her eyes. She was smiling. She was so pretty. He was almost lost in her eyes as he heard her soft voice saying, "Yes, Charlie, I'm sure."

He called Angie and told her he would not be home. He then talked to the girls and told each one that he loved them and would see them the next night. He put his cell phone back in his pocket.

Beverly's apartment was only a one bedroom, but had a sofa in the living room- kitchen combination. The bath was off the bedroom. It was really designed for one person. Charlie had never been inside and was surprised how small it was.

Charlie always kept a set of underwear, shirt, socks and a shaving kit, just in case he had to stay out. Over the years, he had stayed out maybe three times. This time, it was not because duty called. This time it was different. He placed his small bag down next to the sofa and sat down.

Beverly went to the bathroom. She returned in a few minutes and said, "You go first. I'll take my shower after you.... Is that okay?"

Charlie was out in ten minutes and watching TV as Beverly went to take her shower. She came out wearing a bath robe and bare foot. She sat next to him on the couch. He could smell her bath soap and perfume. It was nice. She put her feet under her and turned to face him. Neither spoke.

After a long pause Charlie said in a very soft voice, "Beverly, first of all I really appreciate you letting me spend the night with you." He looked into her pretty eyes and knew what he wanted but was going to keep his promise to her. He cleared his throat and continued. "I promised you that I would not touch you again. I know things are different now with my upcoming divorce. I don't know what you expect from me, but hope you understand where I am coming from now."

She was silent for a long moment and then said, 'Well Charlie I know how strange this is for us. You are the most important person in my life and I do love you. I do understand what you are saying. All I want to do now is to help you get through this awful time."

Charlie looked at her and nodded with tears in his eyes. "Beverly, you are very special to me and I want us to always be there for each other."

Beverly leaned over and kissed Charlie on the cheek. "I can sleep on the sofa and let you sleep in my bed."

"No, Beverly. Just being here is enough. The sofa will be fine for me."

Beverly stood up and said, "Please wake me if you need anything tonight." She went to her bedroom.

Charlie watched her walk away and sat looking into the empty room, wondering what his future was going to be.

Beverly was in and out of the shower the next morning and had breakfast ready when Charlie came into the small kitchen area. They sat across from each other and both smiled.

Beverly frowned then and said, "Charlie, I know this is so sudden and really unexpected for you. Are you going to be, okay?"

"Well, first of all it's the girls. I know they all three love you and you love them, but Angie will always be their mother."

He stood and then kissed her on the cheek and then looked at the kitchen clock. "Six fifteen. Just enough time to get ready to leave for work." They left at six thirty.

Lawrence McBride died at six that morning. Beverly's cell rang just as they were leaving the apartment. The nurse on duty had a note to call her if anything changed in his condition. Mr. Bernard's friend was not just brain dead. He was gone in body and soul. They went to the station. When they arrived, Sammy Willis called them into his office.

"Guess you heard about McBride?" Sammy said.

"Yeah, they called us on the way in," Beverly said.

Sammy looked at them and said, "Guess some guys want to be together no matter what."

Beverly looked at Charlie then at Sammy. "What do you mean, Captain?"

"Nat Bernard was found dead in his truck early this morning. He was parked in front of McBride's store. Seems they both died about the same time."

Beverly remembered telling him she would call him, and the strange feeling she had about not talking with him again. She sat and said nothing, letting her thoughts take over.

Charlie put his hand on her shoulder. "You okay, Beverly?"

She turned quickly to face him. "Oh, sorry, I was just lost in my thoughts.... thoughts about both of these older gentlemen."

Now, the department had the task of trying to find out about the lady, the naked lady in the woods, as she had been labeled. She had no I.D. of any kind and apparently the only person, locally, that knew anything, was Lawrence McBride. Well, he wasn't around now to question. So, where did they go from here? They had already run her finger prints and came up with a zero. No record on file. It might go in as an unsolved identity. The cause of death was known, however. It wasn't a homicide that was for sure. It would be one of those cases that wasn't exactly active, but kept open, just in case any clues did crop up in the future.

Now, the next question was the caller, the caller that had sent the pictures and had accused McBride of killing the lady. They knew they had to find this guy, and felt that they would. He had promised to call again and he was overdue.

Beverly had visited the funeral home that had the bodies of the two old gentlemen. She suggested a joint funeral for them, and since no family members were known of, they agreed. She and Charlie attended the services. It was very touching, with the preacher talking about the friendship between two men that had lasted for so many years. The preacher said it was very fitting that they had both gone together to meet their wives and be in heaven together, forever.

Outside the funeral home, Beverly saw the young man they had seen at the hospital. He had the camera again, with the strap around his neck. He made eye contact with her and smiled. She felt sure he must be the caller. That would be confirmed later that night.

Beverly was home, alone when her phone rang. It was him.

"I saw you at the funeral...you knew it was me, didn't you?"

Beverly hesitated, waiting to respond with the right answer. Then she said, "Oh, yeah, my partner and I have known about you for a while now."

She waited then he said, "What do you mean, you have known about me?"

She could tell that he might be a little edgy. she really got to him. "We have cameras too." She could hear him breathing with a sound like, anger, heavy exhaling. She pushed. "So, when do we get to meet with you?"

The phone went dead. Beverly felt good. She knew she had him on the defensive.

Beverly wanted to call Charlie, but decided against it. He was at home tonight with his three little girls, and of course, his wife, Angie. She sat and looked at the phone, wondering what the future was going to be for Charlie.

Then, there was her relationship with Angie. After all, she and Angie had become friends on their first meeting. She had kept their kids and actually felt like a part of their family. Would she see the girls in the future? How could she leave Charlie and take his girls away from him? It was crazy and so hard to believe.

Charlie was at home and yes, he was enjoying being with his three daughters. But his family was fractured, and he felt like the girls knew it.

Angie was there in body only. It was obvious her thoughts were elsewhere. Charlie played cards with the girls. They loved to play poker with their dad. He would finance them and then refinance them when they lost the money, he had given them. They laughed and had a great time. When their bedtime came, they all three left for the bathroom to get ready. They knew their dad and mom would be in to say goodnight.

After saying goodnight to the girls, Charlie and Angie went to the family room and sat next to each other on the couch. Charlie thought how many times they had loved and kissed on this couch. Now, it was just a vehicle to use for conversation. And, a conversation that was not going to have a good ending.

They spoke softly, not wanting the girls to hear. "So, Angie, I think we have some issues to resolve."

She made no comment, but did turn to face him. He looked at her and thought how much in love he had been with her, and now, he wasn't sure she ever loved him. She had said she thought she loved Arnold Stephenson. Her expression told him nothing, nothing at all. He was sure he wanted to talk it out and tonight was as good as any to talk it out.

"Well, it seems you have nothing to say, Angie. So, I'll start this. We have to first of all think about the girls. Their future is our responsibility and we must make a life for them that is as good as it can be."

"Charlie, I know this comes as a shock to you and in some ways, it is to me. I had not seen Arnold in years, as you know. Also, as you know, Arnold and I had four years together and, well, when I saw him in New York, it just came back. He and I have a connection, a bond."

Charlie looked away and said, "And we don't have a connection, a bond?"

"I'm sorry, Charlie. I know this hurts you and I also realize that we have a responsibility for the girls. So, yes, I do want to resolve this and hopefully, tonight."

"Well, Angie, I'm listing. After all, you have had more time to think about this than I have. It seems I just got in on the last act, so to speak

"Well, I'm going to be honest with you, Charlie. I'm going to be very honest. I want to move to New York. I want to be with Arnold. I do love him and I think he will want to marry me after a while. And, if you are wondering, yes, I will live with him even if he doesn't want to marry me."

Charlie shook his head, and then said, "Well, that explains where you want to live. Now, let me tell you something, and you can take this to the bank. I will fight you to the bitter end if you try to take our girls to New York. I will not stand for it.... period!"

Then the big shocker... She smiled and said, "I wouldn't expect you to feel any other way. I don't want our girls to grow up in that city. They belong here in Memphis, their home, their home with their friends and Beverly. Charlie, I'm not dumb. I know when I move out;

Beverly will be here with you and the kids. She could even learn to love you, even though you are a little old for her."

Charlie was staring at her with his mouth open. "These are your children....my God, Angie. You can just move away and not even think about them? What kind of mother are you?"

She paused, looked down at her folded hands and said, "Not a very good one, I guess."

Charlie got up and walked out of the room. He went to the kitchen and opened the fridge and got a beer. He opened it and sat down at the kitchen table, took a big swig and set the beer down hard on the table. He couldn't think of anything else to say to Angie. She had shown her colors and they were dark. Had she ever loved him and the girls? How could she not love the girls, even if she hated him? He heard Angie walking down the hall to their bedroom. He would never sleep with his wife again. This was all so sad, strange, and very weird.

Beverly's phone rang again. It was then eleven. She thought it would be the "Caller" again. She slowly picked up the phone and listened before answering. Then she heard Charlie say, "Beverly, are you there?"

"Yeah Charlie, I had no idea it was you, everything okay?"

Charlie sighed. "Well, no....Angie and I had a talk tonight and it was so unbelievable, I mean, you just would think she was a different person."

Beverly wanted to be with him as she listened to him. She could feel his pain. It was so unfair. "Charlie, I just wish I could help you.... I'm just so sorry this is happening to you."

"I know you do Beverly, and I really do appreciate your concern." He hesitated for a long moment then continued, "It meant so much to me with us being together, you know at your place."

"Oh, Charlie, I'm glad....and I want to be with you. It's just the family, you know, Angie, the girls. It's all so strange. What would she think if she knew you stayed with me?"

Charlie closed his eyes and said, "You'd be surprised, Beverly."

They sat in silence then Beverly said, "Maybe we can discuss this some more tomorrow, but since you called, I have some info."

"Oh, and what's that?"

"The caller, He called me tonight. It was him at the funeral today. I think I have him worried." She then told Charlie how she had handled him on the phone.

Charlie laughed and said, "Now, sounds like you are the stalker." They both laughed and said goodnight.

They both thought they would never hear from the caller again...and they never did.

Charlie went to the guest bedroom and lay awake until four in the morning. He would be up in an hour and start another day as Sergeant Charlie Baker....soon to be single and a single parent.

The next morning Beverly and Charlie filed the naked lady in the woods in the inactive file. It would still be available, but not worked on a regular basis.

These inactive files were reviewed every month, just as a reminder and to check for clues. Charlie and Beverly were going to have a rather dull day in the office. Besides filing the naked lady's file, they had a lot of old files to review and be prepared to recommend if they should be filed in cold cases or closed.

They had lunch again at the Italian restaurant. This time, Beverly ordered for both. It was a light salad with low calorie dressing and water. Charlie made a face and made a sign with thumbs down. Beverly laughed and grabbed both of his thumbs.

She kept looking into his sad eyes and knew something more was bothering him. "Charlie, you know I will always be with you and help you anyway I can. Please tell me what is so upsetting. I know it's Angie, but is there more? Have you discuss visitation rights?"

Charlie's expression was strange. She had never seen him look so concerned, almost a lost look. He did manage a slight smile and said, "The girls were the main topic and you will not believe what Angie wants regarding them. He closed his eyes and said in a whisper, "She wants me to have Total rights."

"Total rights, what are you saying?"

"She wants the girls to stay with me and she is going to move to New York with Arnold."

Beverly could not speak as she sat and stared at Charlie and thought, how could any mother not want her own children, children she gave birth to. After thinking this she finally said, "So, what does this mean for me. Will I get to see the girls?"

"Angie thinks you will eventually move in with us."

Beverly's eyes were now bulging. "Are you serious?"

"Beverly, I'm serious and Angie is serious about leaving her own children."

They both sat in complete silence. Both feeling so confused, but still thankful they had each other and knowing they would both be there for the girls.

They finished their lunch and went back to the office. They finished their day finishing up more paper work.

They were getting ready to leave just after five. Everyone was leaving. Beverly sat at her desk and looked up at Charlie as he stood up. "Charlie, I think we need to talk with Angie."

"We? You think you should talk with Angie?"

"Charlie, after what you told me at lunch, I think we must talk with her together. I can't believe she will leave her girls, but it seems she is going to leave them."

Charlie sat back down and covered his face with both hands. Beverly sat and waited.

Sammy walked past them on his way out and told them good night. It wasn't unusual for officers to work past five when they had more to complete.

After Sammy left Charlie looked at Beverly and said, "Well, I do know the love you have for the girls and they love you just like a member of our family. I agree that their care is the most important thing in our lives right now."

Beverly smiled and felt so warm knowing how much love she shared with the girls. "Well, then do you agree that we both need to talk with Angie?"

"Beverly, you are so special and I am so blessed to have you in my life. I know you are right. It just seems so strange." He paused and then said, "I guess the sooner the better. What do you think about tonight?"

Beverly thought before speaking and then said, "Maybe you should call her first."

Charlie took his cell from his pocket and called Angie.

Beverly listened as Charlie told Angie he was bringing her home to have dinner with them.

The three girls were so happy to see Beverly. They had not seen her since returning from New York. The three gave her hugs and told her they loved her.

Charlie looked at Angie as she watched the girls gathered around Beverly and wondered what she could be thinking.

After the girl's greetings to Beverly, she looked at Angie and thought about what they would be talking about later on. Angie opened her arms to Beverly and they embraced.

They stood back and Angie said, "Welcome, it's good to see you, Beverly."

"It's good to see you also, Angie. Welcome home."

Angie had always kept frozen pizza in the freezer and knew everyone there would be happy with that for dinner. They were soon eating and the girls telling Beverly all about their trip to New York, The Big Apple they kept calling it. It was a happy and fun time for them.

Beverly helped Angie clean up the kitchen and it was soon time for the girls to clean up and get ready for bed.

At nine all three adults went to the girl's bedroom and kissed them goodnight.

Angie had no idea why Beverly was there other than to have dinner and see the girls. She would soon learn the real reason for her presence.

The three adults were sitting in the family room when Charlie finally spoke. "Angie, I have asked Beverly to join us tonight for a reason other than dinner and a visit."

Angie looked surprised for a moment and then looked at Charlie and said, "You told her, didn't you?"

Charlie looked at Beverly and then at Angie and said, "Yes, Angie. She knows everything we have discussed." He looked down at his hands and said in a choked voice, "I even told her what you want to do about the girls."

Angie shook her head and said, "Well, she would know at some point. I guess it's best to know sooner rather than later."

Beverly could hardly look at Angie as she spoke. She had known Angie for five years and truly loved her, cared about her. This was just impossible to believe.

Angie then looked at Beverly and said, "Well, I am sure you think I am a terrible person, Beverly."

Beverly really didn't know how to answer her. She looked at Charlie and then at Angie. "I am truly at a loss for words. I would never believe you two would separate." She then looked at Charlie and continued. "You and Charlie are like family to me, you know that."

Everyone was silent for a long moment. Angie broke the silence with a stunning comment. "Well Beverly, I'm sure you will soon or later be more than a friend. You and Charlie will take care of these girls. I know you both love them."

Beverly stood up and pointed her finger at Angie and said, "And you can just walk away from your husband of fifteen years and three loving little girls. You asked me a minute ago what I think of you, well I think you are a self-centered cold-hearted bitch."

Beverly stared at her for another moment and then walked down the hallway to the guest bathroom and slammed the door behind her.

More silence with Charlie and Angie. They both sat staring into space. Finally, Angie said, "Well, I told you Charlie, you and Beverly will be excellent parents to your girls."

"My God, Angie, they are your girls too. Are you completely crazy? Have you lost your mind?'

She did cry then and said, "You would never understand. Arnold and I were meant to be together. I love him and am giving up everything and everyone to be with him. You can call me crazy or whatever you want."

Charlie frowned as he stood up and said, "I think Beverly described you best. I am going to take Beverly home and I will not be back tonight."

He walked down the hallway and knocked on the guest bathroom door. Beverly opened the door and he said, "Let's go. Our discussion here is over. I'll take you home."

They walked out the front door without another word to Angie. She made no effort to look up at them or speak to them.

When they arrived at Beverly's apartment, Beverly put her arms around Charlie and held him close for a long moment and then said, "Charlie this discussion with Angie has been totally unbelievable and I know you have to be totally exhausted. I know that I am. Now, you need to get some rest and my sofa is not the place for that." She paused and looked deeply into his sad eyes and continued. "We both need rest and I want us to both sleep in my bed. Please believe me, this is not about having sex."

Charlie knew she was not thinking about sex. He smiled at her and said, "Beverly James you are so special to me and my family. I am so thankful to have you as a part of my life. You know I Love you."

After such a stressful time with Angie they were thankful to have each other and felt at peace sleeping in the same bed.

The next morning would be a new beginning for Charlie and Beverly. Neither one was sure what they should do next. Again, the girls were their most important concern. Charlie knew they must get a lawyer involved to arrange for the divorce. He knew Angie would accept a no-fault divorce and as she had told him would give up her relationship with their girls.

They were both happy it was Saturday, no work today. They did have work many times on Saturdays when they were on a case, but nothing was pressing at this point. They had completed all of the backlog of paper work yesterday.

Charlie had gotten up first and made the coffee. He was sitting at the small table with a cup when Beverly walked in. She kissed him and said, "Thanks for making coffee. Maybe you'll be making breakfast one day."

Charlie laughed and said, "Don't count on it. Coffee is my limit."

Beverly was laughing as she filled her cup and sat down with him. "What about the week end? Won't the girls be wanting to do something with you?"

"I'm glad you asked. I was thinking about taking them to the park and maybe a movie. Would you like to go with us?"

"Well, what about Angie? How can we tell the girls that I am going and not their mother?"

Before he could answer his cell buzzed. He saw Angie's name on the display. He looked at Beverly and said, "Hello, Angie." He sat and waited. After a long moment he said, "Angie, are you still there?"

She started crying and trying to talk, but he could not understand her. She finally slowed her voice and said, "I have some bad news, Charlie."

"Bad news? What is going on?"

"It's Arnold."

"Arnold, what about Arnold?"

"Oh, God. He's dead."

Charlie sat in complete silence and then said, "how, what happened?"

"Oh, Charlie…He took his own life." She then cried uncontrollably.

Charlie covered his phone with his hand and said, "Arnold has killed himself."

Beverly looked at Charlie and said, "Oh God, what else can happen?"

Charlie shook his head and then moved his hand from the phone and spoke to Angie. "Angie, please try to calm down. I know this is awful. Please try to stay calm. I will be there in a few minutes."

He was surprised when she responded. "Thank you, Charlie. Will you bring Beverly with you?"

"Do you want me to bring her?"

She only said yes and ended the call.

Charlie and Beverly were soon on their way to the Baker home. When they arrived, Angie was sitting on the couch where she had been when they left the night before.

They both stood before her and she slowly looked up and said, "I know both of you must hate me."

Charlie stopped her with, "Now, Angie this is not the time to discuss our feelings. You know how I feel about Arnold, but I am truly sorry that he took his life."

Angie looked up at him and said, "Why do you care what happened to Arnold? He meant nothing to you. I'm sure you hated him. I'm the one who is sorry he is gone. I loved Arnold."

Charlie knew any more conversation about Arnold would be of no good to anyone. He then sat next to her and said, "Now, what can I do? What do you want to do? Do you want to go to New York?"

Angie covered her face with both hands and said, "The only thing I want to do is to die?"

Beverly looked toward the kitchen and saw the three girls walking toward them. She went to them and stopped them before they could reach the family room area.

They had heard their mom crying and were all three upset. Beverly opened her arms to them and said, "Come on girls, let's go to your bedroom."

They all three looked toward the den and then turned and went to the bedroom with Beverly.

They naturally wanted to know why their mom was crying. She had to try to comfort them. She actually told them the truth that an old friend of their mom's had died.

After telling them they all three continued to look at her and then Kimberly said, "Is that all you know about her friend?"

Beverly cleared her throat and said, "Yes, that's all I know now." She knew they would learn more later, but knew this was the best answer at this time.

Charlie was still sitting with Angie wondering what he needed to do to help her. She had made it very plain that she was going to give up her marriage and all three girls to be with her lover, Arnold. Now, that Arnold was gone, he wondered what this could mean for their family. Would she stay with them? There was no reason to go to New York.

They both had sat in silence after Charlie had asked her what he could do for her. He knew Angie had to be in shock, but could not believe she wanted to die.

He finally placed his hand on her arm and said, "Angie, I want to help you. Please talk with me."

She slowly turned her head to face him as tears filled her red eyes. "Charlie, you are a good person and a very kind and loving father to our little girls. I will never expect you to love me after what I have said about leaving you and the girls."

Charlie was truly at a loss for the right response as he continued to look into her eyes. He could not believe he could find it in his heart to ever love her again, and now there was Beverly.

She continued to look into his eyes also and said, "Well, am I right? You don't have to answer that question. As I said, I would never expect you to love me again."

Charlie cleared his throat and asked in an almost whisper, "And if the situation was reversed would you love me again?"

It was a long moment before she answered. She looked down and closed her eyes. She then opened her eyes and looked again into his eyes and said, "Charlie, that would never happen. You are a loving dedicated husband and father."

He knew she was not going to answer his question and wanted to try to help her. They had known each other since high school and been married for over fifteen years. He did have feelings for her, but no longer the love he had for all of their years together.

He tried again. "Angie, we both feel the same about our future life together. I never wanted us to separate, but I have accepted this. We need to decide what you need and I truly want to make it work out for us, for the girls."

Angie remained silent as she slowly got up and turned to look down at Charlie. "I have nothing else to talk about. I'm going to bed and do not want to be disturbed. You and Beverly can take care of the girls."

Charlie sat and watched her walk down the hallway to their bedroom, then he thought, used to be our bedroom. It was mid-morning and Saturday. It looked like she was going to spend the day in bed. He didn't know what to do.

Charlie heard the girls talking in the kitchen and walked in to find them having cereal and fruit bowls with Beverly. They all looked at him as he stood there smiling at them.

Beverly finally said, "How is Angie?"

"She's resting right now and really does not want to be disturbed. She is very upset."

The three girls were looking concerned, knowing their mom was so upset.

Charlie then looked at all three and said, "Girls, please don't worry about your mom. She has to rest for a while. She lost a good friend and needs some time to get over it."

They all three seemed to understand and went back to their breakfast.

Charlie and Beverly exchanged glances, both wondering what could be coming next in their lives.

Beverly finally smiled at Charlie and said, "Charlie, let me show you something in the den."

He followed her, not having any idea what she was talking about. When they got into the den he said, "What's going on?"

"Charlie, I think it would be best for the girls to go out for a while. I would like to take them to the park and lunch at McDonald's and maybe a movie. Would that be okay with you?"

Charlie was so impressed with her concern for the girls. He smiled and wanted to hug her but resisted and said, "Oh, Beverly that's so kind of you. I agree they need some time away from here right now."

Beverly had a spring in her step as she went back to the kitchen and told the girls they were going to the park and have lunch at McDonald's. They were all three smiling at her.

Beverly and the girls had been gone for two hours when Charlie decided to check on Angie. What he found was a total shock to him. Angie was lying face down on the bed and only wearing her underwear. He called to her and got no response. Finally, he placed his hand on her back and shook her. Still no response. Then, he saw the problem, an empty bottle of sleeping pills. It appeared that she had taken all of them. She did use them at times when she had problem sleeping. He checked her pulse and could feel it, but it was slow. He immediately called 911 and the medics were there in twenty minutes.

Charlie followed the ambulance to the hospital in his cruiser. Beverly had used his personal car to take the girls. He waited in the ER waiting area and was told by an attending nurse that they would let him know how she was as soon as they could check her over.

It was twenty minutes before the nurse came to the door and asked him to follow her. They walked down the hall and then into an empty room. She then said, "The doctor will be with you in a few minutes." Before he could ask anything, she was gone.

He was a young doctor and introduced himself to Charlie. "Mr. Baker, I am doctor Jim Stevens." He paused and then said, "Your wife is not doing well."

Charlie could not wait. "What do you mean? Is she going to be, okay?"

"Well Mr. Baker, as you know she took an overdose of sleeping pills. She could survive from that, but it's her heart. She's had a heart attack and may not survive. We now have her in ICU on a ventilator."

Charlie was almost to upset to speak and he said, "So, what are her chances?"

"Well, it's always difficult to predict how a patient will recover from a heart attack."

Charlie asked the obvious question. "Can I see her?"

"We have limited visitation in ICU, but you can see her for a few minutes. Please wait here and I will make the arrangements for you." He paused and then reached for Charlie's hand and said, "I'm sorry to have to give you this news. I hope she will recover."

Charlie had no choice. He sat and waited. He wanted to call Beverly, but decided to wait until he knew more.

She looked awful. Her complexion was ashen looking to him. Her eyes were closed and had the ventilator hose in her mouth. She had various monitors on her and he briefly looked at her blood pressure and heart rate. He thought they looked okay, but wasn't sure. He was ushered out after being there for no more than five minutes.

It was now three in the afternoon and he wanted to call Beverly. He went outside to get a breath of fresh air and called her cell.

He heard her sweet voice as she answered. "Hey, Charlie."

He wasn't sure how much to tell her. "Where are you all now?"

"We're at the park and have been on the swings, slides and played in the sandbox. We're having fun, Charlee."

He had never in his life felt like he did at that moment. His wife could be dying and her lover Arnold had killed himself. As he was having these thoughts, he heard Beverly again.

"Charlie, are you still there?"

"Yeah, I'm here. When are you bringing the girls home?"

"I can come now or whenever it is the best time for you."

He thought to himself, there won't be a best time.

She again waited for him to respond. "Well, what do you want me to do?"

He paused for several seconds and then said, "Let me call you back, okay?"

"Okay, just let me know, and something else, Charlie."

"What, Beverly?"

"I love you." She ended the call.

Charlie went back in the hospital and asked for doctor Stevens. The receptionist told him she could page him. He waited and he was surprised to see the young doctor come into the waiting area. He went directly to Charlie and took his hand. "I was just getting ready to call you, Mr. Baker."

"Is there any change? Is she still, okay?"

The doctor looked round the room and saw that there were no other people and said, "It's not good. It appears that her heart is failing. We don't expect her to live much longer. I'm sorry, Sir."

Charlie was shaking with fear. "Are you telling me that she is dying?"

"Yes."

"I want to be with her now!"

The doctor led Charlie to the ICU without another word. They both stood by her bedside and watched her heart monitor showing her heart rhythm slowing and then in a few minutes went to flat line. Charlie had watched his wife die. The ventilators was still breathing for her, but she was gone.

The doctor placed his hand on Charlie's shoulder and again said he was sorry. He left and Charlie stood there alone looking at his dead wife. He slowly sat in the only chair in the room and cried.

The nurse he had first met came in later and asked if she could call someone for him. He looked at her and shook his head.

"No, thank you. But, what about a funeral home? Can you call a funeral home?"

"Yes Sir, I just need the name of your choice."

Charlie gave her the name of a local funeral home they had visited over the years and then went outside again and called Beverly.

It was now five and Beverly had been wondering when he would finally call. She answered. "Well, it's getting close to dinner. Are you ready for us to come home?"

He could hardly speak and starting to sob. "Oh, Beverly...She's dead."

"What? What are you saying Charlie?"

"Angie overdosed on sleeping pills and died at the hospital a few minutes ago. Oh, God. What am I going to do, Beverly?"

"I'm with the girls you know. Where are you now?"

"The hospital. Please take the girls home and I'll meet you there." He closed his cell and went to the parking lot.

Beverly and the girls arrived first as the park was only a few blocks away. The girls were all happy with their day out with Beverly. They all ran into the den, looking for their mom. She heard them calling for her.

Kimberly came back to Beverly and said, "We can't find mom."

Beverly wasn't sure how to talk about Angie. She hugged Kimberly and said, "Your dad is on his way home. I'm sure he will know about her."

They were all four in the den when Charlie walked in. He stopped just inside the den as all three girls rushed to him. Kimberly was first to speak. "Where is mom, Dad?"

Charlie looked at Beverly and then said, "Let's all sit down."

Kimberly, Jodie and Becky sat next to each other on the couch and looked up at their dad. Beverly was standing next to him.

He cleared his throat and said, "Your mom was very sick and had to go to the hospital this morning." He hesitated and looked at Beverly. She wanted to cry, but knew she needed to stay strong for the girls.

Kimberly again couldn't wait. "Daddy, what is wrong with Mom? Is she going to get well?"

Charlie went to them then and knelt down to look directly into their sweet little eyes. "Girls, your mom is not going to get well." His eyes were filled with tears as he then said, "She died and has gone to Heaven."

All three girls were looking at Charlie with complete shock. Then the crying began. Beverly then was on her knees helping Charlie console each of the girls. Everyone cried.

It was several minutes before the girls began to calm down. They were still crying, but more in control of their emotions.

Kimberly was always the one to speak for the girls, being the oldest. She looked at Beverly and said, "Will you stay with us, Beverly?"

"I will always be here for you three girls. I love you all so much."

Kimberly stood and hugged Beverly.

Charlie and Beverly were with the girls trying their best to console each one. It was a very sad and stressful time for everyone. They helped each girl get ready for bed. They wanted nothing to eat. Charlie and Beverly sat on the edge of their beds and continued to comfort them until they finally fell asleep. It was a little after ten.

Beverly walked out quietly and went to the den. She felt Charlie needed some private time with his girls.

Beverly had called Sammy, their boss that evening and told him about Angie dying. He was very sorry to hear of her death. He asked was there anything he could do and Beverly told him not really, but thanked him.

Sammy was quiet for a moment and then said, "Beverly, I know how close you are to The Baker family and know they need you now. I want you and Charlie to take a couple of weeks off and hopefully get some arrangements made for the family."

Beverly was surprised, but knew how compassionate Sammy was. "Oh, Sammy I know this will mean so much to Charlie and It certainly does to me. I will tell Charlie, and again thanks for your love and support." They ended the call.

She had not had a chance to tell Charlie about Sammy until later that night. He was surprised like she had been and also knew how much Sammy thought of his family and Beverly.

Angie and Charlie had both requested in their wills that they be cremated at death. He knew this was what Angie wanted. They had both requested no funeral service with only a private ceremony with family. He explained all of this to Beverly.

After sitting in silence for so long Beverly finally spoke. "So, you will need to go to the funeral home tomorrow and sign the necessary paper work?"

Charlie looked at her and nodded. "Yes, I hope you will be okay staying with the girls."

"Charlie, please don't ever say or think that. I will always be here for the girls. You and I had this conversation a few days ago. I told you I would be here and I am here...,I love these girls and I think their daddy is very special."

Charlie's emotions took over and he cried. This had been so sudden and so many strange things had happened to him.

Beverly held him against her and wanted to console him the best she could. It was a very sad time for both of them.

Charlie knew he had to call Mary, Angie's sister in New York. She was the only living relative. She, like Charlie and Beverly could not believe what Angie had done. She had heard about Arnold taking his life, but never thought Angie had that kind of feelings for him. After listing to Charlie, she knew it must be true. Charlie told her that he wanted her to not come to Memphis. Mary really wanted to be there, but did understand. Hopefully she could attend the family service when they decided to have it.

Beverly went to the guest bedroom later and Charlie went to the master bedroom. Sleep did not come until early morning hours.

They were both up before seven even after both having a sleepless night. Beverly made the coffee and they both sat at the kitchen table and enjoyed the caffeine boost.

"Can I make something for you to eat Charlie?"

He looked at his watch and said, "Maybe when I get back. I'm going to the funeral home and get the arrangements made."

Beverly understood and said, "Take your time. I'll get the girls up and make breakfast for them."

He stood up and said, "I don't know how I could handle this without you, Beverly. We are so blessed to have you in our lives."

"I feel so blessed to be a part of your lives. Now drive carefully. We'll see you afterwhile."

Charlie never liked going to a funeral home. This was his worst visit so far. The director was very kind and patient with Charlie. It was Sunday, but the director had agreed to meet with Charlie. He had all the necessary paper work ready and Charlie simply signed his name a few times and all was done. He advised the director that the family would have a private service at a later date. They agreed to hold the ashes until the service. Charlie left feeling he had done what Angie would have wanted him to do.

The house was quiet when Charlie walked in. He stood in the foyer and listened. After a moment he heard Beverly's voice. He slowly walked to the doorway of the den and saw Beverly standing in front of all three girls. They were seated on the couch with their heads bowed. Beverly was praying with her head bowed. He only heard the last few words of her prayer as then she said, "We ask your blessings on these three girls. In Jesus name we pray. Amen."

He had never heard Beverly pray, but knew she believed in God and was a Christian. They had just never discussed religion. He and Angie were both believers, but very rarely attended church. It was such a special moment for Charlie as he watched his three girls raise their heads and look at Beverly. They truly loved her and he was so thankful for her.

After another group hug with Charlie and the girls, Beverly made a special breakfast for everyone. They all sat around the kitchen table and enjoyed scrambled eggs, biscuits, bacon and gravy. This was so different for all of them to eat like this for breakfast, but this was a different time. A time of change was coming for everyone around this table.

Beverly said another silent prayer, thanking God for allowing her to be a part of this special family. She promised God in her prayer that she would be there for them as long as she lived.

The two older girls went to clean up with showers and got dressed. Beverly helped Becky, the five-year-old get ready. They had no idea where they were going, but Charlie had told them they were all going out for a ride.

They went to Graceland, Elvis Presley's home place. Charlie had toured the home with Angie, but the girls and Beverly had never been inside. The girls really knew nothing about Elvis, but did enjoy touring the house and the two planes Elvis had used. Beverly did know about Elvis and had loved his music and some of the movies Elvis had been in. They finished the tour just before lunch time and Charlie knew the girls would love going back to McDonalds even though they had just been there the day before. They did enjoy the outing and no one mentioned Angie.

The got back to the Baker home at two that Sunday afternoon. Charlie suggested that the girls should take a nap and they all three seemed to be ready for one.

After the three girls were soundly sleeping, Charlie gently closed their bedroom door and he and Beverly went to the den and sat next to each other on the couch.

Charlie smiled at Beverly and said, "I've been thinking about a change of scenery for all of us."

"What? Are you thinking about moving?"

"No, not move, just a trip. The girls have never been to Florida and with this cold weather here in Memphis I think they would love the warm weather and get to see the ocean. What do you think?"

She smiled and wanted to hopefully get him to have a little fun and said, "So, when will you all be back?"

He couldn't resist as he leaned over and kissed her. "Well, maybe you could consider going with us. What do you think?"

They both knew she would always be with them and did enjoy a moment of fun together.

Charlie called the school principal and told him they were going to keep the girls out of school for a week. The principle understood and wished them a good and safe trip.

Monday morning Beverly was on the phone with condos in Panama City Beach, Florida. Charlie had asked her to make the arrangements. She found the perfect arrangement for them. It was on the fifth floor overlooking the swimming pool and the ocean as far as the eye could see. She had looked at the settings on the website. They were going for a week and would leave Tuesday morning and drive. Beverly had an SUV that had room for seven and this gave them plenty of room. Everyone was excited and ready to go.

They arrived in Panama City Beach at five the next afternoon. It was a four-bedroom condo and had plenty of room for all five. Charlie and Beverly were hoping they could have a late-night visit, but would have to wait to be sure about that. It was great just being there and having the beautiful view from the balcony. After getting unpacked, they all went to the local Walmart and stocked up on groceries.

They had a late dinner with some of the snacks the girls liked and then took a walk on the beach. They were back in the condo just after nine and everyone was ready for bed.

Charlie and Beverly made sure the girls were in bed and kissed them good night. They then got a glass of wine each and went to the balcony and listened to the ocean as the waves rushed against the shore. It was so different and so very peaceful. They talked very little, but both were having a lot of thoughts about their future. They both believed their futures were going to be good for the entire family, their new family.

The week in Panama City Beach was good as Charlie had hoped for. The girls loved the beach and were in the pool every day as well. They took in all of the amusement parks and didn't miss any rides, taking some of them more than once.

After a week on the beach, they were ready to make the 500-mile drive back to Memphis. Everyone had nice tans and great memories of their first visit to see the ocean. They did stop for lunch in Georgia and a couple of other stops at rest areas for restroom needs. They were back home at six that evening. It has been a long day and everyone was happy to be home. They had snacks for dinner and the girls were soon in bed.

Charlie and Beverly sat on the couch and looked at each other. Beverly finally said, "You had a great idea. We both know this will not be easy for the girls to get over, but this will help them to start the process."

"Well, I sure hope so. I know they did enjoy the beach and we had very little discussion about Angie. Each one did make comments about their mom, but their comments were very brief and again, I think being there helped them to accept this new life we are all going to have."

Beverly yawned and then said, "Well, I certainly agree with what you just said. We still have a lot of adjusting for all of us and I know we will make it work."

Charlie looked at her with a very serious expression. "Beverly, I need to know you can handle this. We both know that marriage cannot happen in the near future." He paused and then said, "Also, I'm not sure we can have the physical relationship we both want and need from each other."

She knew he worried about this and looked back over the couch to be sure no one was in the hallway and then kissed him. "Charlie, please believe me. I am here for you and the girls and as I said a few days ago, if we never marry, I will be okay. I just want to continue to be part of this family, okay?"

He was so impressed with her and truly loved her. She was like a God send for him and his girls. He really believed it was meant to be for her to be a member of their family. He pulled her to him and kissed her. "Beverly, I can never put it into words how much you mean to me. I do love you and know that the girls and I are truly blessed to have you in our lives."

She kissed him back and said, "Okay, Super Dad, it's bedtime."

They both stood up and embraced and then went to their separate bedrooms.

Sammy had told them to take two weeks off and they were now in the second week. Charlie or Beverly wasn't sure what they should do about next week. All three girls were back in school this week. Becky was in her first year of kindergarten and Kimberly and Joey were in grade school. They all three were in the same school and rode the school bus back and forth. Charlie and Beverly knew someone had to be home with them in the mornings and afternoons when they got home from school. So, it was decision time and they knew arrangements had to be made.

It was already Wednesday with only two more days of school this week. They decided to discuss it, but first decided to take advantage of being alone since Angie's death.

Their love making was good, but they both felt some guilt and both talked about it. They knew they were in love, but this was all so strange. They both felt with time everything would feel right.

They both took showers and then met on the old faithful couch and started the discussion. Beverly wanted to talk first. "Charlie, I have only been with the police department for five years. You, on the other hand, have been over fifteen years and do have three children to support."

He frowned at her. "Well, sure I know that. So, what are you saying? You are surely not thinking about leaving your job."

"Now Charlie, we both know this is totally different. Not many will ever have this kind of arrangement. And, don't interrupt me now." She was frowning at him. "I have thought about this a lot when we were in Florida and I have decided to quit my job and take care of these girls. We have both agreed that us being together was meant to be."

Charlie could not control is emotions and started crying. She placed her hand on his back and waited.

After a long moment he looked at her with tears running down his cheeks. "Beverly, I don't know what to say. You are so special."

They hugged and sat in silence for a long time and finally Beverly said, "Charlie, I want to tell Sammy in person. This is not something to talk about on the phone."

He smiled at her. "I completely understand. So, when do you want to see him?"

She looked at her watch and said, "I'd like to go now, if that's okay with you."

They kissed again and she went to the bathroom to freshen up and then left.

Sammy was surprised to see Beverly walking into the general office area. He waved at her and motioned for her to come in. She went in and sat across from him as she had done so many times in the past.

Sammy was usually smiling, but was frowning now. "Beverly, I hope everything is okay with Charlie and the girls."

"Oh Sammy, they are all doing fine. We all went to Florida and it seemed to help them." She paused and then said, "It's me I want to talk about."

"Oh God, you're not sick, are you?"

She did feel a little sick, knowing what she was going to tell him, but continued to smile. "Sammy, I know this will come as a shock to you, but I'm going to be leaving the police department."

"So, what are you going to do, Beverly?"

"You know what I'm going to do, Sammy. I'm going to take care of three little girls."

Sammy was emotional knowing that he was going to lose Beverly. He was so touched knowing how she was going to dedicate her life to these little girls and Charlie. He finally said, "Beverly, I am going to miss you and I know you well enough to know you are going to miss your job." He paused and became teary eyed and then said, "I am so impressed with your love and concern for these three little girls."

They embraced and both softly cried for a moment and then Beverly said, "Thank you Sammy. Please take care of Charlie." She turned and walked out without another word.

Beverly went to her apartment and gathered up some clothes and personal items. She knew she would be giving up her apartment and moving in with her "New Family."

Charlie was waiting for Beverly when she walked in. She went directly to him and they hugged each other for a long time. "Well, how did it go?" Was Sammy surprised?"

She stood back and smiled with teary eyes. "Well yes, but he was very understanding and said some very nice things to me."

Charlie was not surprised at Sammy having nice things to say to Beverly. He knew how much he would miss her, just like he would miss working with her.

Beverly was now smiling at Charlie and said, "Oh yeah, I asked Sammy to take care of you Superman."

This was a major step for both of them. Charlie was thinking what kind of partner he would have and Beverly was thinking how her daily life was going to be so different. But they had both agreed to this arrangement and they both knew they would make it work.

The three girls were home a little after three and all seemed happier than they had been. Being with their friends at school. They all hugged Charlie and Beverly. It was beginning to feel more like a family each time they hugged these sweet little girls. They were soon having snacks and sitting in front of the TV, watching their favorite cartoons.

The rest of the week was very organized with Beverly preparing meals and helping the girls with homework and other personal needs. Everyone was naturally sad with the loss of Angie, but as the days passed it became easier. They would never forget their loss, but as the old saying goes, time will heal all wounds.

Monday morning was very strange for Charlie and Beverly. For the past five years, they had met at the police office or he had picked her up at home. Now, it was Monday morning and Charlie was leaving. He got to the door and turned back and said goodbye for the third time that morning to Beverly and the girls. They all waved and smiled calling out goodbye to him.

When Charlie arrived, he was going to get a surprise he could have never expected. He went to the coffee pot as usual and sat at the desk he and Beverly had used for five years.

Sammy soon came in and walked by Charlie and said, "Good morning, Charlie." He smiled and then said, "It's good to have you back. I need to see you in my office."

Charlie had expected this meeting as he knew he would be assigned a new partner. He sat across from Sammy and said, "Beverly told me about her meeting with you. I really appreciate you understanding and the kindness you extended to her."

"Well, I sure don't have to tell you how much she has meant to this department. She is truly one of a kind and will certainly be missed by everyone here."

They sat in silence for a long moment and then Sammy said, "Charlie, I'm sure you think I want to talk about a new partner for you."

Charlie looked a little puzzled and said, "Well yes, I can't imagine discussing anything else, Sammy."

Sammy laughed with his big belly laugh and said, "Oh, really?"

"What are you saying, Sammy? Hope you don't want me to retire or leave."

"Charlie, this timing could not come at a better time for you."

Charlie frowned and said, "Sammy are you going to tell me what in the hell is going on?"

"I know I am taking too long to tell you, just having a little fun in my last days on the job."

"Last days? Man, you are driving me crazy."

"Charlie, last week the mayor offered me an early retirement package that I really can't refuse. I'm not at retirement age, but this will give me and my wife some years while we are young enough to travel, enjoy life."

Charlie was surprised to say the least. "Wow! This is a surprise. Have they appointed anyone to take your place yet?"

Sammy looked very serious and said, "Yes, and the mayor has given me the authority to name my replacement. I told him of my choice and he was very pleased and totally agreed with my choice."

Charlie was sitting there wondering who this choice could be. "Is he someone I know, Sammy?"

Sammy was enjoying playing with Charlie. He smiled and said, "I have his name on the letter I sent to the mayor. Here take a look."

Charlie could not look up as he read the name Sammy had given to the mayor. It was his name, Charlie Baker. Following his name Sammy had stated that Charlie was the only person he would consider to take his place. Charlie looked at Sammy and then stood and reached across the desk and shook his hand. "Sammy, I can't begin to tell you what this means to me. I thank you from the bottom of my heart, Sammy."

"Well, Charlie you're welcome and very deserving. I am looking forward to working with you for the next month and know we can have a smooth transition. Congratulations, my old friend. I know you will do a great job. I am so proud of you."

Sammy walked around the desk and hugged Charlie. "Now, you need to get out and clean out your desk so you can move in here with me. But first you need to call Beverly. I know she will be as proud of you as I am and this entire department."

Beverly cried and like, Charlie couldn't believe the news about his new position. She was so proud of him. This would make their new family much better with Charlie having an office position and able to be home every night with his "New Family."

The month with Sammy was over and Charlie Baker was sitting at his desk thinking how everything had worked out for him and his girls. He knew he and Beverly would marry at some point, but they both knew it needed to be when the girls felt right about it. He knew it would happen. They were happy as a family now.

The new Baker family had now been together for five months. School was out for the summer and Beverly had a lot of activities with them during the week days. The weekends were fun filled for the entire family.

The big surprise came at dinner one Saturday evening. They had all had a fun day going to the mall and a movie. As Beverly was picking up the dishes, Kimberly was helping her. She was starting to put a dinner plate in the dishwasher and looked at Beverly and said, "Beverly, you know how much we love you."

Beverly smiled and handed her another plate. "Honey, I do know and you know I love you girls too."

"And our dad, do you love him?"

Beverly was truly at a loss for words as she looked at Kimberly and only smiled.

"Well, does your smile mean you love Dad?"

Beverly was not prepared for this discussion. She and Charlie had agreed they would talk with the girls when they felt the time was right. Could this be the right time? She then looked directly into Kemberly's eyes and asked, "If I do love your dad, how would you feel about that?"

Kimberly didn't hesitate. "I would like that; I would like that a lot. And you know what else?"

Beverly spoke very softly as she asked, "No, what else?"

"If you love our dad, we think you should marry him and be our mom."

Beverly cried as she took Kimberly in her arms. After a long embrace she said, "Your dad is in the den now. Let's go ask him, okay?"

Charlie was on the couch watching the news. He looked at Beverly and Kimberly as they walk in and stood in front of him. "You all got the kitchen cleaned up fast."

"We're not finished, Dad?"

Charlie looked at Kimberly and then at Beverly. "What's going on? You both are smiling."

"Charlie, yes we are smiling. Kimberly wants to tell you what she told me."

He again looked at Kimberly and said, "Okay, Kimberly what did you tell Beverly?"

Kimberly looked at Beverly and then back at her dad. "I told her that if she loves you, we think she should marry you and be our mom."

Charlie was as shocked as Beverly had been. He looked at Beverly and said, "And what did you say, Beverly?"

"I said let's ask your dad."

Charlie became emotional as he stood up and opened his arms to Beverly. "I think we should do what our girls want us to do. What do you think?"

Kimberly was jumping up and down as she said very loud, "Say yes, Beverly, say yes."

They soon had all three girls in the den and told them that they wanted to be sure this was what they wanted. They all were so happy and excited and gave hugs and kisses to their dad and then soon to be their new mom.

A few days later they married. They wanted a simple wedding, but wanted the girls involved and Charlie and Beverly's co-workers. It was held in a small church where Charlie and Angie were members. All three girls were flower girls and Sammy came with his wife and was very pleased to be asked to give the bride away. After the wedding, they had a reception at the Holiday Inn. It was a great evening for everyone.

Beverly was now able to sleep in the same bed with her husband. Their first night together as man and wife was very special. They did have sex, but knowing they were married made it so very special for both of them.

It was time for school to start again and the girls were looking forward to being with their schoolmates. They all loved school and were very good students. Beverly was so impressed with all of their desires to learn. She was always there to help with homework and giving her advice and suggestions. Charlie had told her that Angie had never really taken an interest in their school work. Beverley's involvement was a blessing for the girls.

A few nights later, after the girls were in bed asleep, Charlie and Beverly were watching TV. He looked at her and said, "Well, tomorrow is Kimberly's birthday and she will be ten years old."

Beverly smiled and said, "Yeah, it doesn't seem possible. When I first met her, she was only four years old."

They both sat in silence for a long while and then Charlie laughed and then said, "I was just thinking about her birthday and her being our first born." He turned to look directly into her eyes and then continued. "Beverly, I've never told anyone about Angie's pregnancy."

"Pregnancy? What do you mean, Charlie?"

He closed his eyes and said in an almost whisper. "She never wanted to have children. When we married, she wanted me to have a vasectomy. I told her we should wait and maybe she would change her mind. She never did. When she learned she was pregnant she wanted to have an abortion. I finally convinced her to have the baby and told her if she didn't want it, we could consider giving it up for adoption. After Kemberly was born I was so thankful she accepted her."

Beverly had sat listening to Charlie. "Well, then you all had two more."

Charlie laughed and continued. "Yes, and after two more. She insisted that I have a vasectomy and I did. I will always remember her saying that she had never wanted to be a mother."

"But she seemed to be loving to the girls."

"Well Beverly, Angie was not a good mother. She did love our girls, but always put her wants and needs first. I never told her but always knew she did not have the love of a mother."

"Oh Charlie, I'm so surprised. I hope the girls never felt her lack of motherly love."

"Well, I guess we will never know, but you know what is so good now?"

"What is that, Charlie?"

Charlie leaned over and kissed her and then said, "They finally have a mother with true motherly love. Beverly, I am so thankful to have you and love you with all my heart."

Beverly held Charlie and cried. She knew this special relationship was meant to be.

They went to bed and enjoyed making love and knowing how much they meant to each other and three very sweet little girls. They would have a birthday celebration for Kemberly tomorrow.

Beverly was always up and made breakfast for Charlie. It was Saturday and usually a day off, but Charlie had a meeting with the county attorney about a case. He would be back by noon in plenty of time for Kemberly's birthday party. The girls were still sleeping and Beverly was going to bake a cake later with the girls.

Charlie was home just after noon and Beverly and the girls were busy in the kitchen. The kitchen table was full of bowls and all of the ingredients to make a cake. All three girls were having a great time helping Beverly.

Charlie stood looking at them and was so happy to have this family and knew his girls were just as happy and loved their new mom. He could still hear Kimberly saying she wanted Beverly to be their mom.

Beverly had also made pizza for lunch and they were soon all having a slice with soft drinks and looking forward to having cake and ice cream for Kimberly's birthday.

When they had finished their pizza, Beverly looked at Kimberly, Jodie and Becky and said, girls I am so thankful to be a part of your lives and want to thank each one of you for wanting to call me mom. I thank God for allowing me to be in this family as your mom and wife of you dad." She stood up and continued. "Now. We have a present for Kimberly in the den, so you all have seats in there and your dad and I will bring the cake and ice cream so we can all celebrate together.

It was a special moment for everyone and they all knew this was the beginning of a new life for the Baker family.

She Had No Home

2009

It was the hottest day of summer and I had just finished breakfast. As I got ready for my morning walk, I heard sounds coming from the farm next to mine.

I walked toward the sound. It was a sander I was hearing, an electric sander. A man and woman were sanding the corners of a barn that had been painted white. I found this odd that someone would sand off the paint on a barn. I had painted pieces of furniture white and then sanded the edges to give the piece a look of wear. In years past, many pieces of furniture were originally painted white. After many years of use, the paint was worn off. Now, these two people were sanding the edges of the huge barn. Did they think people would believe this to be an old barn?

The woman stopped her sander and turned to face me. "Good morning," she said. "You live around here?"

I must have looked shocked as I stared at her, then at the man. "Well, yes. I live just over there," I said as I pointed back toward my farm.

Then I saw her. She wasn't more than five years old. She had been looking up at me and I had not noticed her. She had a little white dog in her arms. The dog was just as cute as she was. I knelt down and touched the little dog on the head. "Is this your little dog?" I asked.

She smiled and held it out, offering it to me. "Would you like to hold him? His name is Sparkle," she said as she waited for me to take the little dog.

Sparkle was very light and soft. He seemed to be a cross breed, with some Poodle influence. I looked at her and smiled before saying, "Sparkle seems to like me. Does he like everyone?"

She seemed embarrassed as she tucked her head and said, "He likes everyone until they are not nice to him."

The lady was now standing next to the little girl. Placing her hand on the girl's shoulder she said, "Would you mind taking her home? It's just too hot out here for a little girl."

Before I could answer, the little girl said, "Yes Mister, would you please take me home?"

Take her home? I couldn't think of a good answer, but I did want to help, so I said yes.

Then the obvious question, "Where do you live?" I asked.

Before she could answer the woman said, "she'll tell you. She can go now. Will you take her please?"

She held my hand and I held the little dog in my other arm as we walked away from the painted barn. To my surprise, there was a large brick building between my farm and the painted barn. It appeared to be five or six stories high. I had never seen it before and could not believe it was actually there, but it was.

We entered on the ground floor and found a day care center for children. The room was large and the floor was covered with toys and games of all types and sizes. There was a young lady attending to some of the children playing a board game. She stood as she saw the little girl and me. "Oh, good morning, have you brought Anna to stay with us today?"

I didn't even know the little girl's name. I looked down at her then back at the young lady. "She asked me to bring her here. Is this where her parents leave her?"

"Oh no," she said. "We haven't had Anna here before, but she did come in this morning and left her baby carriage."

I was getting more confused by the minute. "Her baby carriage?"

The lady smiled and looked down at Anna. "Well, it's actually a carriage for her little dog, Sparkle. Right, Anna?"

Anna pointed toward the corner of the large room and said, "There it is, next to the window." She ran to the small wooden carriage and pulled it back to where we were standing.

"Sparkle loves to ride in his cart. Can we go now, Mister?"

Again, I had the obvious question, "Where are we going, Anna?"

Anna placed Sparkle in the carriage after taking him from me and said, "Please come now, I am sure we will find out soon."

The lady smiled and said, "It's okay, she'll tell you where she needs to go."

Reluctantly, I took her little hand as she led me to the back of the room. We walked directly to a small door on the back wall of the play room. Anna moved quickly, pulling Sparkle in the carriage with her other hand. "We need to go in here," she said.

The small door opened from the bottom, sliding up like a window. It was a small elevator, much like a dumbwaiter. She stooped and stepped inside, pulling Sparkle with her. I had to get on hands and knees to enter. The door came down and the small elevator started to rise. When the door opened, we got out, again with me on hands and knees.

We were at the end of a long hallway facing a large plate glass window. From there I could see my farm and the white barn with the two people still sanding on the corners. We turned and walked down the hallway to a standard size elevator and descended to the ground floor again.

As we walked outside, the day was still very hot and sunny. Anna pulled Sparkle in the little carriage which she called a cart. I held her hand and continued to walk, not knowing where we were headed or for that matter, where she lived. We walked for several minutes and I could not wait to know where we were going. I stopped and knelt down and said, "Anna, this is so very strange. Please tell me where you live. I need to take you home. You mother told me that you would tell me where you live." I waited.

"She is not my mother," she said as she reached into the carriage and picked up Sparkle. "Sparkle has no mother either."

"The lady and the man at the barn are not your parents?"

"No, they are not my parents. I don't know who they are, Mister."

She handed Sparkle to me and said, "He wants to live with me and I want to live with you."

I held Sparkle and looked into her cute little face. "Anna, you need to be with your family. Do you understand, Anna?"

Her smile was sweet as she looked into my eyes and said, "I understand that you are my family now. Can we go home now, Mister?"

When I woke up, I quickly dressed and went outside. There was no white barn and no five-story building anywhere near my farm. Only the same houses and fields that had been there the day before. I knew it has been a dream, but I had to look to be sure.

I turned to walk back toward my house, and saw the little carriage. It had been painted white with sanded edges to make it look old and worn. It was one I had painted for our antique booth. Then, I knew this was why I had the dream.

Five Will Die By: Bob Austin and Grandson, Greg Austin

July 25, 2009

He looked like a killer. His eyes were almost as yellow as those of a wild animal. He was strapped to the table where his life should end within the next fifteen minutes. His execution was scheduled for twelve midnight. But, before he was to be put to death, he was allowed one statement to the gallery of people on the other side of the glass. They had gathered there to watch the killer of their loved ones. Loved ones he had brutally killed by stabbing and slashing their bodies. This would not bring their loved ones back, but they would have the peace of mind, knowing for sure, that this horrible monster would soon be dead. Most of them hoped that his soul, if he had one, would go directly to hell.

Both of his arms and legs were strapped to the flat bed. An IV had already been placed in his arm and all that was left to do was to place the poison into his veins at exactly midnight. The guard tilted his bed to about a forty-five-degree angle and allowed him to face the glass. He could not see the people on the other side, sitting in the dark. He was very visible to them, however, in the brightly lit room. He glared at the glass and slowly raised his upper lip, showing his crooked brown-stained teeth. Then he smiled before saying, "I know who you are and I know why you came. You want to watch me die. I do deserve to die, but not today." He paused and laughed for a few seconds then said, "No, not today. I'm not the one to die today, but I do promise you this, five of you will be dead within the next three days. There will be three women and two men. Yes, you will die, but I will live."

The guard lowered his bed back to a flat position as he looked at the clock on the wall. Only five minutes left. The attending physician placed the syringe in the shunt in the killer's arm and watched the second hand on the clock. The hand made three revolutions and then at two minutes before mid-night, the phone rang. It was the governor of the state. He had ordered a stay of execution. The killer would not die today.

As he was being loosened from his restraints, he turned his head to face the glass, and said, "I told you that I would not die today."

The shock of hearing the governor's decision caused a loss of concentration by the guard and the doctor. In that moment of shock and disbelief, the killer made his move. He grabbed the syringe from the doctor's hand and stabbed the guard standing next to the table. Then leaped off the table and took the wounded guard's gun. The killer shot the doctor as his would-be executioner was reaching for the door handle, trying to escape.

The only two people left in that brightly lit room were in a state of shock as the killer turned to face them, pointing the loaded weapon. The guard seemed to be losing his ability to stand up as he held his wounded arm. He had removed the syringe but was still holding it in his hand. The other remaining person in the room was the Warden. He was tall and lanky and his look was one of fear. Everything happened so fast, he had no time to react. Before he knew it, the killer had the gun to his head.

"Why are you doing this? You have a stay of execution. You know there's no way you can escape from this maximum-security prison," the Warden said as he surveyed the room, looking from the wounded guard to the dead doctor lying next to the door.

The killer glared at the Warden and said, "I made a promise and for once, I intend to keep it. You are going to be my ticket out of this place."

The twelve people in the gallery could not believe this man who had killed so many, was still alive and now on the move. They began to wonder if the promise he had made was going to come true. They all looked around and worried that they could be one of the five to die. Their thoughts were given way to the sound of gun shots from inside the building.

As Alice Burns was walking away from this horrible scene, she wondered if the man who killed her mother had actually been looking through the glass at her. She was just twenty-four and had only come to see the life of this maniac end, but now, she was worried for her own life.

Five years ago, Alice Burns came to visit her widowed mother during her Christmas break from college. The front door was open when she arrived, and Alice knew something was wrong. She ran into the kitchen and immediately saw a trail of blood leading into the dining room. Alice screamed as she saw her mother lying in a pool of blood with large cuts across her body. She had looked up at the open window just in time to make eye contact with the killer. Seeing those yellow eyes tonight had reminded her of that same man jumping out of her mother's window years ago.

She knew his name was Charles Markum. She knew he was psychotic. She knew he had killed other people, but she did not know why.

Going down the long dimly lit hallway, Charles Markum had believed his freedom was only moments away. He had fired three warning shots into the ceiling of the hallway, hoping to intimidate the guards he knew would be trying to capture him.

After being in this prison for so long, Charles knew his way around. He had always had an escape route planned, but never was given the opportunity to execute it. Now, with the Warden as his hostage, his plan was going to be easier than he had thought.

"Mr. Markum, I hope you realize that you are making a big mistake," the Warden said. "And if you do kill me, there will be no more stays of execution for you."

Charles only laughed as he thought about killing the Warden after he was free from this place. He had no intentions of letting him live. As they entered the garage, Charles said, "Get out the keys."

"What keys?"

"You know what keys, the keys to your car."

Charles held the gun on the Warden as he started the car and headed for the main gate. The guard on duty had already been alerted of the escape, with the Warden as hostage, and quickly opened the gate, allowing them to pass through.

After driving for about twenty minutes, Charles Markum felt he could make it on his own. It was time for the Warden to die.

Leaving the Warden's body beside the road, Charles was free to keep his promise. He knew he had three days to fulfill his promise to the five people, and he didn't want to waste any time. He started the car and sped off into the night. Charles Markum was on the loose…. again.

Alice Burns went home after the terrifying ordeal at the State Prison. She locked all of the doors and sat alone…. scared, in her darkened living room. Her thoughts went back to the time when she knew her mom was dating again. She remembered her mom talking about *Charles*, but she never got to meet *Charles*. She sat and held her head with both hands and thought, "Surely this could not be the same *Charles*." Charles Markum was a monster. Charles Marcum had killed her mom and she had seen him as he went out the dining room window.

Those yellow eyes. They were the same today as they were then.

The trial had been long, and she had attended every moment, knowing that Charles Markum was guilty. She had felt relieved knowing he had been convicted and would be put to death. Now, today, after years of waiting, he was out and free again. Charles Markum was free to kill five people as he had promised. Alice knew she had to be one of the five he planned to kill. She also knew there were other family members that had lost love ones because of this crazed killer.

The sound of her phone ringing seemed almost deafening to her as she turned to look toward the hallway. She slowly got up and walked to the phone and stood beside it for a moment before answering. It continued to ring. Reluctantly, she picked it up.

His voice sounded like it had today as he said, "I don't know if you will be number one or number five." He hesitated, and cleared his throat. "But I do know you will be one of the five."

Alice slammed the phone down and screamed. She had no idea how he could have gotten her phone number, but he had. This would be just the beginning of her nightmare.

After calling the local police, Alice felt a little safer. The Police Department had agreed to place an officer in front of her house. She slept very little and her thoughts were constantly about Charles Markum.

She awoke to her phone ringing. She looked at her bedside phone, knowing it had to be Charles Markum.

But it wasn't. She slowly picked up the phone and listened. She knew the line was open and waited. Then she heard a strange voice. "Miss Burns?" It wasn't Charles's voice.

"Yes?" She waited.

"This is Captain Joe Clarkson with the Police Department."

"Oh, Captain, I wasn't expecting *you*."

"Just a call to see if everything is okay with you."

Alice was relieved to hear a friendly voice. She was sure it was Charles again. *Maybe,*

She thought, *Charles was scared off by the presence of the cruiser in front of the house.*

Alice lay there, wondering what this day had in store for her. She didn't have to wait long to find out. The phone rang again. She picked it up promptly. This time she did answer, "Hello."

"Only four to go."

It *was* Charles. Alice waited and tried to think of what to say to this monster. She had never allowed anyone to take control of her life and she didn't intend to let Charles Markum be the first one. "Charles Markum, I am not afraid of you. I think of you as the lowest of all people I have ever known or heard of. Now, you may think that you can get away with your plans. Well, you are mistaken, Mr. Charles Markum."

"Well, Miss Burns, you sound like you have all of this figured out. I don't know what you think you can do to me. You will be much easier to kill than that slut mother of yours."

Alice was furious. She knew talking with him was a waste of time and would only upset her more. She decided to end the call. "Charles, I am sure we will meet face-to-face very soon, and I am looking forward to it." She hoped her comment would convince him that she was not afraid of him, even though she truly was afraid.

The next call came that night at eight-fifteen.

"Two and three are down, with two to go."

"I think you are just trying to scare me."

"Well, think whatever you want. Your time is getting closer and closer."

The line went dead.

The morning of day two, the newspaper came with headlines of Charles's escape.

Alice quickly turned to the obituaries and found three names of people that were at the execution: Patrick Simmons and Dale and Donna Scott, all killed yesterday with large cuts across their bodies.

The ringing of the phone took her away from the paper. She knew who it was…. "Hello."

"I saw you pick up the newspaper from your front porch. Did they spell the names of your friends correctly?"

Alice turned to look out the front window and for a split second, she saw the shadow of a figure of a man between two houses across the street. She knew it had to be him.

The morning of the final day came peacefully. No calls from Charles and no more information from the police. Alice wondered if person number four was still alive. She thought the fourth person could be Susan Alexander.

Susan's mother had also been a victim of Charles's. She decided to call Susan. The phone rang.... too long. Alice was about ready to hang up when she heard a man's voice.

"Hello?"

"Yes, is Susan there?"

"I'm sorry," he laughed. "She's not able to come to the phone just now.

Alice knew it was him. No one's voice was as cold as his. "What have you done to Susan?"

"Well, I guess you can count, she was number four."

Alice was at a loss for words. She held the phone and looked into the receiver, wishing she could reach through the line and kill him.

"There is only one left to die.... locking your doors won't help you."

He hung up.

Alice immediately told the policeman in front of her house about the call. He dispatched one of his fellow officers to Susan's residence. They knew Charles would be gone by then, but they had to go to the scene.

Captain Clarkson had sent an additional officer to Alice's home. The additional man and the officer that was already there were stationed inside the house. One stayed upstairs with Alice and the other one took his position in the basement. After an hour the officer with Alice decided to check on his partner in the basement. Alice heard him call out for him. There was no response, so the officer went down to check on him.

Alice waited. There was no sound coming from the basement. She went to the top of the stairs and called out, "Officer? Is everything alright?" More silence. She ventured slowly down the wooden steps. She paused and listened again, still no sound. "Are you okay?"

She took two more steps, looked down and saw the bloody bodies of the two officers, lying next to each other. She crouched next to the first one as she heard a noise to her left. She looked up and saw him. The yellow eyes of the monster glared into hers. He smiled as he slowly started toward her.

"You look so much like your mother; it's funny how my blade will kill both mother and daughter."

"You were right about one thing Charles, five people will die," Alice said as she grabbed the gun from the dead officer's holster. "And you are number five."

Charles charged at her, but the bullet caught him in the chest, his body fell at her feet.

Alice slowly climbed the stairs and went to the kitchen phone. She told the officer on duty what had happened. He advised her to stay calm and wait for them to arrive. She sat down at the kitchen table knowing her nightmare must be over now.

She knew she was wrong when she heard the basement door open.

Carl Jordon

June 29, 2010

Carl Jordon was sitting on the front porch of his old general store. He had just purchased a new Case double x knife at a local dealer. It had cost him $125.00. He was using it to whittle as he sat in his favorite rocking chair. His thoughts went back, back to his youth when he could have bought this same knife for just $ 4.50. "My how things have changed," he thought as he continued to whittle on a piece of cedar, he had picked up at one of his friends' homes.

His thoughts were disturbed as he heard the sound of a small engine approaching his store. Carl looked to his left and saw what was making this noise. It was a young man riding a small motorcycle. As he came closer, Carl could see that he was not wearing a helmet. Carl detested people using bad judgment and not wearing a helmet was proof to Carl that this young man wasn't very smart. He went back to his whittling, thinking that this young man was just passing by. To his surprise, he pulled in to his parking lot, stopping just a few feet from the front porch.

Carl looked at him and slowly closed his new Case knife and put it in his front pocket. The young man smiled and got off his motorcycle.

"Do you sell gas here?"

Carl thought he must have a problem. His gas pumps were only a few feet from where he was standing. Carl had already thought the young man wasn't very smart… no helmet.

"Well, yes, I sell gas. Those are gas pumps right over there."

His visitor turned and looked at the pumps and said, "Oh, I didn't see them."

Carl thought he must have some kind of problem. How could he not see the gas pumps?

The young man nodded toward his motorcycle and said, "I would like to fill up."

Carl stood up. "I'm not self-service, I do the pumping." He hesitated. "I don't take no credit cards, just cash."

"I have cash. Will you fill my bike for me?"

Carl walked to the pumps and motioned toward the motorcycle. "Pull it over here and give me a deposit."

"A deposit? What do you mean?

Carl stood next to the pump, hand on the nozzle. "I require a deposit before I pump…I'll give you your change when I'm done."

Carl noticed the tattoos on the young man's shoulders and upper arms as he turned to face him. His right arm had a spiral from his shoulder down to his elbow. A woman's face was tattooed on his left arm. Carl had never liked tattoos and associated them with undesirable characters.

The young man pulled a twenty-dollar bill from his front pocket and handed it to Carl.

"I hope this will satisfy you, old man."

His actions, the tattoos and now his disrespect, were too much for Carl. He took a step toward his customer. "You know son, you can go down the road about five miles and get your gas. I don't have to listen to this kind of talk."

He looked down at the gravel parking lot, then back to meet Carl's eyes.

"I'm sorry, sir. I am out of line here. I didn't mean to offend you."

Carl waited in silence, glaring at this intruder. He found his voice again and finally said, "All right, then. Bring your motorcycle over here and I'll hold the twenty until we are done."

After filling is tank, the total was $6.23.

Carl replaced the fuel cap, giving it a firm twist. "Do you want your change, or do you want something inside."

He turned and looked toward the store and said, "What do you have, anything to eat?"

"Yeah, I've got sandwiches and drinks. Come in and look around."

Going directly to the refrigerated show case, he pointed to a ham and cheese sandwich. "I would like one of those and a soda."

As he sat and ate his sandwich, he noticed a plaque hanging on the wall. Looking closer, he could see that it was a Bronze Star for bravery.

"Is that you're award?"

Carl went to the plaque and took it down and ran his finger over the upper edge, removing a thick coat of dust.

"Yeah, this is mine. Got it for bravery in the Korean Conflict, they called a conflict. It was a war, really. We lost a lot of good young men over there." Carl looked at the plaque holding the Bronze Star and said, "I'd rather have some of my buddies back rather than this Bronze Star."

The young man laid his sandwich down and walked over to take a closer look. "May I see it, please?"

Carl stared at the young man and said, "You may see it, but you have no idea what it took to receive this. You young people have no idea."

As his visitor held the plaque, Carl saw tears filling his eyes. He was surprised by his display of emotion.

"Do you have someone in the military? Carl asked.

He turned and looked at Carl for a long moment then said, "No sir, but I do know how it feels to be there."

"You do?" Carl asked with a sound of sarcasm.

"Well, I didn't get a medal like you, but I did see a lot of action."

"You saw action?" Carl's face revealed his doubt.

"Yes, I just finished my third tour of duty in Iraq."

Carl was more than embarrassed as he placed his hand on the young man's shoulder and said, "I think you and I have a lot to talk about. First of all, I need to apologize to you for judging you simply on your appearance. I need to remember that we are still at war and it's truly young people like you that are protecting our country. Too many times, older folks like me tend to think we have all the answers and know how people should look and act."

"I noticed you looking at my tattoos," the young man said. "I'm sure you don't approve of them, am I right?"

Carl smiled and said, "Well, I have never had one and during my life, I always felt like they were worn by undesirable people."

The young man placed his left hand on his right shoulder and said, "This spiral tattoo represents the many twists and turns I knew I would make during my tours of duty. I wasn't sure there would be an end to my journey as there is no end to these spirals." He then placed his right hand on the tattoo of the woman's face on his left shoulder. "This is an image of my mother. She was with me during my darkest hours and helped me keep my faith each time I placed my hand on her image."

"So, you had these done in Iraq?"

"No, I had them done after my first tour."

Carl was now having a better understanding of the meaning of these tattoos.

"I'm sure your mother was pleased to see her image and to know how much it meant to you."

The young man was silent as he handed the Bronze Star plaque back to Carl. He looked up and met Carl's eyes and then said, "I am sure she would be, but you see she died just a few days before I finished my second tour."

Neither spoke as the young man stood. He extended his hand and said, "My name is Jeremy Martin. It has been a pleasure meeting you sir."

Carl held his firm handshake and placed his left hand on Jeremy's shoulder. "I am also glad to meet you too, Jeremy. I hope you will forgive me for my unkind remarks about you and your actions."

Jeremy smiled and released Carl's hand. "There's nothing to forgive, sir. I am sure we have different feelings about each other than when we first met."

Carl slowly slipped his hand into his pocket and pulled out the Case knife.

"I want you to have this knife. It's a Case double X. I have always used Case double X knives; they are the best, in my opinion." He held out the knife for Jeremy to take. "My name is Carl Jordan and I'm almost eighty years old, but I still know what is going on in our world. I know about you young men and women that have volunteered to protect our country. I also want you to know that our brief meeting today has changed my thinking and hopefully will make me a better person. So, Jeremy Martin, when you hold this Case knife in your hand, I hope you will remember our meeting and the positive impact you made on an old veteran."

Carl Jordon stood on his front porch and watched as Jeremy Martin rode away, then said a prayer for his safety.

"Corki" A True Story.

January 15, 2008

I have always thought of writing about our little Welch Corgi, "Corki."

Today, January 15, 2008, I will begin to put down some of the thoughts I have had about her and the many pleasures she gave us during her short life. I used to tell everyone how Corki and I had conversations. We could talk without speaking aloud. She understood more than most dogs, and she had a way of communicating that was unbelievable. It was her eyes. She would look directly into your eyes and tell what she was thinking, or what she wanted. I will always remember her big brown eyes, never blinking, but always communicating.

She brought us more pleasure that I could ever explain. We had been without a pet for several years and really had not seriously thought about getting another one. Too much responsibility, we thought. Then, it happened. One Saturday morning, Wanda, my wife and I visited a pet shop. We were just looking around. We had heard a lot of bad things about pet shop pets and had talked about getting our next pet from a breeder, if we decided to get one.

We left this pet shop with our new dog that same day. It was love at first sight. She was in a small cage, all alone. We had never seen a Welch Corgi. We had heard about the Queen of England and her dogs, but knew little about them. I made eye contact with her only after being in the pet store for a few minutes. She was three months old and so very cute. "What kind of dog is this?" I had asked the pet store manager. He explained all he knew about the breed and that he had a friend who owned a Corgi. He told us his friend's dog was the smartest dog he had ever been around. Everything he told us about these dogs sounded wonderful. But it wasn't what he told us that captured my attention. No, it was her eyes. Those big brown eyes that spoke to me. I loved her then, and now after she has been gone for over two years, I still love her.

We had a wonderful relationship with Corki. Like most dogs, she became part of our family. Everything we did involve her. While at home, she was always by me or Wanda every awaking moment. She loved to be with us and really never let us get too far from her. She had a bed she loved and slept in it every night, and a lot during the day. It seemed that she was always listening. Many times, when we were talking, she would come in to join in our conversation when a subject that she was interested in came up. She would always hear us say we were going somewhere, or we were going to make popcorn, or we saw a deer or a cat outside. When she appeared, she always had that question in her expression. Her head slightly tilted to one side and again those bright brown eyes. She would seem to say things like: "Are we going to the store? Or did you say you are making popcorn.... Where's the deer?"

Corki and I made many miles around our small farm. We walked most mornings and both enjoyed the time together. I will always remember her running ahead of me and stopping to look back, making sure I was following her. We made the same route each morning, her always leading the way. Our small pond was our first stop. We had to chase the frogs and many times run the resident squirrels back up their favorite tree. This was also a place to rest and Corki would usually decide when it was time to go. If I started too early, she would bark and give me a stern look, saying: "I'm not ready yet!"

We made regular visits to our veterinarian and Corki always checked out fine. She had her regular worm shots and annual rabies shots. She had blood work done when she was six months old before she was spaded. The next blood test was done before having her teeth cleaned. She was then seven years old.

I took her to the vet and left her. She was to be ready that evening. Then, I received the call that shocked me and Wanda. The blood test showed her to have kidney disease. We had noticed her being more tired and having less energy in the past year or so. We just thought she was getting a little older. The vet told me she would only live for another six months and there was really no treatment for kidney failure in dogs. There were, however, special diets that would prolong her life. And maybe, just maybe, reverse the disease.

Wanda and I cried. I could not remember feeling like this about a dog. It felt like we were losing a family member. We had hopes of her regaining her health, but it was not to be.

We kept her on the special diet and cooked her special foods for almost a year. Her last week was very bad. She could not eat much at a time and spent most of her time in bed. We knew the time was near and decided to not let her suffer more than necessary.

On July 23, 2005, our little sweetheart went to heaven. We had her cremated and keep her ashes in our bedroom, near where her bed used to be.

We are thankful for the eight years of pleasure she gave us and we will always remember those big brown eyes, silently speaking to us.

Life in a Nursing Home

September 5, 2011

Her day began at five that morning, like all mornings. She is a single mother with three children. She has a boy fifteen, a boy ten and a little girl two. Taking care of three children isn't easy for anyone. Mary's world also includes her mother. It's true, her mother does help her with the kids, but she also needs and request some attention from her daughter.

Mary smiles as she leaves her modest home, kissing everyone as she walks out the front door each morning. As she drives the twenty miles to her job, she thinks about all of the residents that depend on her and the aids that work for her. Her job is very stressful, but she has chosen this profession and loves helping others. Mary is an LPN and knows her job very well and takes it as seriously as anyone can. She is the Charge Nurse on hallway 25 at a local Nursing Home and Rehabilitation Facility. She has many bosses, but answers first to the Director of Nursing; an RN who has more than thirty years of experience, most of it in nursing homes. The boss everyone must

keep satisfied is the Director of the facility and a very
"hands on person". Nothing happens in his facility that
is not known by him, either directly or indirectly. And,
any infractions will always be addressed with the person
involved. Everyone at the nursing home is well aware of
his involvement.

Mary, like everyone else, understands the chain of
command and respects the authority they have. She
knows, however, there are others that she must be aware
of and their demands. Their demands are many times
more critical than her bosses. Her first concern is the care
and safety of the residents…and their request, and yes,
their demands. She can, most times, satisfy their request
or demands. The one group that keeps her upset and
unsettled the most are the families of the residents. Many
times, they have just enough information to cause total
confusion and misunderstandings that are completely
unnecessary. When one of these family members
questions her, she becomes defensive and has a difficult
time handling their complaints. Most of this is because
she feels that she is doing the best she can and finds it hard
to believe the family member has the nerve to complain
when they only know part of what is going on. It usually
takes her a day to get over one of these confrontations
with a family member. Her first response is to give the
person as simple an answer as possible and hope they will
accept her answer. When they don't accept her answer,
she becomes very defensive and many times refuses to
continue discussing the situation with the family member.
She will usually walk away, claiming she has to attend to

another resident, but most times she goes to her supervisor and complains about the family member. After she has a day to get over the confrontation with the family member, she shows no signs of being upset and is back to doing her job as always. She is cheerful and shows only signs of her genuine desire to help everyone she encounters during the day.

No one can possibly understand the stress and constant pressure the nurses have. It is with them from the second they walk in until the last second, they walk out at the end of their shift. It really doesn't end there either. The awareness of that need around them is gone, but as they drive home, or trying to go to sleep at night, many of the issues of the day continue to be relived in their subconscious. So, it really never goes away. Most of these dedicated people want to keep these thoughts in their minds. They feel responsible, these patients depend on them and they know it. So, from my involvement with these dedicated people, I have learned and accepted the responses and reactions of these dedicated people. I can never imagine trying to take this responsibility and handle it like they do. The next time you have a disagreement or misunderstanding with one of these dedicated people, please think about what you have read here and take a step back and make sure you have all the facts before attacking someone who is doing their best to care for and protect your family member. There are always two sides to every story, and without knowing both sides, we cannot truly understand the situation. There could be a problem on one side or both sides, but we must always

Robert H. Austin

remember that everyone makes mistakes and many times these mistakes are because of misunderstandings. Listing to both sides of any disagreement will usually result in good understanding for both sides.

The Homeless Miracle Man

July 2009

He was sitting on the shoulder of the road. The morning sun was warm to his dirty body. His mangy dog was lying next to him, scratching and passing gas. The sound of cars and trucks only added to his already severe headache. No one seemed to notice him or if they did, gave no sign of concern for his apparent need. His clothes and shoes were nearly worn out. His old army coat was full of holes and his pants had both knees worn through. One shoe had completely lost a heel and the other had no shoelace. He had a ragged toboggan pulled over his ears and down below his eyebrows. As he sat there thinking and wondering what would finally become of him, a stranger did stop. At first, he thought he was just hearing things, as he did many times. Then, he looked up to see a young girl standing over him. She smiled and looked at his dog. She bent down to pat the dog's head and said, "What's his name, Mister?

She looked to be in her early teens. She was dressed in jeans and a cotton sweat shirt. Her hair was blond and cut

263

short for a girl. Her blue eyes seemed to pierce through his as he looked at her. The sun was just over her shoulder and made it hard to see her face very well. Her eyes however were different. They seemed to shine through the bright light. He turned toward his dog, cleared his throat and then said, "Skippy. His name is Skippy. Only has three legs, that's why I named him Skippy."

She sat down next to Skippy and continued to pat him on the head. She looked up again into his dark eyes and said, "This poor animal is starving. I can see his ribs. Do you ever feed him?"

He looked ashamed as he also looked at the dog's rib-cage. She didn't have to tell him about starving. He and his dog were both starving. He knew the last meal he had was from a garbage can behind a McDonalds the day before. It had made him sick and he still felt dizzy from whatever it was. Skippy had licked around the dumpster and found a stale French fry or two. They could both use some good food.

She nudged him with her hand on his shoulder and said, "You didn't answer me, Mister. When did you feed him?"

The dog growled for the first time. The girl jumped back and glared at the skinny dog. "What's the matter with him, I'm not going to hurt him."

"He ain't worried 'bout you hurtin' him.... it's me he's worried 'bout. He thinks you're tryin' to hurt me."

The girl wasn't sure the dog was worried about the man, but she was sure it was hungry. She was sure the man was hungry also. She only had a five-dollar bill in her pocket. She slowly took it from her pocket and handed it to the man and said, "Please get something to eat and promise me that you will feed your dog also."

She didn't remember what happened and would never know why she was hit. The car swerved for some reason and lost control and caught her with the left headlight. She was thrown fifty-two feet before landing on the guard rail. The homeless man and his dog were the only witnesses to the hit and run. His memory of the event was of no help to the officers investigating the scene. He couldn't remember the color of the car or anything to describe how it looked. The officers finally gave up and left the man and his dog still sitting on the shoulder of the road. They took pictures of the scene and made the required measurements. It appeared to be a hit and run that would never be solved. There was no evidence at the scene.

Three weeks after the hit and run, the teenage girl was still in a coma. Her mother and dad had kept a vigil at her bedside since the first day. They were there with her around the clock, taking shifts of twelve hours each. The doctors gave them little hope for her recovery. The last CT scan had shown very little brain activity and they had been advised that she could soon become brain dead. The only hope they had was for a miracle and they prayed for one every day.

The fourth week after the girl had been hit, a strange thing happened. It was three in the morning and the girl's mother was awakened by the sound of a strange voice. She sat up quickly from the roll-away bed she had been sleeping on and saw a very filthy man bent over her daughter. He was wearing a ragged old army coat and had a toboggan pulled down over his ears. The girl's mother wasn't afraid and couldn't understand why. This was so unnatural, but it seemed peaceful as she watched this man bent over her daughter. His voice was very low and his words where not clear. She could not understand anything he was saying, but it seemed almost like a prayer. He stopped speaking and placed his dirty weathered hand on the girl's face. As he did, the room illuminated with a bright light, causing the girl's mother to cover her eyes. After a few seconds the light was gone and the man was lying on the hospital room floor. The girl's mother stood and walked to the foot of her daughter's bed and could not believe what she was seeing. Her daughter had sat up and was smiling at her mother. The girl looked down at the man lying in the floor and said, "He told me that it should have been him and his dog."

The mother found it difficult to speak. She finally said, "Oh, darling, you are awake. Thank God."

"Mother," the girl said. "God sent him to bring me back."

The mother looked down at the poor dirty man and said, "Do you mean him?"

"Yes," she said as she also looked down at the lifeless body. "He told me that his dog died last night and now he was ready to give his life to me so I may live."

The mother knew this had to be the man the police had told them about. Her daughter had been next to this man and his dog when she was hit. Now, he had come there and given his life for her. This had to be the miracle they had prayed for. She smiled at her daughter and said, "Honey, this man gave his life for you just like Jesus gave his life for all of us." She paused then said, "We do have angels here on earth and you had the opportunity to meet and talk with one."

They Met at His Funeral

January 2001 (A true story)

She stood next to his casket and thanked each one for coming to pay their respects for her husband. There were many family members as one would expect and a lot of friends, they had both known over the years. Some family members had driven over a hundred miles to attend the funeral. I was there with my wife and two small children. My parents and grandparents were also attending from the same town.

I have always enjoyed watching and listening to people. As I stood near the casket, I heard most people saying the same things to my great aunt Lena. Her husband and my great uncle Rob had been a part of my life since I was born. They lived in Union City, Tennessee and we would see them at least once a year from the time I could remember. We were from Bowling Green, Kentucky and would make the annual trip to Union City, always in the summer. One of the reasons was because school was out and we could stay over longer than a week end. We all enjoyed staying at Uncle Rob and Aunt Lena's home. She

269

was the county librarian and Uncle Rob was semi-retired, working in a small paint store until his sudden death. The other reason we enjoyed visiting there was Reel Foot Lake, located near the Mississippi River. The lake had been formed by an earthquake during the late 1800's. When the earth had opened up from the earthquake, the river ran backwards and filled in the large opening. Anyway, we always made at least one trip to the lake during our visits…and always caught fish. We would take them back to Uncle Rob and Aunt Lena's house. But they were not cleaned in the house nor were they cooked inside the house. Aunt Lena would not allow fish to enter her house until they were ready to be served. She detested the smell of the fish being cleaned or cooked. So, my grandfather, Uncle Rob's brother-in-law would cook the fish in an iron skillet setting on a charcoal grill in the detached garage. I'm sure if the garage had been attached, he would have been outside.

I was thinking about all of these things as I stood near Uncle Rob's casket, listening to Aunt Lena express her gratitude for each comment made about her husband. They had been married for over fifty years and never had children. I never knew why and never asked. It wasn't talked about in our family.

I am writing all of this to simply tell about Mr. Tommy Wilson. I had never heard of Mr. Wilson and no one in the funeral parlor seemed to know him. He moved slowly through the crowd and waited his turn in line to speak to Aunt Lena. As he got closer to the front of the line he moved back, giving others his place. It became obvious that he wanted to be the last one to speak to Aunt Lena.

Finally, after everyone had moved away from the coffin and took seats in the large room, he stepped forward and took Aunt Lena's hand. She smiled sweetly and looked into his sad eyes.

His first words got my attention. As he held her hand he said, "Mrs. Harrigan, you don't know me." He paused, looking down at Uncle Rob's body lying in the coffin. "My name is Tommy Wilson. Your husband and I were special friends."

I will never forget Aunt Lena's remark as she held Mr. Wilson's hand. She said, "Oh, Mr. Wilson, I have never met you, but I do know you."

Mr. Wilson looked at her with an expression of shock. "But, how would you know me, Mrs. Harrigan?"

She smiled and released his hand. "I know that you lost your wife just five years ago and I know you and your wife Shelly had two children. Tommy, Jr. and a lovely daughter, Betty Ann. Tommy, Jr. is a game warden and Betty is married to a policeman here in Union City. Both of your children gave you and Shelly four wonderful grandchildren. They are all grown now and living away. Some in Nashville and others in the state of Texas, I believe."

Mr. Wilson was at a loss for words. Tears came in his eyes as she finished telling him all about his life and family. He finally said, "But, how?"

Aunt Lena turned to look at her dead husband and said, "Rob and I talked about you every night before going to sleep. His stories of you, Mr. Wilson and your family were so comforting to hear. I could hardly wait for the latest news about Tommy Wilson. I'm so glad to get to meet you. You'll never know how much your friendship meant to Rob." She paused again and then looked back into Mr. Wilson's eyes and said, "No. Mr. Wilson, we've never met, but I have known you since you and Rob first met."

Who will drive the truck?

August 14, 2013.

How often do we hear someone talk about people going to college and getting a degree? It is the topic of conversation for most high school students, their teachers and parents. Education is important for our future and becoming more necessary with each passing generation. All of the high-tech jobs now require a college degree. A degree is required for most entry level jobs at most major companies. So, it goes without saying that a college degree is a must for most people. But who will drive the truck?

Now, I'm not advocating that skipping college is the thing to do, but I do believe that college isn't for everyone. There are millions of people in the world with no college degree and a lot of these people do very well in their life. Some only make minimum wage and just get by, living from pay check to pay check. Some, however, do start at the bottom and work their way up in industry, becoming top managers and sometimes presidents of companies. Still others start their own business and are successful. These are the lucky ones.

Robert H. Austin

This leaves the labor level people who work as servers in restaurants, factory workers, retail clerks, cashiers, construction workers and many others, including truck drivers. Now, to the real reason for this short story. What makes these people any different from the true professional people? Is it money, position, prestige, power? Are these professional people better people? Do they love their families any more than the non-professional people? Are they better citizens? Do they have more love for their country? Is their God any different for these people? The answer is an easy one. Having a position of power and respect doesn't make anyone a better person. The love and kindness come from within and no level of education can change what a person really thinks and feels. We are all the same inside. It's a shame that some people feel that position and education level make them a better person and even worse, some of these people think they are superior to those with less position and education.

Johnny Miller was just ten years old and in the third grade. He, like so many, had a best friend. His best friend was Billy Stevens. Johnny and Billy always played together at school recess. They both loved sports and were looking forward to junior high school where they could play on a real team. It didn't matter to them whether it was baseball, basketball or football. They just wanted to play on a team, and be on the team together. These two best friends had not visited each other at their homes. They were just friends at school.

Just a week before school was out for the year, Johnny's mother asked him what he wanted to do during the summer break. He thought for a few seconds and then told his mother that he would like to spend some time with his best friend, Billy Stevens. His mother thought for a few moments then asked if Johnny knew Billy's parents. Johnny had never met them and had no idea who they were. She then asked what he would do with his best friend. That was easy for Johnny. It was to play ball and have fun. He wanted to invite Billy to their home the week after school was out. His mom had agreed and was looking forward to meeting Johnny's best friend.

Billy Stevens did come to visit Johnny on the first Saturday after school was out. Johnny's mother had called Billy's mother and gave the invitation. She had called the school to get Billy's parents phone number. Billy's mother took him to Johnny's house and came to the door with him. She met Johnny's mother and they chatted for a brief moment. Johnny was going to spend the day, and his mom would pick him up at five that afternoon.

Johnny's mother liked Billy the moment she met him. He was very polite and said, "Yes ma'am and no ma'am." She was impressed with this young man and was happy her son had such a nice little boy for his best friend. Johnny's mother made sandwiches for the boy's lunch and talked with them as they ate. She wanted to learn about Billy's parents and what his father did, what profession was he in? When she asked Billy about his parents and his father's job, she almost choked on her food as he smiled and told her that his dad drove an over the road truck.

Both boys were concerned about her near choking on her food. She recovered and told them that she was okay, but did need to be excused as she need to make an important phone call. After she left the table, Billy told Johnny that he hoped his mother was okay. Johnny smiled and said that she was okay and not to worry. He and Billy were both very compassionate and loved everyone. They had no concern for a person's position in life. They never thought about it. Johnny's father was a district judge and his mom was a lawyer, but hadn't practiced after marring Johnny's father twelve years earlier.

The two boys had a wonderful day together and were planning their next visit as they waited for Billy's mother to arrive. She did arrive at five, as promised. She spoke to both boys and asked about their day. She could see how happy they were as they sat on the porch swing and smiled at her. She then looked toward the front door and asked about Johnny's mother. She wanted to thank her for taking care of Billy.

Johnny went into the house to find his mother. He found her lying on her bed with a wash cloth on her forehead. He asked if she was okay and she told him that it was just a headache. She told him to tell Billy's mother that she would talk to her later, but needed to rest now. Johnny tried his best smile as he told Billy's mother that his mother said she would call her later, but wasn't feeling well at the moment. Billy and his mother left after asking Johnny to tell his mother that they hoped she would soon be feeling better.

That night after dinner, Johnny's mother and father asked him to sit with them in the study. They never sat in the study. It was always in the den and watch TV. He wondered what could cause his parents to want to sit in the study. This had never happened. But what Johnny Stevens heard that evening would change his life forever.

His father, The Judge, opened the discussion, or as Johnny remembered it, the "Order." Johnny was never to see Billy Stevens again and for sure, never invite him to their home. When he asked why, they both told him, and in no uncertain terms.

A Truck Driver...A Truck Driver! For the rest of Johnny Miller's life, he would never forget those three words...A Truck Driver! He could not understand then and thirty years later he still could not understand or accept his parent's attitude.

Johnny still saw his friend at school and did go to his home on two occasions. He made the excuse that they could have more fun meeting at the ball field, and they did until they both graduated from high school. Billy Stevens went to college and then to law school. He defended hundreds of people who couldn't afford a lawyer's fee. He didn't care, he had enough income from the ones who could pay those with a formal education and were known for their power and control of others. His best friend, Johnny Miller, didn't go to college. He knew education was important, but owning his own construction company with over 300 pieces of heavy equipment and more contracts that he could handle made him happy. He made a lot of money and a lot of jobs for his construction workers. He didn't drive a truck, but he never made any difference in people, no matter what position they had in life. Both of his parents died after Johnny was successful, but never understood why he chose the life he had.

So, there will always be the Johnny boys and the Billy boys. College isn't for everyone and it's not always because of what their parents did or requested them to do.

Jim's Choice

Sept. 7, 2010

They met in a small coffee shop in downtown Louisville, Kentucky. He was a law student, and she was a waitress. Jim Miller had been told that he would be a lawyer for as long as he could remember. His father was a lawyer and had made a good life for Jim and his mother. They had all of the things anyone could need or want. Jim had never questioned his destiny and knew that he would be a lawyer, just as his parents had told him.

Veronica Sullivan had no idea what her future held for her. She was raised by a single parent, a lonely and sad mother, pregnant too early in life. Veronica felt happy knowing she had a job and enough money to afford a small apartment near her place of employment. Her mother had died just two years before, and now Veronica Sullivan was a sole survivor.

Veronica and Jim became friends during their first meeting. Jim was under stress most evenings when he entered the small coffee shop and sat at the counter. Veronica knew what he wanted and always greeted him with a hot cup of coffee and a warm smile. He always returned her smile and slowly sipped his coffee. They never spoke for the first few minutes. Smiles and warm looks of friendship were their silent conversation. After he had drunk half of his coffee, he would look into her pretty brown eyes and softly say, "Thank you, Veronica."

It was always the same every evening and Veronica waited for the moment he would say, "Thank you Veronica." She would pause and say, "You're welcome, Jim."

Three months had gone by since their first meeting, and they both knew most everything about each other. Jim felt sorry for Veronica, knowing how she had to struggle just to make ends meet, but he had no idea how content she was with her life. She, on the other hand, felt sorrier for Jim. She knew he was living a life that had been programmed for him. At least she could choose what she wanted to do, and what she was doing was just fine with her.

They had never talked about seeing each other outside the coffee shop, but, on that night, three months after their first meeting, that would change. As Jim finished his coffee and a tuna salad sandwich, he asked her for a date. She was shocked and found it hard to speak. She had thought how nice it would be to have a date with him, but never thought he would ask her, an uneducated waitress.

Jim waited as she blushed, turned away, and then returned with the coffee pot. She filled his cup and said, "Jim, we have learned a lot about each other over the past few months, but I never thought you would be interested in me."

He frowned as he said, "I don't understand. Why do you think I would not be interested in you, Veronica?"

"I'm just a waitress working in a small coffee shop. You are going to be a lawyer someday, maybe a judge, or who knows what else."

Jim reached across the counter and took her hand. As he held her hand, he looked deeply into her eyes. "Veronica, I've never known anyone with more knowledge about human behavior than you. I know you are not formally educated, but you have an ability to read people and understand their needs and desires." He paused and then continued. "I would love to spend more time with you and hopefully get to know you better. I would love to take you to a nice restaurant and spend an evening with you."

Their first date was fun for both of them. They had a wonderful dinner and then went dancing at a small club in downtown Louisville. Jim took Veronica home, and she invited him in for a nightcap. As they talked and finally kissed, she couldn't resist his advances and welcomed him to her bed. Sadly, Jim never asked her out again, and she saw him less frequently after their night together. Veronica could not get him out of her mind. She had never had sex before, and had always thought it would be because she was in love. She felt she was in love with Jim Miller and wanted to be with him…to spend her life with him. She was totally obsessed with him, but knew in her heart that the love affair was totally in her mind and not in his.

Ten years later, Veronica had never married and had dated fewer than ten men. Most were one-night stands and ended with anger and frustration for her. It seemed to her that they all wanted the same thing. She had submitted to a few, but soon found it disgusting and stopped dating. Her thoughts of love and a relationship were always about her first love, Jim Miller. Her life had remained the same the past ten years. She was still a waitress, however, now working in the Galt House in Louisville and making a good living with some generous tips during The Kentucky Derby and other annual events.

Jim Miller had become a judge and a much respected one. He had married into the family his parents had suggested and lived a miserable life with a wife he didn't love. He had worked with many different people as a lawyer and now a judge. Their names were impossible to remember, and he found it difficult to trust anyone. He felt he was being used by everyone he encountered. It was all about his position, and no one truly cared about him. He needed more in his life. He had no one to love and no one to love him. While he trusted no one, he knew he needed that trust now more than ever in his life. As he sat in his chambers late one evening, his thoughts went back to ten years before when he first met Veronica Sullivan. She was honest and kind and understood people. She had a gift that no one could be taught, and she could be trusted. He had to find her and talk with her. Was it trust he wanted from her, or was it more?

Veronica had no idea who was calling in the middle of the night. She looked at her clock radio before answering her phone. It was 3:00 a.m. She let it ring for another moment and then picked up the phone. Her voice was thick with sleep, and it almost sounded like a man's voice. Then she heard his voice.

"Veronica, is that you?"

She rubbed her eyes with her free hand and said, "Yes, who is this?"

"It's Jim...Jim Miller."

She didn't respond. She sat in complete silence as she heard him. "It's me, Jim Miller. You remember, I used to come to the coffee shop, and we talked." He paused. "Talk to me, Veronica, please."

"It's been a long time, Jim. I'm sorry...I should not call you by your first name. I should say Your Honor, Sir."

After a long pause, he continued. "You will never have to call me anything other than Jim. I have regretted never seeing you again after our first date. My life has been miserable since becoming a lawyer and a judge. I have no love in my marriage, and my only happiness is my work. I have no one to love and no one to love me."

She was sitting up, holding the phone firmly against her ear, listening to him. She had wanted him from their first meeting, but knew he was from a different world, a world she had no place in and could never live in even if she had the chance. Now, after not seeing him for over ten years, he was crying on her shoulder as he had done during their conversations in the coffee shop. "What was all of this about?" She wondered.

"I know where you live, Veronica, and I want to come to your apartment tonight."

"What?"

"You heard me. I know this sounds crazy, but I must see you tonight."

"Well, it's not night, it's three in the morning, Judge."

"I'll be at your door in thirty minutes. I know you will not turn me away."

The phone line was dead as she started to speak. She replaced the phone and went to the bathroom. She must look her best for her early morning guest.

The warm smile that Jim Miller had remembered was not present when Veronica opened her door. She looked older, but still attractive. She looked more mature than the twenty-something she was ten years before. She had never told him her exact age when he had asked her on their only date. She had only said "twenty-something." He had thought he must have been five or six years older. He was twenty-eight then and just a few months from graduating from law school.

He stood, waiting for her to invite him in. Without a word, she stepped back and waved her arm toward the inside of her home. Jim slowly walked in and stood in the middle of her modest living room. He remembered how they had kept silent each time they met, and the memory was made fresh again as she left the room and returned with a cup of coffee. As she handed it to him, the warm smile from ten years ago returned. He slowly sipped the hot liquid and looked into her moist, brown eyes.

"Thank you, Veronica," he said.

Her voice cracked as she replied. "You're welcome, Jim."

She had dreamed of this day for the past ten years, but never, in her wildest dreams, thought it could happen, but it was happening. Jim Miller was standing in her living room, cup of coffee in hand, and looking into her sad eyes. This was not the Jim Miller she had known and loved so long ago; this was the Honorable Judge James Miller. He was one of the most respected judges in the state of Kentucky.

Her voice was different now, slower and softer. "I can't begin to tell you how excited I am to see you, Jim." She hesitated. "You said it's okay to call you Jim?"

His voice sounded different to her, also. "I want you to always call me Jim, Veronica."

"Oh, Jim," she said as she touched his arm. "I can never tell you how much I've thought of you over the years. I do want to show you something."

She turned and walked through the living room door as he followed her. She opened the door to her bedroom and switched on the light. Three of the four walls were covered with newspaper clippings chronicling Jim Miller's career since his graduation from law school. Judge Miller was in total awe. He could not believe the time and dedication it must have taken to collect and compile all of this information.

"Veronica, I am amazed at this collection. I can't imagine anyone caring so much for someone they knew for such a short time and so long ago."

Veronica smiled as she looked at the newspaper covered walls.

"I always knew you would be an important person someday, and my love for you has kept me interested in your career. I am so very proud of you, Jim."

He wasn't sure what she meant about her love for him. Was it romantic or just an infatuation because of his successful career?

"Veronica, I'm not sure I understand your feelings for me." He gazed at the newspaper clippings and sighed. "All of this is impressive to most people, but, to me, it's a life of misery."

Veronica stood in silence and waited for him to continue. He sat his empty cup down on the nearby dresser and turned back to face her. He opened his arms as she walked into them and felt the warmth, she had dreamed of over the past ten years.

As they stood holding each other, a young boy walked into Veronica's bedroom. He looked at Veronica then at Jim and asked, "Mom, who is this man?"

Veronica looked up at Jim and gave him her warm smile from so long ago.

"Jimmy, this is your daddy. I have always known he would come to see us some day."

Jim Miller was speechless. His gaze went from the newspaper clippings on the wall, to young Jimmy and then settled on Veronica.

"Would you ever have told me had I not come to see you?"

Veronica continued to smile as she turned and took their son's hand and pulled him into their embrace. Jim's choice had been made for him and now he did have someone to love and knew he would be truly loved for the first time in his life.

Well, this concludes my short stories. I have always loved hearing short stories and trying to write some. This book of short stories is my fourth book to published. They are all published by iUniverse and are also available on Amazon and Barnes and Noble. The titles include: The Shoebox, The Saloon, Total Commitment and this Book of Short Stories.

Printed in the United States
by Baker & Taylor Publisher Services

Printed in the United States
by Baker & Taylor Publisher Services